Simulacrum
by Rian Darcy

Clasp Editions
an imprint of
Circlet Press, Inc.
Cambridge, MA

Published by Circlet Press, Inc.
39 Hurlbut Street
Cambridge, MA 02138

www.circlet.com

First paperback edition: December 2012
ISBN 978-1-61390-070-3

Contents

Chapter One

Normal people didn't get excited about murder. Of course, normal people didn't get phone calls in the middle of the night from the city's chief homicide detective, either, but even if they did, Shaun was pretty sure they wouldn't be smiling about it.

The thing was, after two years as a desk jockey in the Cybercrimes Division of the LAPD, Shaun was itching for a chance to do some fieldwork. It wasn't that he didn't like his job—he was good at what he did, and he'd always liked computers—but he was trapped in a world where an exciting day at the office consisted of stumbling across a new email scam. Tonight, though, that was going to change.

Or so he thought.

Shaun looked up at the building where he was supposed to be meeting Detective Hudson and wondered if he was about to be the ass-end of a joke. He'd never worked a homicide case before, but he'd always imagined that a real life crime scene would look a lot like they did in the movies, complete with coroner's vans and news crews. The real thing wasn't that glamorous. The building itself was a typical Los Angeles apartment block: crumbling stucco, a red tile roof, and a shopping cart parked on the scraggly front lawn. An AC unit was buzzing away in a third floor window, trying to combat the August heat, while a couple of teenagers shared a cigarette on the balcony, watching Shaun and muttering to each other in Spanish. The building was otherwise quiet. There wasn't even a patrol unit outside, just Hudson's retired police cruiser.

Shaun checked his t-shirt to make sure he hadn't spilled any coffee on it while driving, then ran his fingers through his short brown hair and braced himself for whatever was waiting inside.

The entry door had been propped open with a cinder block. Shaun toed it out of the way before stepping into the lobby and easing the door shut behind him. A television blared away in one of the downstairs apartments, and the laugh track seemed to follow him as he made his way upstairs. He still wondered if someone was fucking with him, but when he spotted the yellow crime scene tape stretched over a door at the end of the hall, he heaved a sigh of relief. The door was unlocked, so he opened it and ducked beneath the tape to step into a sparsely furnished living room.

"Mason?" Hudson shouted from elsewhere in the apartment. "If that's you, get your ass in here."

Shaun found her in one of the bedrooms, which had been turned into a home office with a desk, two bookshelves, and a Simulated Reality tank. The tank was empty except for the Epsom Salt solution that would keep a user afloat, but the interior lights were still on, and the touchscreen on the side of the tank displayed the 'Ready For Use' message. If it wasn't for the numbered marker the coroner's office had left on the floor beside the tank, Shaun would never have guessed that someone had died there.

As sick as it was, the sight of that little plastic number gave him a glimmer of hope. There had been five Simulnet-related deaths in L.A. County over the last six months. According to the equipment that monitored a user's vital signs when they were in the tank, all of the victims had suffered massive seizures. Shaun's gut had been telling him that there was more to the deaths than equipment malfunctions (and judging by some of the conversations he'd over-heard at work, he wasn't the only one who felt that way), but since there had been no evidence of foul play, the coroner's office had ruled the deaths accidental. After all, no one had ever been mur-dered through Simulnet before. The fact that Hudson was at the scene, though, meant that Homicide had finally been called in. Shaun just couldn't figure out why the place was so empty.

"Hey, am I late to the party or something?" Shaun asked. "Where is everyone?"

Hudson didn't reply right away; she was busy frowning at her mobile phone. Shaun knew better than to interrupt, so he just stood there and watched her. She must have been pretty when she was younger, he thought, before smoking, middle age, and her job had taken their toll on her looks. After a few minutes of typing, Hudson switched her phone off and tucked it into the pocket of her blazer. Then she narrowed her eyes at Shaun and announced, "I'm about to ask you to do something illegal."

Shaun's eyes widened. Hudson had a reputation for pushing boundaries, but she also had a reputation for being a good cop. She'd put in eighteen years with the FBI before signing on with the LAPD. No one knew for sure why she'd decided to make the switch, but everyone assumed it had something to do with the medal in the display case behind her desk. Shaun couldn't imagine her asking someone to do something illegal. "Is this some kind of test?" he asked.

"No, Mason, it's not a test." Hudson flashed him a wry half-smile. "That's why I need you to promise me that even if you say no to what I'm about to ask, this conversation stays between us."

"Okay." Shaun drew the word out. He couldn't shake the fear that this was a pop quiz he was doomed to fail.

"Here's the deal: forensics finally found something we can use." Hudson gestured to the tank. "Someone set up a data trap on the victim's Simulnet line. It logged the addresses of all the places she'd been visiting and kept tabs on network activity. The logs show a huge spike in data transfer right before she died."

"And that's probable cause to open an investigation?"

Hudson shrugged. "It's close enough. We're not sure what caused the surge, but since the data was coming from an outside source and not the tank itself, that should at least keep the damn coroner's office from calling this another accident. It'll be manslaughter at best."

While Hudson talked, Shaun wandered over to the desk and sorted through the papers strewn across it—bills mostly, and a few receipts, but the thing that caught his eye was a grade report from the local university. Shaun pointed to the name at the top. "Sarah Poulson? Is that her?"

Hudson nodded.

Shaun scanned the list of classes—Women's Studies, Gender Issues in Economics, and Biochemistry—then the list of grades. From the looks of it, Sarah had been a straight 'A' student. She would have gotten along with his sister.

Hudson's phone rang while Shaun was going through the other paperwork on the desk. She answered it with a curt greeting, then scowled, flapped her hand at Shaun, and disappeared into the living room.

Shaun took that as permission to keep poking around.

Nothing on the desk struck him as being out of the ordinary, though he did notice that a few of the bills were addressed to someone named Keith Larson. The bookshelves were overflowing with college textbooks and paperback thrillers, but nothing overtly personal, so Shaun turned and left the room. On his way out, he spotted Hudson in the kitchen, pacing and muttering into her phone, but he didn't stick around to listen to what she was saying.

The master bedroom was tidy in the bland sort of way that results from two people with differing tastes trying to find a compromise. A man's watch was lying on one nightstand, and the other nightstand was cluttered with photographs. One snapshot in particular caught Shaun's eye: a photo of a young, blonde woman, sitting on a picnic blanket and smiling up at the camera. She looked happy.

The photo reminded Shaun so much of a similar photograph on his shelf back home that he had to look away. He tried to busy himself with sifting through the contents of the nightstand drawer: a half-empty tube of lip balm, a few hair elastics, another paperback novel, and a band-aid still in its wrapper. Something rattled near the back of the drawer. It turned out to be a brown pill bottle with Sarah's name on it. The label was for an antidepressant prescribed by a Dr. R. Greene, and the bottle was half empty.

"Mason?"

Shaun jerked and almost dropped the pill bottle, which he stuffed back into the nightstand drawer before calling, "In here!"

Hudson came into the room looking harried and annoyed. She

darted a glance at the open drawer but didn't mention it. "Sorry about that," she said. "I hate taking calls in the middle of meetings, but it was important."

"Everything okay?" Shaun asked.

Hudson pressed her lips together in a tight line. "Just dealing with someone hellbent on being uncooperative. Don't worry about it."

"You still haven't told me what you want me to do."

"Your job." Hudson sighed and pushed her hair back from her forehead. "Look, I can already tell you that this case is going to turn into a bureaucratic nightmare. The Chief's office has been on the phone with the feds all night, squabbling over who has jurisdiction. Until they get that settled, I've got an office full of Homicide detectives sitting around, twiddling their thumbs."

Shaun understood the problem. Simulated Reality was still a new technology, and there had been a lot of back-and-forth over who, if anyone, should enforce the handful of laws that existed for it. Simulnet was technically an extension of the Internet, so the feds argued that it should fall under their jurisdiction. Unlike the Internet, however, which existed as a worldwide network, Simulnet was split into regional clusters. A basic monthly fee allowed users to access their local clusters—the Los Angeles County cluster, for example—but if they wanted to access other regions, they were charged an additional rate. Because of the way Simulnet was divided, local law enforcement wanted to claim jurisdiction over their regional clusters. The debate had been raging for almost two years.

"While these morons are busy fighting over who gets to play in the sandbox, people like Sarah Poulson are dying," Hudson said. "I need you to go in under the radar and get a head start. The sooner we find the person responsible for this shit, the better."

Shaun nodded and scratched at the back of his neck for a moment while he thought. Although he'd been waiting for an opportunity like this for a long time, nothing was turning out the way he thought it would. Finally, he said, "I don't know. I mean, don't get me wrong, I've got no problem helping out, but I'm not sure how much I can do. I don't have a ton of field experience, and I've got even less experience investigating things I'm not supposed to be investigating."

"Oh, I doubt that. As I hear it, you made quite a name for yourself at Cal Tech."

Shaun flushed. By some stroke of luck, he'd managed to keep himself out of prison long enough to get into college—not that he was a bad kid, just curious, bright, and easily bored, which, as it turned out, was a dangerous combination. By the end of his freshman year at Cal Tech, he'd discovered the thrill of joyriding through faculty email accounts, and by his sophomore year, his fellow students were paying him a hundred bucks a pop to snag copies of upcoming tests off the university's FTP server. He'd never officially been caught.

"Don't look so surprised, Mason; it's in your file. Or did you think we just hire people off the streets without doing background checks?" Hudson said. "Anyway, it doesn't matter if you're a little wet behind the ears. You're not likely to get spotted where I'm sending you." She paused for a second and stared at him, like she was trying to decide whether or not she could really trust him. Then she pulled a small, portable hard drive out of her pocket and held it up so he could see it. "This is a copy of all the logs from Sarah Poulson's line—all the addresses she visited, all the data fluctuations, everything. As far as anyone outside this apartment is concerned, this doesn't exist, got it?"

Shaun nodded and took the drive. It felt heavy in his palm, despite being smaller than his thumb. "I'm happy to have a look, but I'm pretty sure I won't find anything on here that forensics wouldn't catch."

"You're not analyzing the drive, you're using the addresses in those log files to start an investigation inside Simulnet."

Shaun's heart lodged itself in his throat. "Inside Simulnet?"

"You can say no," Hudson told him.

Shaun stared at the drive in his hand. "Y'know, having me ask around on the streets is one thing—at least we'd be able to pretend we had jurisdiction—but you're asking me to dive straight into contested territory. Do you have any idea what would happen to me if I got caught?"

"At the very least, I'd disavow all knowledge of your independent investigation and suspend you for a month. Depending on how this turf war with the FBI ends, it's possible you'd be interfering with a federal investigation too, so you'd be looking at a couple years in prison for that. Then there are all the lawsuits you'd probably face from privacy advocacy groups..."

"Lawsuits? Count me in." Shaun flashed her a quick, nervous smile and pocketed the drive. That was how he made most of his decisions: split-second before he could talk himself into backing down. His ex-girlfriend had hated that about him—which was probably one of the reasons she was his ex, he thought—but he knew that if he tried to make his choices any other way, he'd never get anything done. Committing to something this important made him feel jittery, so he took up pacing beside the bed. "Anything else you can tell me before I get started? Was she connected to any of the other victims?"

"None so far. The killer doesn't seem to be targeting his victims based on who they are in the real world," Hudson said. "I've been doing some research in my downtime, and the only link I've been able to find between them is that they were all regular Simulnet users."

"So you're thinking they might be connected inside Simulnet?"

"People aren't always the same in Simulnet as they are in real life," Hudson pointed out.

Shaun knew exactly what she meant. Despite the fact that he worked with computers for a living, he didn't log in to Simulnet very often—he'd always preferred the real world—but whenever he did log in, he was always amazed by the number of beautiful people roaming the streets (not to mention the scores of dragons, elves, and goblins who could be found strolling through the park on Sunday afternoons). By contrast, Shaun's avatar was an exact replica of his real world self; he didn't have the money or inclination to create anything more impressive.

"I'll need you to take a leave of absence while you're working on this; I don't care what kind of excuse you use as long as your story is solid," Hudson said. "According to your file, you've got five days of sick time and two weeks of vacation time. I hate to make you use them this way, but I need you focused on this investigation, not getting distracted by shit at the office."

"Fine by me," Shaun said. "I have to be honest, though: for a tech guy, I haven't exactly spent a lot of time in Simulnet. I mean, I log in once or twice a week, but I usually stick to the entertainment districts."

Hudson's lips tightened and she glanced away, like she was suddenly uncomfortable meeting Shaun's gaze. "That's why you're going to have a guide."

"You're giving me a partner?" Shaun asked with a frown.

"Something like that." Hudson took out her phone and pressed a few keys. Shaun's phone buzzed in his pocket, and Hudson explained, "I just sent you the address of a cafe in Stackston. I need you to log in and meet him there at nine."

Shaun checked the string of numbers in the text message, then tucked his phone away and asked, "How will I recognize him?"

"You won't, he'll find you. He's good at that." Hudson sighed and checked her wristwatch. "You should go home and get some more shut-eye before your meeting."

Shaun wasn't sure he'd be able to sleep, but he nodded anyway. "Should I call you later with an update?"

"No, it's better if we only talk about this when we absolutely have to. I only want to hear from you if you're in trouble or if you've found a major lead. And I'm not just looking out for my own ass, here; the cleaner I keep myself in all this, the easier it will be for me to help you if you get caught."

"Got it," Shaun replied. He hoped he sounded less nervous than he felt. The idea of diving into the investigation without backup was as terrifying as it was exciting.

Shaun turned to leave, but he paused at the door and glanced over his shoulder. Hudson had already turned her attention back to her phone. Part of him knew he should just be grateful for the chance to finally do something worthwhile, even if was unofficial, but curiosity won over common sense and he asked, "Hey, why did you call me? I mean, of all the people in my department, why the new guy?"

Hudson glanced up from her phone and eyed him for a second, then said, "You know, believe it or not, you didn't end up on the LAPD's payroll by accident. It's not like someone left you on our doorstep in the middle of the night and we took pity on you. You've been looking for a chance to prove yourself, so go do it instead of standing around, wasting my time with stupid questions."

Shaun grinned. "Yes ma'am."

Shaun left Sarah's apartment feeling jittery, but lack of sleep caught up to him on the drive home, and he barely managed to crawl into bed before he was sound asleep. A few hours later, he was startled awake by the sound of his mobile phone buzzing its way across his nightstand. He reached for it without opening his eyes and answered with a bleary, "Yeah?"

"Shaun? Are you still in bed?"

"Kim?" Shaun mumbled, then sat straight up and blurted, "Shit, what time is it?"

The sound of his sister's laughter made his heart constrict. Sometimes he forgot how much he missed her. They were fraternal twins, and although they'd had their share of arguments, they'd been inseparable for most of their childhood. Now, though, they hadn't seen each other in person for almost two years. Kim was finishing her graduate work in France, and even though they met on Simulnet whenever she had the time and he had the money, it just wasn't the same.

"It should be eight o'clock there, unless I screwed up the time difference again," Kim said. "Why are you still in bed, you slacker? Don't tell me you had another late night."

Shaun hesitated. No matter what answer he gave, it was going to be the wrong one. If he said no, she would know he was lying. If he said yes and didn't offer an explanation, she would assume he'd been out partying. Finally, he settled for telling the truth. "Just up late working on a new project—you know, the usual boring stuff."

"Another project, Shaun?" Kim sighed. "Didn't you just finish working on that virus tracker or whatever?"

"Yeah, well, you know how it goes. I'm still the new kid, so when they ask me to do something..."

"You know, I wish you'd take the rest of your life even half as seriously as you took your job."

Shaun sighed. They'd been having this argument since high school. It was amazing, he thought, that they could be alike in so many ways, yet so different went it came to what they wanted out of life. Kim liked stability and predictability; her main goals at the moment were to finish school, buy a house, and settle into a lifetime career of teaching at UCLA. Meanwhile, Shaun's plans for the future included hanging a towel rack in the bathroom and tackling the pile of laundry in his closet, and he liked it that way. Kim lived her life in the someday, and Shaun lived his in the now.

"You know I only nag you because I love you, right?"

"God help the poor guy you end up marrying."

"Don't be a dick," Kim replied, but she was laughing.

Shaun smiled, relieved to have wormed his way out of getting lectured. "Anyway, what about you? Anything exciting happening out there? Have you cloned any giant, dinosaur-eating ferns yet?"

"You really believe I work in Jurassic Park, don't you?" Kim replied with a snort.

"Just remember you promised to name that fern after me," Shaun replied as he flopped back among his pillows and yawned. There was a long silence, and he frowned. Uncomfortable silences usually meant Kim was trying to find a way to broach the real reason for the phone call.

And sure enough, a few seconds later, she said, "So, Julie called the other day."

Shaun groaned and stuffed a pillow over his face. So much for dodging lectures.

"She asked about you," Kim went on, oblivious to Shaun's misery. "She didn't come right out and say it, but she hinted that she's not seeing anyone."

"You should have asked her out, then."

"Don't be an asshole. You know she'd give you another shot if you stopped being such a stubborn prick and called her."

Shaun heaved a sigh and shoved the pillow away. "Kim, nothing's changed since we broke up. I'm not gonna see her and suddenly want to get married."

"It's not like she's going to expect you to propose the first time you have drinks together."

Actually, Shaun wouldn't have been surprised if that was exactly what Julie expected. During the last three months of their relationship, every time they'd gone out together and the evening had ended without a marriage proposal, she had gone home angry. Shaun had tried to psych himself up and convince himself that after four years of dating, getting married was the logical next step, but he just couldn't do it. Eventually, Julie had given him an ultimatum: propose or leave. Shaun left.

"Look, at least think about giving it a try. It's been what? Six months? Maybe all you guys needed was some time apart to cool off."

Shaun sighed. "If I promise to call her, will you promise to stop bugging me about it?"

"Only if you actually call her."

Shaun rolled his eyes.

"Look, I'm really not trying to be a pain, it's just that Julie was really good for you. You seemed so—" Kim was interrupted by a man's voice, rattling something off in French. She sighed. "Damn it. Hey, look, I actually have to go. We're headed out to the field tomorrow and Professor Rigel wants to have a meeting before dinner so we can plan for the morning."

"That's okay, I should get my ass outta bed and get going anyway."

"I won't have reception out there, but I'll call you when I get back to town, okay?"

After making Kim promise to call as soon as she got back, Shaun hung up and covered his face with his hands. He felt anxious, the way he always did whenever he knew Kim would be unreachable. It wasn't just his protective brotherly instincts that made him worry; he relied, more than he liked to admit, on knowing his sister was just a phone call away if he needed her.

Shaun sighed and rubbed his eyes with the heels of his palms, then glanced at the framed photo on his nightstand. It had been taken from above, just like the picture of Sarah, but the girl in this photograph was much younger—twelve, to be exact—with dark hair and a shy smile. She was wearing light blue pajamas and kneeling in a sea of crumpled wrapping paper. Shaun reached over to touch the frame before crawling out of bed.

After downing two cups of instant coffee, Shaun ambled into his living room, made sure the front door was locked, and booted up his SR tank. The tank's interior lights flickered on, and the on-board computer whirred as it ran through its self-check routines. While Shaun waited, he plugged the drive Hudson had given him into one of the tank's ports so that the files would be accessible from inside Simulnet. The float solution inside the tank was fresh— he changed it once a week whether he'd used the tank or not— and after a few minutes of being warmed by the climate control system, it was was exactly 98.6 degrees. When the tank's control screen gave him the 'System Ready' message, Shaun shed his clothes and climbed inside.

The interior lights went dark when Shaun closed the hatch, and the inside of the tank was lit only by the bluish glow of the secondary control screen. Shaun selected the address of his apartment in Simulnet, then fitted the transmitter unit over his head. The transmitter worked by manipulating brain waves with sonic pulses, but it looked so much like the cap from an electric chair that Shaun always imagined he could feel a shock when the metal made contact with his body. Once everything had been adjusted and calibrated, Shaun reached up and tapped the login button on the control panel, then lay back and closed his eyes.

When Shaun opened his eyes again, he was lying on the futon in his Simulnet apartment, in exactly the same position he'd been in when he logged out. He stayed where he was for a few minutes while he waited for his body to adjust. Slipping into an avatar made his skin feel tight, like the full-body equivalent of squeezing his foot into a shoe that was half a size too small.

Eventually, the disorientation passed and he sat up. Unlike his real world apartment, a spacious one bedroom in North Hollywood, his Simulnet apartment consisted only of a tiny living room, a walk-in closet, and a transport chamber that had been programmed to look like an elevator. It was an absurdly simple living space, especially in Simulnet where even the poorest of users could own mansions, but Shaun didn't spend much time there, so he didn't see a point in making a ton of improvements. The apartment served its purpose: a quiet place for him to go when he wanted to log off.

"Welcome home, Sir."

Shaun smiled. Winston was one of the only additions he'd bothered with: an artificial intelligence program responsible for keeping the apartment secure and managing Shaun's messages while he was offline. Having a butler, even an artificial one, made him feel a little like Bruce Wayne.

"You have no messages," Winston informed him. "May I be of any assistance?"

"Not right now, but thanks," Shaun replied as he pushed to his feet.

"Very well, Sir."

Shaun stretched, then went to change out of the suit he'd been wearing. The last time he'd logged in had been for a blind date with one of Kim's friends from college. She'd been nice enough, but it turned out that Kim was the only thing they had in common, and Shaun wasn't comfortable basing a relationship off of his sister—actually, he wasn't sure he wanted a relationship at all.

After changing into jeans and a T-shirt, Shaun tucked his phone into his pocket, then made his way over to the transport chamber. The control panel came to life at his touch, and he entered the address of the cafe where he was supposed to be meeting his new partner. The doors of the chamber slid open, and Shaun stepped inside. Technically, the chambers weren't necessary since avatars could be teleported from one location to another, but the human brain wasn't wired to accept instant shifts in reality. True teleportation triggered all sorts of nasty side effects, ranging from vertigo and nausea to full-blown psychotic breaks, so the chambers had been designed to give the illusion of travel.

The doors opened again a few seconds later, and Shaun stepped out of the chamber into a Moroccan-themed coffeehouse full of low couches, layered rugs, and piles of overstuffed cushions. The only other customer was a blue-skinned woman who didn't look up from the book she was reading, so Shaun ordered a coffee from the perky elven girl behind the counter and then wandered outside to sit at one of the tables on the sidewalk. The warmth from the coffee soothed his nerves, and since he had a few minutes to kill, he busied himself with examining the scenery.

It was early afternoon in Stackston, and cooler than it had been in the real world. The hosting company that managed the neighborhood had pre-programmed its weather and streets, but the buildings had been designed by users in a hodgepodge of different styles, ranging from classic to outright absurd. The restaurant next door to the Moroccan cafe looked like a scale replica of the Parthenon, and across the street, a giant white cube with no windows had been plopped down beside a thatched cottage. The clashing styles gave the city a surreal, bewildering quality.

Someone bumped into Shaun's chair and startled him out of his thoughts. He looked up just in time to see a winged cyborg levitate past his table, followed by a petite blond girl with a me-chanical spine. Shaun watched them go and wondered if he'd ever get used to being in a world where there was such a thin line be-tween man and machine. Sometimes it appealed to the little kid inside him, the fledgling computer geek who'd had a poster of The Terminator above his bed and spent hours drawing robots, but then he remembered that those things could only happen online and his excitement ebbed. Simulnet made a million things possible, but none of it was real.

Shaun sighed and took his phone out to check the time. It was ten minutes past nine, and his partner still hadn't arrived. He peered through the window of the cafe, but it was still empty except for the blue-skinned woman who'd been there when he ar-rived. Shaun sighed and drummed his fingers on the table.

Five minutes later, he took his phone out again and scrolled through his address book until he found Hudson's name. Just as he was about to press 'call', however, a softly accented voice said, "Me being late doesn't qualify as an emergency."

Shaun jerked in surprise and almost dropped his phone.

A dark-haired man seemed to have simply appeared in the chair across from him, already slouched in his seat with his head bowed over a chunky old laptop. His bony, ring-adorned fingers were flying over the keyboard, and the toe of his boot was tapping out a restless beat against the sidewalk. There was a row of silver earrings in his ear and a tattoo in what looked like Chinese on the back of his wrist. He wore a black tweed jacket and a layer of scarves wrapped around his neck.

Shaun gaped.

The man didn't look up, but his fingers paused over the keyboard. "You're staring."

Shaun was taken aback. That was hardly the greeting he'd been expecting—not that he really knew what he'd been expecting—and for a second, he didn't know how to respond. Finally, he cleared his throat and replied, "Sorry, it's just, you startled me. I didn't even see you sit down."

"I know."

"Oh," Shaun said. They hadn't even been talking for ten whole seconds, and he could already feel the conversation slipping out of his control. After another uncomfortable pause, he prompted, "Uhm, are you the one who's supposed to be meeting me?"

"Yes."

"Okay." Shaun drew the word out, then squinted and said, "Sorry, I don't think I caught your name."

The man finally looked up from his laptop. There was something odd about his face, like each of his features had been borrowed from a different race. He looked like he hadn't slept or eaten properly in weeks; there were dark circles under his eyes, his cheeks were hollow, and his skin was pale. When he focused his unnaturally blue eyes on Shaun's face, the intensity of his gaze made Shaun want to physically recoil. After a long silence, the man said, "Lore."

"Lore?" Shaun repeated.

"My name."

"Oh! Sure, sorry." Shaun tried to break the tension between them by offering a sheepish grin, but when Lore didn't react, he felt a twinge of annoyance. Normally, he had no problem getting along with people, even the disagreeable ones, but so far this conversation had been one strikeout after another. He didn't get the impression that Lore was purposely trying to be difficult, but the effect was the same. Still, he managed to keep a polite smile on his face as he said "So, Lore, huh? I'm guessing that's not your real name."

Lore didn't reply; he just sat there, looking at Shaun. It was unnerving to have his full attention and have no idea what to do with it.

"Right. Well, nice to meet you. I'm Shaun Mason." Shaun stuck his hand across the table for Lore to shake.

Lore just stared at Shaun's hand before turning his attention back to the laptop. "I know."

"I see." Shaun gritted his teeth. "So you're my new partner, then?"

"I don't like rhetorical questions."

Shaun finally ran out of patience. "Look, man, what's your problem?"

"My problem?" Lore quirked an eyebrow.

"You've known me two minutes and you're already being a dick," Shaun replied. "Are you always like this, or did I manage to do something to piss you off sometime between when you sat down and when I noticed you?"

Lore stared at him for a moment, as if considering, then sighed almost politely and said, "We need to be clear on one thing from the start: I'm not here to socialize. I don't like you or dislike you. I don't engage in small talk because it's a waste of time. I'm here to do my job and to help you do yours. Everything else is superfluous." He held Shaun's gaze for what seemed like a few seconds too long, then turned back to his laptop.

It was the look that did it. There was a flash of wariness in Lore's otherwise neutral expression that made Shaun back down. It vanished as quickly as it had appeared, but Shaun recognized it immediately; he'd seen it before, on the faces of victims who'd been hurt so badly it was either shut down or break apart. Shaun wondered what Lore's story was.

"I need the log files," Lore murmured. He seemed to be talking to himself, but when Shaun didn't say anything, he glanced up and arched an eyebrow.

"Oh, shit, yeah, hold on." Shaun fumbled with his phone and then flicked through the menus until he found the files from the drive Hudson had given him. "What address should I send them to?"

Lore stopped typing long enough to give Shaun an email address, then went back to whatever he'd been doing.

Shaun sent the files on their way, then set his phone aside and folded his arms on the table. In a hesitant tone, the verbal equivalent of approaching a dangerous animal, he said, "Okay, so, I know you're not big on chit-chat, but I figure if we're gonna be working together, we should know something about each other."

"Your name is Shaun Mason. You spent most of your academic

career earning high scores on all of your standardized tests but average grades in all of your classes. You graduated from UCLA with dual Bachelor's degrees in Computer Science and Criminal Justice. You applied for a job with the LAPD two years later, after repeatedly and unsuccessfully applying with the FBI. You have a twin sister called Kim and an ex-girlfriend called Julie." Lore looked up and stared straight into Shaun's eyes. "I already know more about you than I care to know about most people."

For a moment, Shaun was uncharacteristically speechless. It wasn't until Lore looked down at the laptop again that he was able to mentally shake himself and reply, "Okay, I'm impressed. Did Hudson tell you all that, or did you dig it up on your own?"

"I research people before I agree to work with them. You should do the same."

"I didn't even know your name until just a few minutes ago. I figure if Hudson is cool with you—"

"Then you already know everything you need to know about me," Lore interrupted.

Shaun blinked.

"Have I insulted you?" Lore asked. He didn't sound apologetic, but it didn't seem like he was trying to pick an argument, either. If anything, he sounded curious.

Shaun considered the question. Lore was prickly and aloof, but Shaun couldn't shake the feeling that there was more to him than he let on. And since Shaun loved both challenges and puzzles, he flashed Lore his most irritating grin and replied, "Nah, we're good."

Lore eyed him for a moment, then nodded and turned his laptop around so Shaun could see the screen. "I ran reverse look-ups on the addresses in the log files. Two are private addresses, but I found names for the other four."

Shaun was taken aback by the abrupt change of subject, but he just went with it and leaned in to read the list of names: "Platinum, Der Kampf, Anguish Arts, Oubliette—they sound like S&M clubs or something."

"Most of them are." Lore spun the laptop back around and

resumed typing. "They're all in the Okui District. Sarah may have been a regular in the neighborhood."

"Y'know, I didn't know her or anything, but she doesn't strike me as the type who'd be into that sort of thing."

"Everyone is different in Simulnet." Lore peered at Shaun over the edge of the laptop screen. "That's a side effect of anonymity."

"So what are you like in real life?"

Lore stared at Shaun for a moment more before standing abruptly and snapping his laptop closed. "Meet me at Oubliette in twenty minutes."

"Sure, but I need the—" Shaun broke off when his phone buzzed. It was a text message from an unknown number, containing the Simulnet address for Oubliette.

"Twenty minutes," Lore said. He picked up his laptop, then turned and strode into the cafe. Shaun watched him through the window as he went to the transport chamber and stepped inside. Their eyes met when he turned around again, and Shaun waved. Lore didn't return the sentiment.

Once the doors had shut, Shaun sighed and shook his head, then took a sip of coffee that he promptly spit back out again. Amazing, he thought, that almost anything was possible inside Simulnet, yet his coffee had still gone cold.

Shaun went back into the cafe to have the barista reheat his coffee, then leaned on the counter while he waited and looked around the coffeehouse. When his gaze landed on the chair where the blue-skinned woman had been sitting earlier, he frowned. She'd left her book. Once the barista had come back with his coffee, he went over and picked the book up, and arched an eyebrow at the title: 'Simulacrum and Simulation' by Jean Baudrillard. Curious, he flipped the book open to the first page, only to find it blank—as was the page after that, and the page after that. Shaun put his coffee down on the table and used both hands to flip through the pages. They were all blank, right up until very end where someone had scrawled a message on the inside of the back cover: 'Don't believe everything you see.'

"What the fuck?" Shaun said out loud.

"Is there a problem, Sir?"

"Huh?" Shaun looked up to find the barista watching him. He offered her a reassuring smile and replied, "No, sorry. There's no problem." Then he turned his attention back to the book, frowned, and muttered under his breath, "I don't think so, anyway."

Chapter Two

The address Lore had given Shaun was for a public transport chamber across the street from Oubliette. As soon as Shaun stepped out of the mock phone booth and saw the line of people waiting to get into the club, he understood why Lore hadn't sent him straight inside: his jeans and T-shirt would have been a flashing neon sign that he didn't belong. Oubliette's customers used the same mix of avatars as everyone else—everything from scantily-dressed model types to satyrs with ocular implants—but even though the neighborhood looked like it had just survived a war, the people milling around outside the club may as well have been the patrons of a five star restaurant. Shaun was surprised; he'd toyed with bondage before, but S&M clubs had always conjured images of leather chaps and bull whips, not three piece suits and little black dresses.

Shaun scanned the crowd. When he didn't see Lore anywhere, he stuffed his hands in his pockets and leaned against the transport chamber. The longer he waited, the more jittery he felt. He was equal parts nervous and excited, like a little kid about to go off to summer camp and spend two blissful months away from the watchful eyes of his parents. This was hardly his first time at a nightclub—he'd been sneaking into bars with fake IDs since he was fifteen—but an S&M club on Simulnet was a far cry from the trendy Hollywood spots he usually frequented.

Someone cleared their throat next to him, and Shaun wheeled around to find Lore standing there. Shaun pressed a hand to his chest and let out an embarrassed chuckle. "Jesus, that's the second time today. You're like a ninja or something."

Lore thrust a paper-wrapped package in Shaun's direction. "You'll need to change."

Shaun was too surprised to react for a moment, but then he took the package and said, "You know, you could have just told me there was a dress code. I'm pretty good at dressing myself these days." He eyed Lore, who was wearing a smart black suit with a blue tie. He'd done away with his mantle of scarves, and Shaun spotted another tattoo peeking out from underneath his collar.

"You're staring again."

Shaun snapped to attention, then offered a sheepish grin and a muttered apology. He'd never met anyone so adept at throwing him off his guard, but he actually sort of liked it. Being around someone who could surprise him was a nice change of pace.

There was a narrow alley directly behind where they were standing, and Shaun jerked his head toward it. "Hey, want to keep a lookout for me while I duck in there and get dressed?"

Lore followed and stood at the entrance of the alley with his back to Shaun. The bluish glow from a nearby streetlight made his hair look more purple than black, and the light glinted off the earrings in his ear. His arms were crossed, and he was drumming his fingers against his elbow, but it seemed more fidgety than impatient. Shaun wondered if he was always like this.

While Shaun wriggled out of his jeans, Lore glanced over his shoulder and said, "There's an ID patch built into the coat. It should mask your user ID if anyone tries to scan you."

"Doesn't that violate terms of service?"

"Probably."

"Oh good, first day on the case and I'm already breaking rules." Shaun tried to sound annoyed, but he had a feeling the effect was ruined by the smile on his face. There was nothing quite like the thrill of doing something you weren't supposed to, and it had been a long time. Once he'd finished changing into the suit, he said, "Okay, you can turn around now. How do I look? A little bit Tony Stark, a little bit James Bond?"

Lore gave Shaun a once-over, then turned and headed back toward the club without a word. Shaun hurried to catch up and wondered why Lore's stride seemed so much longer than his despite the fact that they were almost the same height.

"Hey, who am I supposed to be, anyway?" Shaun asked. "The name on the ID patch, I mean."

"Stephen Malone."

"Better than John Doe, I guess."

As soon as they'd taken their place at the end of the line, Lore's posture changed like someone had flipped a switch that forced all of the tension out of his body: he tucked his hands into his pockets and slouched a little, then tipped his head ever-so-slightly to the side. Even his expression seemed to relax, and he actually smiled at a group of girls who giggled their way past him.

Shaun knew he was staring again, but he couldn't help it; he'd never seen anyone snap into character so quickly before.

They made it through security without a problem and stepped through the front doors into a cozy lobby area. The room had been decorated with black walls, plush red couches, and a gleaming oak bar. Well-dressed club-goers were milling around, sipping cocktails and chatting with one another.

"Are you sure this is an S&M club?" Shaun muttered. So far, Oubliette reminded him more of an upscale bar in Hollywood.

Lore nodded toward another set of double doors. "Through there."

The main room was decorated in the same style as the lobby, but it left no doubt as to what the club was really about. Sex was everywhere: sprawled over couches, kneeling in chairs, tied up on the floor, and even hovering in midair. There was no music, just the background noise of conversation and laughter, and the sound of riding crops on bare skin. Only a handful of people were fully dressed. Shaun was hardly a virgin, but the sight of all those naked bodies made him feel like an enthusiastic teenager all over again; he couldn't decide where to look first.

"This way." Lore seemed completely unfazed by what was happening around them.

Shaun followed Lore to the bar, where a group of men were sipping their drinks and watching the room. They were in their late forties or early fifties, and attractive enough to be movie stars. Shaun couldn't stop staring. When Lore handed him a glass, he took a sip without looking and almost spit it back out again. "Jesus, what is this?"

"Club soda. Given your inexperience with anything stronger..."

"Inexperience? I've been drinking since I was fourteen." Shaun made a face and took another sip. It made his nose wrinkle. "God, this shit is vile."

"Then don't drink it." Lore set his drink down on the bar. "Wait here."

"What? Where are you—?" Shaun began, but Lore was already weaving his way across the room, back toward the lobby. Shaun cursed under his breath, then surveyed the crowd while he tried to decide whether he should stay where he was or try to mingle. He sighed and lifted his glass, then remembered what was in it and plunked it back down onto the bar.

The group of men at the other end of the bar had dispersed. Only one of them, a tall man in a khaki suit, had lagged behind to talk to a younger man with slicked-back hair and sharp cheekbones. They were standing close together, with their heads bowed and their arms touching. Neither of them seemed to have noticed Shaun, so Shaun edged closer to see if he could overhear their conversation.

"...can't tell my wife anything anymore," the older man was complaining. "She'd cut my balls off if she knew I came to places like this."

The younger man stroked his arm. "That's a shame, but plenty of people come here to explore fantasies they can't talk about with their significant others. Why don't you tell me one of your favorites—Paul, was it? Tell me something you'd never be able to tell your wife."

"I'm not sure that's a good idea. I didn't really come here to meet anyone."

"Don't get coy." The younger man let his hand glide down Paul's chest to his stomach. "I've seen you here before, and I've seen what you do. Now, why don't you tell me what you want so we can have a nice time?"

Paul's smile was predatory as he leaned in to whisper something into the younger man's ear. When the younger man pulled away a minute later, he was blushing, and he kept his gaze on Paul's face as he sank to his knees. Paul leaned back against the bar and reached down to card his fingers through the younger man's hair.

Shaun knew he should probably look away, but he was fascinated. He'd experimented with other men before, during his freshman year of college, but even though he'd enjoyed the sex and the guys had been nice enough, he'd never been able to form emotional attachments to any of them. Only a handful of men had caught his interest since then, but his crushes were mostly sexual and always fleeting, so if anyone bothered to ask, he always said he was straight. That didn't stop him from being curious about what was happening next to him, though.

The younger man had unfastened Paul's trousers and freed his cock, and was lapping at the tip while Paul tugged on his hair. Shaun swallowed and shifted his weight from one foot to the other, and when Paul murmured, "put it in your mouth," he felt his cheeks turn red. What Paul and his partner were doing was tame compared to some of the other things happening around them, but for some reason it was affecting Shaun more than he would have imagined. Maybe Kim was right, he thought; maybe he just really needed to get laid.

Thinking of his sister put a damper on Shaun's libido, and he finally looked away to stare at the rows of bottles behind the bar. Paul was whispering something, but Shaun did his best to ignore it. He was so distracted that he didn't even notice someone had slid up to the bar beside him until the person's elbow brushed his. The contact startled him, but he tried to play it cool as he glanced over to find a man his own age smiling at him.

"Does this drink belong to someone, or are you here alone?"

"Ah, no, it's my friend's."

"What a pity."

Shaun didn't reply.

The man's smile faltered. "You're new here, aren't you? I'm pretty sure I'd remember seeing you around before."

Before Shaun could answer, someone put their hand on his

shoulder, and he twitched away. When he realized it was Lore, though, he forced himself to relax, and stifled a surprised grunt when Lore's arm slid around his shoulders.

"Hey, sorry for taking so long." Lore gave Shaun an easy smile. "I ran into an old co-worker in the lobby. Speaking of which, it looks like you made a friend of your own while I was gone."

The man who'd been chatting with Shaun now looked distinctly uncomfortable, and he made a dismissive gesture with his hand. "No, no, I was just saying hello. I didn't realize he was with someone."

"Oh, we're not—y'know, we're not with each other," Shaun said as he jerked his thumb back and forth between himself and Lore. "We're just—y'know, we're here together, but not like that. It's a friendly kind of together. We're just friends."

The man didn't look convinced—in fact, he was smirking by the time Shaun was finished speaking—but he didn't question it; he just raised his glass to Shaun and Lore and said, "Well, then I hope you have a great night of not being here together."

As soon as the man was out of sight, Lore's smile disappeared, and Shaun ducked out from underneath his arm.

"Where the hell were you?" Shaun demanded. One of the two men at the other end of the bar—Paul, probably—growled something under his breath, and Shaun fought the urge to look over at them.

"Looking at the visitor's logs."

Shaun glared at him. "That's why you ditched me? To go look at the visitors logs?"

"I didn't take you for being skittish."

"I'm not skittish! I just don't like it when my so-called partner prances off to god-knows-where and leaves me sitting here by myself, looking like I don't know what the hell's going on. I know I'm not exactly a seasoned pro, but I'm not here to just stand around and look pretty."

Lore raised an eyebrow. "I didn't take you for having control issues, either."

"I don't have control issues!" Shaun threw his hands in the air, then sighed and rubbed his eyes. "Look, did you find anything or not?"

"According to the club's records, Sarah's user ID has only been logged here twice."

Shaun frowned. "So she wasn't a regular, then."

"That doesn't mean she wasn't a regular," Lore pointed out. He took a sip of his drink before putting his glass back down on the bar and saying, "Ask around."

"What?"

"Ask around about Sarah."

Shaun scowled. Lore was really starting to toe the line between being endearingly eccentric and purposely irritating. "Sorry, but you don't get to ditch me without warning, then come back here and then immediately start giving me orders."

Lore's expression was infuriatingly blank.

"That's not how this partnership thing works; you don't get to boss me around," Shaun said. "Besides, you're apparently the actor here, so why don't you do it?"

"Because I'll be speaking to the bartender."

Shaun opened his mouth, then closed it again. Then he looked away, scratched at the back of his neck, and muttered, "Oh."

"Start with her." Lore inclined his head toward a blonde woman who was standing at the end of a couch, watching one man tie another man's wrists behind his back.

Shaun hesitated for a moment, then took what was supposed to be a fortifying swig of his drink only to remember that what he was drinking was both non-alcoholic and disgusting. After making a face and dropping his glass onto the bar, he shoved his hands into his pockets and moved toward the woman. He was so distracted by his nerves that he didn't realize Paul and his partner had finished until he practically ran them over.

"Shit, sorry," Shaun apologized when he and Paul collided with each other. He offered an embarrassed grin. "Guess I should pay more attention to where I'm going, huh?"

Paul smiled and waved him off before throwing an arm around

his partner and leading him away. "Have a good night."

Shaun watched them go, and tried not to blush when the younger man glanced back over his shoulder and gave him a smoldering once-over. When the two men had disappeared into the crowd, Shaun mentally shook himself and wandered over to where the blonde woman was standing. She glanced up as he approached, smiled at him, then went back to watching. Shaun stopped right next to her, close enough that their shoulders were almost touching.

"So," Shaun began.

The woman turned her head to look up at him. "So."

"You know, I never did get the hang of starting conversations with strangers." Shaun chuckled. Once upon a time, when he'd been a gawky teenager, this kind of awkwardness had been genuine. As he'd gotten older, though, he realized that it sometimes worked to his advantage, so he'd started doing it on purpose.

The blonde woman laughed and shook her head. "I'm not very good at it either, so I usually don't even try."

"Well, this is my first time here, so that's not making things any easier."

The woman's eyes lit up. "Oh really? What do you think so far?"

"It's… I guess 'interesting' is the word I'd use." Shaun grinned and shot a glance at the two men on the couch. They were kissing, slow and deep, and moaning into each other's mouths. Shaun looked away. "Truth is, I'm not really into this kind of stuff; I only dropped by because a friend kept telling me I should check it out. I guess she's a regular here."

"Oh? What's her name? I might know her."

"Sarah," Shaun replied. "Sarah Poulson."

"Hmm." The woman pursed her lips, then shook her head. "No, I don't think I know her, at least not by that name. But so many people here use fake names, you know."

Shaun nodded and opened his mouth to reply, but he was interrupted by a low, breathy moan. He glanced at the couple on the couch. Both men were naked, and the man whose arms were tied behind his back was now blindfolded as well. The other man was kneeling behind him, biting down on his shoulder and sliding a hand down between his legs. Shaun shifted his weight and cleared his throat.

"You know, they'd probably let you play with them if you're interested, especially if you told them it's your first time here." The woman smiled again.

Shaun actually considered the offer for a moment before he remembered that he was there to work, not play. He took a step back and flashed the woman another smile. "No thanks, I've got a friend waiting for me. It was nice meeting you, though. Have a good night."

The woman's expression shifted from surprised to disappointed, but she just nodded and waggled her fingers at him before turning her attention back to the two men.

Shaun wandered away, trying to act as nonchalant as possible. His excitement was turning into apprehension now that the investigation was underway. Realizing that any one of the half-naked avatars surrounding him could belong to a murderer had put a damper on his libido.

He wandered through the club, trying to decide who to strike up a conversation with next, and eventually made his way over to a group that had gathered around a young, dark-skinned woman with white hair who was hovering horizontally in midair. Her wrists and ankles had been tied, and she was stretched out on her stomach like invisible ropes were holding her taut. Shaun couldn't see her face, but her shoulders were heaving and her toes were curled, and when the man standing over her brought a riding crop down on the swell of her buttocks, she let out a soft cry.

Shaun was about to move on when he heard someone exclaim, "Oh my god, is that him?"

There was a group of four girls standing behind Shaun, all of them in various states of undress. They weren't watching the girl being whipped, though; they were whispering to one another and staring over toward the bar with wide eyes.

Shaun followed their gazes to the bar where Lore was wrapped up in conversation with the bartender.

"That's not him; it's just someone who looks like him," one of the girls said.

"Are you kidding? Who would be suicidal enough to copy his avatar?"

"Oh my god, you guys, I think he just looked over here. Did he look over here?"

Shaun's curiosity finally got the better of him, and he moved closer to interrupt. "Hey, sorry, but I couldn't help overhearing your conversation and I was just wondering: who is that guy?"

The girls stared at him for a moment before glancing at one other with wary expressions. One of them started to say something, but the girl next to her pinched her arm and she stopped. Shaun frowned, but before he could ask anything else, the girls turned and walked away as a group, occasionally glancing back over their shoulders at him.

Shaun watched them leave, then looked back over at the bar. Lore didn't even so much as glance in his direction.

Hours later, Shaun had made two rounds of the club and walked away with nothing to show for it but a few phone numbers that had been tucked into his jacket pocket. He'd lost track of Lore at some point, and after almost an hour of hanging out by the bar by himself, he'd gotten tired of waiting and decided to leave the club alone.

It was dark when Shaun stepped out onto the sidewalk, though his body's internal clock told him it should be early afternoon. Lack of sleep from had finally caught up to him and added to his disorientation, and all he really wanted to do was log off and go to bed.

"Now you're the one deserting me."

Shaun jerked in surprise, then closed his eyes and sighed. "I swear to god, man, do you have some sort of fetish for sneaking up on people and scaring the shit out of them?"

Lore had been leaning against the wall just outside the door of the club. He pushed away from the dirty bricks and tucked his hands into his pockets as he appraised Shaun. The angles of his face looked softer in the dark. "You're exhausted."

"Yeah, well, sleep deprivation and four hours of pretending to be some sort of kinky social butterfly will do that to you."

"Mm," Lore acknowledged, then pushed his sleeve back to check his watch. "You should log out and rest."

"Yeah, that doesn't sound like a bad idea. You sure you don't mind?"

Lore shook his head. The neon lights from the bar across the street cast shadows beneath his cheekbones.

"Hey," Shaun said, "I was talking to some girls earlier—well, more like I overheard them talking—anyway, I'm pretty sure they were talking about you. They were acting like you were some kind of celebrity or something."

Lore's eyes narrowed and his shoulders stiffened, but then he visibly relaxed again, as if he'd caught himself in the process of an emotional reaction and consciously put a stop to it.

"Well?" Shaun prompted when Lore didn't say anything. "Are you gonna tell me what they were freaking out about?"

"I don't know."

Shaun sighed, but he was too tired to argue the point so he just shook his head and said, "Fine, whatever, I'm going home. Wanna meet up later?"

"We'll meet there." Lore nodded toward the phone booth across the street.

"Sure. What time?"

"Whenever you're ready."

"You gonna give me a number where I can call you, then?"

"No."

Shaun frowned. "So you're planning to just hang out here until I show up again?"

"No."

"Then how are you gonna know when to meet me?"

"I'll know," said Lore.

Shaun huffed a laugh. "What, have you got a data trap on it or something?"

"Or something," Lore agreed. He actually looked amused.

Shaun rolled his eyes. "Man, the intelligence community sure missed out with you. You're closed up tighter than Cheyenne Mountain."

As soon as the words were out of Shaun's mouth, there was another almost imperceptible changed in Lore's demeanor: he turned his head just a little and frowned. He didn't look angry, but it was obvious that something about what Shaun had said bothered him.

"Er, sorry," Shaun apologized. "I didn't mean to, you know, offend you or anything."

"You didn't offend me."

Shaun didn't buy it, but he didn't want to make things worse by pressing the issue either, so he just stuffed his hands into his pockets and said, "Okay then... I guess I'll see you later."

Lore didn't reply.

"Right," said Shaun. He offered Lore an awkward salute, then turned to make his way across the street.

Just as opened the door of the phone booth, he heard Lore call, "Mason."

"Yeah?" Shaun looked over his shoulder at Lore, who was still watching him from the doorway of the club. At a distance, when he was lit by the dramatic glow of orange and blue neon, it was impossible to see the dark circles beneath his eyes and the pallor of his skin. Shaun wouldn't have called him pretty, per se, but he was striking in ways Shaun couldn't explain.

"You didn't offend me," Lore said.

"Hey, don't worry about it." Shaun smiled. "I'll see you later, okay?"

Lore opened his mouth, then paused and frowned before replying, "Later."

Chapter Three

Shaun winced when he emerged from the darkness of the tank into his sunlit living room. In the span of just a few hours, he'd gone from the morning sunlight of the real world to late afternoon in Stackston, then to the darkness of the Okui District, and back to early afternoon. The rapid time shifts combined with lack of sleep had left him disoriented, and he stood next to the tank with his eyes closed, dripping float solution all over the carpet.

When the feeling had passed, he grabbed a towel off the hook beside the tank and dried himself off, then padded naked into the bedroom. He'd left the window cracked, and he wrinkled his nose at the dry heat being swept into the room by the Santa Ana winds. Fire season was starting early this year. It was only a matter of time before the skies of Los Angeles would be brown with smoke.

Shaun sighed and flopped down face first onto the bed. He expected to fall asleep as soon as his eyes were closed, but he just lay there listening to the sound of his own breathing and trying to ignore the thoughts whirling through his mind. This was one of the reasons he had a habit of staying out late, drinking and dancing until he was so exhausted he could barely stand: he'd never gotten the hang of switching his brain off when it wasn't being distracted by other things.

Eventually, he gave up on trying to quiet the noise in his head and instead tried to concentrate on something more pleasant than dead girls and serial killers. Until his visit to Oubliette, Shaun had considered himself pretty well-versed when it came to sex. After all, he'd never been one to do things in moderation. In college, while everyone else had been going through a nightly routine of getting trashed and fumbling around in the dark, Shaun had been spanking his male study partners and having threesomes with girls who handcuffed him to the bed. He'd experimented enough to know what he liked and what he didn't and, given what he did for a living, he'd seen more than enough photos of everything else.

The trouble was, it wasn't the kinkier things he'd seen that were standing out in his memory. Shaun was thinking about Paul and his partner: about the young man on his knees, with his lips stretched around Paul's cock and Paul's fingers tugging at his hair. He was imagining the slick glide of the young man's tongue and the sharp drag of his teeth. The fact that thinking about it was turning him on wasn't unusual—he still looked at gay porn once in awhile, whenever the mood struck—but the fact that he was fixating on it was.

Shaun didn't realize he was touching himself until he had his fingers wrapped around his prick. He paused for a second and opened his eyes, then decided that maybe an orgasm would help him sleep. As usual, he tipped his head back and summoned his favorite fantasy: a brunette he'd seen on the cover of a men's magazine two years ago, who had the brightest blue eyes and the most perfect tits he'd ever seen. It didn't go as planned.

As soon as he relaxed into the rhythm and sensation of stroking himself, his mind began to wander, and instead of wandering to gorgeous cover models, he found himself wondering what would have happened if he'd tried to join Paul and his partner. He wondered if the young man would have tried to suck both of them at the same time, or if he would have ended up on his knees between them, with Paul's cock shoved down his throat and Shaun's buried in his ass. Shaun bit down on his bottom lip and stroked himself a little faster. A few seconds later, he was coming so hard it made the muscles in his stomach cramp.

When the last of his orgasm had rippled through him, Shaun opened his eyes to stare up at the ceiling with a frown. He'd honestly thought he'd gotten all of his experimenting out of his system in college. Apparently, he'd been wrong.

❧

Lore was waiting next to the phone booth when Shaun stepped out of it.

"I need coffee," Shaun complained. He was bleary-eyed and stumbling, despite having just had a two hour nap. He'd been tempted to stay in bed until morning, but as soon as he realized how long he'd been asleep, it had been impossible to drift off again.

"This way," Lore replied as he turned and began walking.

Shaun sighed and hurried to catch up. They fell into stride together as they made their way down the street, past boarded-up houses and dirty alleyways. It was daylight now in Okui, and the greyish sunlight emphasized the layers of grime that clung to the neighborhood. The fact that the sun was out hadn't discouraged people from visiting the district's clubs and bars, though, and it was strange to see so many nicely dressed (and hardly dressed) people wandering through the dingy neighborhood.

"Y'know, I get that this place looks shady on purpose," Shaun said as he stepped around a huge, mud-filled crack in the sidewalk, "but did they have to make it smell bad too? If I wanted to smell garbage and pee, I'd just take a trip to downtown L.A."

"Realism," said Lore.

"Yeah, right. Hey, where are we going, anyway?"

Lore stopped so abruptly that Shaun almost ran into him, and stared across the street at a nondescript building. "A tour. If the victims were regulars in this neighborhood, we'll be spending a lot of time here. You should be familiar with the area."

"Oh," said Shaun. "Wait, victims? As in, plural? How do you know the other victims came here?"

"I only know that one of them came here for sure." Lore began walking again. "The other female victim, Dawn Miller, visited Der Kampf the week before her death. If she and Sarah were both here in Okui before they died, the others may have come here as well."

"But there were no network logs for the other victims. How do you know she was there?"

"Der Kampf keeps visitor logs."

Comprehension dawned. "So you just checked the IDs of the other victims against the club's visitor logs?"

Lore nodded.

"So we might have our first connection." Shaun frowned. "Wait, does that mean you went to Der Kampf without me?"

"Yes." Lore didn't sound apologetic.

"God damn it," Shaun complained. "I thought we agreed you wouldn't do that kind of shit without me!"

"I never agreed to that."

Shaun scrunched his face up in displeasure, but Lore didn't seem to notice.

"How much do you know about Okui?" Lore asked.

"Not much," Shaun admitted. "Some of the guys in my department came here for a bachelor party last year, and I've heard people talk about some of the crazy shit that goes on at the clubs, but I'd never actually been here until yesterday."

Lore hummed.

Shaun waited, but when Lore didn't say anything more, he sighed. "You know, asking that question kinda made it seem like you were leading in to telling me about the neighborhood..."

"Did it?"

"You're doing this on purpose, aren't you?"

Lore came to a halt in front of an adult toy store with a garish, holographic window display, and gestured across the street to a crumbling brick townhouse with powder blue front doors. "That's the administration building for the city's host. Okui is privately owned by a Japanese investment banker, Katou Katsu. He doesn't charge rent on any of the property here, but he's picky about which businesses he'll allow to operate in the area, and he charges a forty percent tax on their profit."

"Forty percent?" Shaun let out a low whistle.

"A small price to pay for not having to worry that your club violates the host's terms of service."

Shaun frowned as they started walking again. "So anything goes?"

"Almost anything," said Lore. "Pedophilia is forbidden, regardless of whether it's real or simulated." His face darkened. "There are private clubs for that."

"Really?" Shaun asked, disgusted. Dealing with child pornography was an unfortunate part of working in Cybercrimes, and it never failed to make him sick. In fact, the first time he'd run data recovery on the hard drive of a pedophilia suspect, he'd had rush to the bathroom halfway through.

Lore glanced over at him. "Compared to the rest of Simulnet's underground, Okui is tame."

Shaun didn't reply; he just nodded and stuffed his hands into his pockets. He knew from experience that new technology would always develop a dark side, but he'd naively hoped that Simulnet's advertising propaganda had been right, and that Simulnet really did represent a safer future.

"This neighborhood gets a lot of tourists who only come here once or twice to fulfill their curiosity—" Lore paused as a black motorcycle zipped past, then led the way across the street. "—but most of the people who visit clubs like Oubliette are regulars."

"Oh great. I'm sure we didn't seem suspicious at all, then. You know, two new guys showing up, asking a bunch of questions... I'm sure it happens all the time."

Lore shrugged.

"How do you know so much about Okui, anyway?" Shaun offered Lore a teasing grin. "You come here often?"

"When I need to."

Shaun was about to ask Lore to elaborate when he was interrupted by his growling stomach. Apparently Lore heard it too because he came to a stop and arched an eyebrow. Shaun chuckled and scratched at the back of his neck. "Uh, you think we could stop for some food? I didn't eat before I logged in."

"There's a noodle shop around the corner," said Lore.

Shaun nodded and followed Lore to an alley between two towering apartment buildings. A group of unnaturally tall, unnaturally pale men with bald heads and long black coats were standing there, passing a pipe filled with something that smelled like licorice. A few of them eyed Lore as he passed, but looked away when Shaun tried to make eye contact with them. Shaun hurried past and resisted the urge to glance back over his shoulder.

The entrance to the noodle shop was in the alley itself, and consisted of a tiny doorway draped with green plastic beads. A lopsided, hand-lettered sign had been duct taped above the door: 'Kim Lee Ramen.' The interior of the shop wasn't much nicer than the exterior, but it smelled good so Shaun was willing to withhold judgment. The restaurant was deserted except for a single employee who was lounging behind the counter: a tall man in a white suit, with bright red eyes and waist-length blonde hair pulled back into a ponytail. He flashed them a lazy smile, and Shaun caught a glimpse of sharp, elongated canines.

"Please, come in," The man purred as he gestured for them to sit down at the counter. There was a flicker of recognition in his eyes when he saw Lore, but just like all the others, he didn't say anything. Once they were settled, he tapped the sticky-looking countertop, which turned transparent to display the shop's menu on a screen below it. "Each single item is three marks, and two items together are five. May I get you something to drink?"

"Water," said Lore.

"I'll have a coffee," said Shaun. While he waited for his drink, he pulled out his phone to check his Simulnet bank accounts. They were separate from his real world accounts, and he didn't usually keep much money in them since he rarely logged in to spend it. Thankfully, he had enough to cover his meal.

The tall, blond man came back with their drinks and took their orders, then brought their food out a minute later. Simulnet restaurants had replicators in their kitchens that were programmed to instantly create any item on the menu. The food didn't have any nutritional value, but it suppressed the hunger center of the brain for a few hours.

Shaun eyed Lore's small bowl of rice as he dug into his ramen, and asked around a mouthful of noodles, "Is that all you're eating?"

"Yes."

"Well, thanks for making me feel like a fat ass," Shaun said with a chuckle. "Though I guess I should just be glad you're eating at all."

Lore paused with his chopsticks hovering over his bowl.

"Shit, sorry, I didn't mean it like that! I didn't mean to say—it's not like I think you don't eat or anything, shit just comes out of my mouth sometimes and—"

"I'm not offended," said Lore. "I just don't understand why you care so much about my eating habits."

Shaun stared at him for a second, then turned back to his ramen and mumbled, "I don't."

"All right."

"Fine."

They ate in silence. A few minutes later, the beads in the doorway were swept aside, and an orc with dark brown skin, tattooed forearms, and a ring through his nose walked into the restaurant. Shaun tried not to stare, but it didn't matter; the orc didn't even glance in their direction as he stepped up to the counter and barked, "Blake!"

The man who'd served Shaun and Lore emerged from the back room. When he saw the orc, he smiled and sauntered over to extend his hand. "Darling! What an absolute pleasure to see you again. What brings you to this side of town?"

The orc didn't even glance at Blake's hand. "You seen Ruby lately?" His voice was gruff and he wasn't smiling.

Blake frowned and shook his head. "No, she hasn't been in for a few days. I thought you had finally given her some time off."

"Damn it." The orc slammed the heel of his palm down on the counter. "She's been no-call, no-show since Tuesday night. I should've known something was going on when she asked to leave early. She never leaves early."

"Maybe she's flitted off with that girl she's been seeing?"

"She would've told me."

The nagging little voice in the back of Shaun's head got louder and louder as the conversation went on, until he finally stopped eating altogether and glanced at Lore, who gave him a barely perceptible nod.

"I'm gonna keep trying to call her, but keep an eye out for her, will ya?" the orc was saying.

"Of course," Blake replied.

As soon as the orc had gone, Shaun caught Blake's attention and said, "Hey, sorry, I couldn't help but to overhear your conversation. I've been trying to track down a old friend of mine, and I think she mentioned a friend named Ruby."

"Oh?" Blake crossed his arms on the counter and leaned against it so that he and Shaun were at eye level with one another. He gave Shaun a smooth once-over, then asked, "And what's your friend's name?"

"Sarah," Shaun replied. "Sarah Poulson."

Blake seemed to think for a moment, then shook his head. "Mm, the name doesn't ring a bell, but Ruby has a lot of friends. It comes with her job, I suppose."

"Yeah? What does she do?"

"She's a bartender at Platinum."

Shaun tried to keep his expression neutral as he took a sip of coffee. Platinum was one of the clubs Sarah had visited right before she died.

"You know, Ruby spends a lot of time in the club even when she's not working. It's possible that some of the regulars there might know Sarah as well. I can give you directions to the club, if you'd like, so you can pay it a visit." Blake offered Shaun a feline smile and dropped his voice to a purr. "Though not, of course, until you've finished your meal. I'd hate to see you leave before you're thoroughly satisfied."

Shaun almost choked on his coffee.

Blake pushed away from the counter with a smirk and sauntered off.

Shaun watched him leave, then ducked his head under the pretense of concentrating on his ramen. When Lore made a soft, almost-coughing sound beside him, he grumbled, "Stop laughing."

"I'm not," said Lore.

Shaun was pretty sure he was lying, but decided it was best to just try and change the subject. Under his breath, he said, "We need to try and find Ruby. It can't be a coincidence that she went missing the day after Sarah was killed."

"I know."

Before Shaun could say more, he was interrupted by a quiet jingling sound. Lore pulled a phone out of his pocket and checked it, then stood without a word and made his way outside. The beads in the doorway clattered as he left the restaurant, and Shaun sighed.

A few seconds later, Blake peeked out from the back room. When he spotted Shaun sitting alone, he lifted an eyebrow and asked, "Do I have you all to myself, then?"

"He's coming right back."

"I see." Blake looked amused. He tucked his hands into his pockets and wandered over to lean his hip against the counter and smirk down at Shaun, who did his best to focus on his meal. "Am I making you uncomfortable?"

"No," Shaun snapped. Then he paused and chewed on his bottom lip for a moment before admitting, "Okay, yeah, maybe a bit."

Blake laughed. "I apologize. I've been told I have a nasty habit of coming on too strong, too early."

"No, no, it's fine—it's flattering—it's just, I'm sort of..." Shaun trailed off, searching for the right word. Having men hit on him had never made him uncomfortable before—he usually just smiled, explained that he was straight, and bought the guy a drink—but for some reason, he was feeling defensive after what had happened at Oubliette.

Blake's smile softened, and he leaned down with his arms crossed on the counter, putting him at eye level with Shaun. "Are you new to this? Men, I mean. I'm sorry, I just assumed that you and your friend were together."

"No." Shaun shook his head. "I'm not new to it, it's just—it's been a long time." Shaun had no idea why he was being this open with a complete stranger, but it felt good to talk about it.

Blake tipped his head to one side. A lock of hair had slipped loose from his ponytail, and it fell over his eye. "You know, lots of people don't figure it out until later in life. You aren't the first."

"Yeah, but it's not like I got drunk and had a one off with someone. Trust me, if it was going to stick, it would have stuck."

Blake gave him a knowing smile. "Ah, you thought it was a phase."

Shaun huffed and looked away.

"You know," Blake purred, "if you ever want to give it another try..."

Shaun sighed and turned to look Blake in the eye again. The offer was tempting, but there were more important things on his mind than sorting out his sexual preferences. "Thanks, but I'll figure it out on my own."

"What a pity," Blake murmured.

They stared at one another for a few minutes until the beads in the doorway announced Lore's return. Blake offered Shaun one last smile before moving away again, and Shaun took a deep breath to calm his nerves.

"Finish your ramen," Lore said as he reclaimed his seat beside Shaun.

"Quit being so bossy," Shaun retorted.

"Then finish your ramen."

Shaun heaved a sigh and rolled his eyes, then promptly did as he was told.

As it turned out, Platinum wasn't an S&M club at all; it was a gay and lesbian bar housed in what looked like a dilapidated old warehouse. The front of the building had been tidied up, however, and decorated with vertical rows of neon tubing that shifted through all the colors of the rainbow. There were a few high-end sports cars and a single-passenger jet parked out front, but the people wandering in and out of the bar were dressed more casually than Oubliette's patrons had been. Shaun could feel the bass from the club's music all the way across the street. The vibrations were a clever bit of programming, Shaun thought, a subtle way of making people stop and take notice of the club without realizing they'd just been advertised to.

"Hey, wait." Shaun grabbed Lore's elbow before he could step off the curb. "Shouldn't we change before we go in? Or does this place not keep logs?"

Lore glanced at Shaun's hand on his arm and replied, "Check your pocket."

Shaun frowned and stuck his hands in his pockets. There was something small and cold in his right pocket, and he pulled it out to hold it up to the light. It was a tarnished silver anchor, no bigger than the tip of his thumb.

"Keep that with you," Lore instructed. "I applied the same identity patch to it that I applied to the jacket you were wearing at Oubliette."

Shaun quirked an eyebrow. "That's a lot of code to pack into something this small."

Lore just hummed in reply.

"Right, well, easier than putting on a suit every time I log in," Shaun said as he pocketed the anchor. Then he made a sweeping gesture with his arm and said, "After you."

Lore led the way across the street. There was a line of people waiting to get inside, though it was only half as long as the line at Oubliette had been. They took their place at the end of the line and waited in silence, right up until Lore slipped an arm around Shaun's shoulders as they followed two winged girls into the club.

"Could you not do that?" Shaun hissed.

"What?"

"This, the arm thing." Shaun tried to shrug Lore's arm off. "People are gonna think we're together."

"They come on to you when they think you're alone."

"So what?" Shaun huffed. "Why do you care? Jealous?"

Lore glanced at him. "It interferes with your concentration."

"Does not," Shaun muttered.

Lore didn't reply, but he did take his arm away. Once they were inside, he gestured for Shaun to follow him to the bar. Platinum was bigger and busier than Oubliette had been, and they had to push their way through the crowd. A layer of fog hovered just below knee level, and the dance floor was lit by multicolored orbs floating overhead. Silver cages drifted in mid-air, and Shaun found himself staring at the naked male dancers inside them, one of whom caught his eye and smiled.

When they got to the bar, Lore pulled Shaun to the far end where there were two empty stools right next to each other.

"I can't believe how busy it is in here," Shaun yelled over the music. "It's not even six, is it?"

"At least a quarter of these people are logged in from their offices."

"People will always find a way to procrastinate at work, I guess." Shaun laughed. After the bartender had come to take their drink order—Shaun ignored the brief amusement that crossed Lore's face when he specified that he wanted regular water—Shaun turned on his stool to look out at the crowd. "So where do you think we should start? The staff? Blake did say Ruby was a bartender here."

Lore nodded, then said, "But not yet."

"Why not?"

Lore's expression made Shaun feel like a toddler stuck in an endless loop of asking 'why.' "Because it would be suspicious for us to march in, order two glasses of water, and immediately start asking questions."

"Right," Shaun muttered, then added, defensively, "I don't usually do fieldwork, you know."

Lore didn't seem moved.

Their drinks came, and they both turned on their barstools to watch the club. The first time Shaun had gone to a gay bar, back when he was sixteen and eager to test out his fake ID, he'd expected it to be a miniaturized version of a gay pride parade, with older men in leather chaps and younger men wearing too much body glitter. He'd been disappointed to discover that for the most part, gay bars looked just like straight bars—at least in the real world. Platinum was an exception.

Just like any Simulnet club, Platinum was full of elves, half dragons, and cyborgs. The difference was that in Okui, the bar's patrons were free to do whatever they wanted with whomever they wanted. Two topless, translucent girls were kissing at other end of the bar, and a few feet away, a black-skinned Shiva was stroking one of his two cocks while a young man with waist-length hair was lapping at the head of the other. When Shaun realized he was paying more attention to the men instead of the women, he sighed and looked away.

"I'm gonna make a couple rounds of the room," Shaun nnounced as he slid off his bar stool.

"Wait," Lore said.

Shaun turned and quirked an eyebrow, but Lore was busy typing something into his phone. A few seconds later, he held it up so Shaun could see what was on the screen: a photo of a young Latina girl with short blue hair and a dazzling smile.

"Ruby," Lore explained.

"Where'd you get that?" Shaun asked as he examined the photo. She was standing behind the very same bar he and Lore were sitting at, with her hands on her hips and her head cocked to the side with affectionate impatience.

Lore made a noncommittal sound and tucked the phone back into his jacket pocket.

Shaun rolled his eyes. "You know, it wouldn't hurt for you to tell me things once in awhile. I'm sure the international-man-of-mystery thing probably works with the ladies, but I'm supposed to be your partner."

The look Lore gave him—a quick glance from the corner of his eye, sharp and inscrutable—made Shaun more curious than ever, but he decided not to push the issue. Work was, for the moment, more important than trying to unravel the seemingly impossible puzzle that was Lore, so Shaun tucked his hands in his pockets and said, "I'll be out there—" he nodded toward the dance floor "—if you need me."

Lore nodded and took a sip of his water. From his relaxed posture and wandering gaze, anyone who looked at him would probably think he was eying up his prospects, but Shaun knew better.

Shaun snorted and shook his head, then made his way out into the throng of people. It was a good thing crowds had never bothered him, he thought, because there were people pressed against him from all sides. Within minutes, he was sweating from the crush of body heat. Someone behind him grabbed his ass, and he looked over his shoulder at a pale, blonde elf. He couldn't tell if the avatar was supposed to be male or female, but it had a great smile and an even greater ass. Shaun considered pulling them over to dance, but before he could work up the courage, the elf waggled its fingers at him and disappeared into the crowd.

Eventually, Shaun made his way to the other side of the dance floor, and by the time he emerged from the crowd, he was so caught up in the energy from the people around him that he didn't even notice the loud boom from outside until someone near the front of the club yelled, "Fire!" The shout caused a commotion near the entrance, and the panic quickly spread through the rest of the club. Most of the crowd probably didn't even know what was wrong, but that didn't stop them from pressing in unison toward the front doors.

Shaun reacted on instinct; he dropped his glass and raised his elbows to either side of his body to keep some space between himself and the people around him. As the crowd shoved past him, he turned and craned his neck, trying to find Lore. Shaun finally spotted him sitting at the bar with his drink in hand, looking completely at ease.

"God damn it," Shaun cursed as he was pushed toward the front of the club.

The crowd burst outside into the street, causing Shaun to stumble. As soon as he'd regained his footing, he looked around and immediately spotted the source of the commotion: one of the cars that had been parked across the street was engulfed in flames.

"Shit," Shaun cursed as he began pushing people out of the way to get closer. "Move—I said move out of the way, god damn it." He made it to the street and darted across it to where a small group had gathered around the car. He made a shooing gesture at them. "Get back, it could go up again."

"It's not gonna go up again, you idiot," a young man said, rolling his eyes. "This isn't real life. The explosion wasn't real; it's probably just a publicity stunt or something."

Shaun gritted his teeth, but he didn't argue. He didn't have time to pick fights. The young man wandered away after a few minutes, and Shaun concentrated on keeping people away from the wreckage until the flames had died down. Then he crept a little closer to peer into the car's interior.

There was a charred body in the driver's seat.

"Fuck." Shaun looked away and rubbed the heel of his palm against his forehead, then turned to scan the entrance of the club, hoping Lore had followed him outside. Unsurprisingly, Lore was nowhere to be found. Shaun cursed again and pulled his phone out of his pocket, trying to decide what to do next. Finally, he sent a text message to Hudson: 'explosion in Okui, looks like car bomb, let me know if any rl victims.'

By the time Shaun was finished sending the message, a group of official-looking men in suits had arrived and were inspecting the smoldering remains of the car. Since there was no governing body inside Simulnet, Shaun assumed they worked for Okui's host, and decided to make himself scarce. The last thing he wanted was for the owner of a privately hosted neighborhood to figure out that there was a cop snooping around.

As Shaun was turning to go back into the club, he spotted something from the corner of his eye: someone was crouched on the edge of a rooftop three buildings away. Shaun paused and squinted to get a better look. The figure looked male, though it was hard to tell beneath the bulk of the black hooded sweatshirt the person was wearing, and they seemed to be watching the aftermath of the explosion. The hair on the back of Shaun's neck stood on end.

Then the figure turned, looked straight at him, and waved.

Shaun was running before he'd even made the conscious decision to do it.

The person in black turned and took off across the roof of the building, headed for the entrance to the stairway. Shaun darted up the steps to the front of the building, praying it would be open to the public, and cursed when he found the front door locked. There was an alley next to the building, and he wracked his brain for a moment, trying to decide whether the person he was chasing would head for the front door or the back door. Finally, he ran back down the stairs and sprinted down the alley, hoping he'd chosen correctly.

The back door burst open when Shaun reached the end of the alley, and the suspect ran down the back steps, then started down narrow street behind the building. Shaun ran after him, cursing the fact that he'd never bothered to have his avatar augmented with speed enhancements. He was actually starting to close the gap between them when two large men in suits stepped out from a side alley and caught him by both arms. Shaun immediately began to struggle; he kicked and twisted, and tried to tug his arms out of this captors' impossibly strong grasps while blurting a half-coherent explanation of why they needed to let him go.

Meanwhile, the suspect kept running for another twenty yards or so, then slowed and turned around so that he was walking backwards. He was a white male with nondescript features and a smug expression. He and Shaun stared at each other for a few seconds before he lifted his hand in a mock salute and then simply disappeared, leaving Shaun to snarl curses at thin air.

"Who the fuck are you? Let go of me," Shaun growled. It occurred to him that he could simply log out and disappear the way the suspect had, but he doubted it would do any good. His captors seemed determined enough to keep a hold of him that he was sure they'd be waiting for him when he logged in again.

The men didn't seem moved by Shaun's struggling. The taller one who was holding Shaun's left arm just said, in heavily accented English, "Our boss wants to see you."

Shaun immediately stopped moving. "Your boss?"

"Mister Katou."

Chapter Four

Okui's administration building was a confusing labyrinth of vaulted ceilings and hardwood floors. Staircases that should have led up to the second story ended in first floor parlors instead, and the hallways were lined with windows overlooking lush gardens that didn't exist when the building was viewed from the street. The sunlit rooms full of gauzy curtains and antique vases seemed to serve no other purpose than to distract visitors from the fact that they were being led deeper and deeper into the heart of an impossible maze.

Shaun was quiet while his kidnappers marched him down the twisting corridors. He tried to keep track of all the different turns they were making, but he was eventually forced to give up. The house hadn't been constructed according to the laws of physics, at least not as he knew them.

Eventually, they emerged from the tangle of hallways into a cavernous office with floor-to-ceiling windows that overlooked a hedge maze dotted with fountains. There was a large desk in the center of the room, and behind it sat a young Japanese man wearing a black suit and a blood red tie. Shaun assumed that was Katou. The man's eyes narrowed when he saw Shaun, and the ruby in his pinky ring glinted as he gestured toward one of the visitor's seats.

One of the guards gave Shaun a push.

Shaun scowled over his shoulder, then stalked over and plopped down in one of the brown leather chairs. Before the man behind the desk could say a word, Shaun said, "Look, Mister Katou or whatever your name is, I don't know what the hell the problem is, but—"

"I'd hoped we could be civil with each other, Mister Mason." Katou spoke without an accent, and his voice was calm but vaguely threatening.

Shaun's heart skipped a beat, and he was a split-second away from asking how Katou knew his real name, but then he thought better of it. Instead, he laughed humorlessly and said, "You have your guys drag me down here against my will, and you're lecturing me about civility?"

"I apologize for the rough treatment. Sometimes my bodyguards can be overzealous in their work ethic."

The guards in question went to stand behind Katou's desk with their hands folded in front of them. Shaun hadn't noticed before, but they were both missing pinky fingers, and he could see the edge of a tattoo peeking out from underneath the cuff of the larger one's sleeve. Shaun wondered why an investment banker needed bodyguards whose avatars made them look like they'd been recruited from the Japanese mafia.

"Why are you in Okui?"

"What?" Shaun dragged his gaze away from the two men to glare at Katou. There was something familiar about him, about the cadence of his voice and the way he lounged in his chair, but Shaun was sure they'd never met before.

"Why is the LAPD poking around in my city?"

"The LAPD? You think I'm here officially?" Shaun smirked and shook his head. "Come on, I can't be the first cop who's shown up in Okui looking for a good time."

Katou's gaze hardened. "Don't make this more uncomfortable than it needs to be, Mister Mason. I'm prepared to play nicely with you despite the fact that we both know you're outside your jurisdiction, so please don't insult me by lying to my face."

"I'd only be outside my jurisdiction if I was here on official business," Shaun replied.

"But you aren't here for leisure either," said Katou. "So if you aren't here on official business and you aren't here for leisure, where does that leave us?"

Shaun licked his lips and glanced back and forth between the two bodyguards, weighing his options. Playing innocent didn't seem to be getting him anywhere. He considered running, but he had no idea how to get back outside. That left him with telling the truth, or at least a version of it that wouldn't implicate anyone except himself: "I'm here about Sarah Poulson, a girl who died a few days ago."

Katou leaned back in his chair and steepled his forefingers against his lips. "I see."

"I think she was killed," Shaun explained. He wasn't sure how much he should give away, so he didn't go into the mechanics of how it had happened.

"And you think the killer may be hiding in Okui?"

"I think he might be coming here to choose his victims," Shaun replied. He realized with a flash of panic that Katou himself might be responsible for the murders, though he knew that was probably far-fetched. Still, he promised himself that if he survived this conversation, the first thing he was going to do was demand that Lore give him a contact number. At least that way, next time Shaun was abducted by bodyguards, he might have a fighting chance of sending a distress call.

Katou's gaze was intense enough to rival Lore's. "What interests you so much about this case that you're willing to risk your career to investigate it?"

"Isn't enough that I'm concerned about public safety?" Shaun replied with a hand pressed to his chest, over his heart.

Katou's expression didn't change.

"I grew up without a father, so I suffer from a need to prove myself?"

Katou's eyes narrowed.

"Fine." Shaun heaved a sigh. "I've applied to the homicide division three times in two years and got denied every time. I figured if I could solve this before the feds did, it would help my chances next time I send my resume in."

Katou didn't look convinced, but he didn't argue. He eyed Shaun before opening his desk drawer and reaching inside. Shaun tensed, half expecting Katou to draw a gun on him, then frowned in confusion when Katou withdrew a thick envelope and pushed it across the desk toward him. Shaun swallowed his nervousness and took the envelope.

The envelope was filled with paper marks bearing an Okui watermark. They'd never really caught on in Simulnet, for the same reason debit cards had all but replaced paper money in real life, but a handful of places accepted them, and they were useful for the kind of transactions you'd rather not have linked to your user ID.

Shaun stared at the envelope full of marks—roughly ten thousand dollars if his math was right—then looked at Katou. "If you're trying to buy me off—"

Katou interrupted his protest with a wave. "I'm not trying to buy you off, Mister Mason. Believe it or not, I don't like the idea of a killer roaming the streets of my city any more than you do. However, one of the things that makes Okui so attractive to small businesses is that I don't involve myself in their affairs unless absolutely necessary."

Shaun was incredulous. "You can't seriously think anyone would leave because you stepped in help catch a killer."

"No, but seeing my men out there roaming the streets, questioning people, would make business owners nervous. None of my employees are what you would call experienced in the art of subtlety; they're enforcers, not investigators."

"So this—" Shaun held up the envelope "—is supposed to be an incentive to keep me working the investigation?"

Katou offered him a thin smile. "Precisely."

Shaun opened the envelope again and thumbed through the bills, counting them. Ten thousand dollars was a third of what Shaun made per year. The offer was tempting, but...

"I'll do it," Shaun said as he tossed the envelope on the desk, "but I'm not taking your money."

"If you're worried I'll use it as leverage against you—"

"No, it's not that," Shaun interrupted, though the thought had actually crossed his mind. "It's just, I started this investigation on my own, and I'm going to finish it on my own. Besides, I'm not going to take money for a job I'm willing to do for free."

"Your pride won't allow it?"

"My integrity won't allow it," Shaun said. The truth was, if he really had started investigating on his own, he might have considered taking the money—he was honorable, not stupid—but since he was working under orders from above, no matter how unofficial those orders were, accepting the money would make him feel like he was crossing a line.

Katou hummed and took the envelope. He riffled the edges of the bills a few times, then pulled out a small stack and placed it on the desk in front of Shaun. "At least take this to cover your expenses. Consider it a reimbursement from a grateful city."

Shaun stared at the money, debating with himself, then reached out to take it. As soon as he had it in his hand, though, Katou grabbed his wrist.

"I know you don't trust me, Mister Mason, and it's probably safer for both of us that you don't." Katou's voice was quiet but his gaze was sharp. "But I mean it when I say that I want your investigation to be successful. If you need assistance of any sort, my resources are at your disposal."

Shaun stared at Katou for a moment before nodding once. When Katou let go of his wrist, he scooped the stack of bills up off the desk and shoved them into his pocket. Then he stood and asked, "Can I leave now?"

"Of course, Mister Mason." Katou leaned back in his chair and gestured to the door Shaun had come through earlier. "Through there, across the ballroom, and through the next door."

"The ballroom?" Shaun repeated, confused. He didn't remember seeing a ballroom on his way into the office.

Katou's expression shifted; he looked genuinely amused. "Yes, Mister Mason, the ballroom."

Shaun frowned and went to the door. Just as Katou had said, on the other side was an enormous ballroom with a gleaming wooden floor and a crystal chandelier. Shaun glanced over his shoulder at Katou, who was still watching him, then walked out of the office and let the door swing closed behind him. His footsteps echoed as he crossed the room. When he reached the other side, he paused with his hand on the doorknob, then opened the door and stared out at a set of broken, blue-painted front steps and the dirty streets of Okui.

"Well, fuck me," Shaun said.

The adrenaline was starting to wear off by the time Shaun got back to Platinum, but instead of feeling relieved, he felt jittery and short-tempered. Hudson still hadn't replied to his text messages, Lore hadn't bothered to come looking for him, and the reality of what had just happened to him was finally settling in. When he spotted Lore sitting at the bar, sipping a drink and chatting with a scantily clad girl with purple hair, something snapped. He shoved his way across the dance floor and stood there glowering at the girl until she said an awkward good-bye and made herself scarce. Lore set his drink down and regarded Shaun with the kind of serenity Buddhist monks spend their entire lives striving to achieve.

"What," Shaun yelled over the music, "the fuck."

Lore quirked an eyebrow.

"Have you been here this whole time?" Shaun demanded. "Did you somehow miss the part where there was a car bomb outside? Did you even bother to wonder where the hell I've been?"

Lore's eyes narrowed, and Shaun didn't realize he'd moved closer until Lore put a hand in the middle of his chest to push him backward. "Calm down."

"Calm down?" Shaun snapped as he shoved Lore's hand away. "I just watched someone get burned to a fucking crisp, then got kidnapped by a guy who probably could've had me killed, and you're telling me to calm down?"

"Yes."

Shaun knew he was too close—his nose was almost touching Lore's—but he didn't move away. He was too angry. He lifted a hand and jabbed his finger at Lore, ready to continue berating him, but Lore caught his wrist and fixed him with a glare that made him physically recoil.

"If you don't calm down," Lore said, just loudly enough to be heard over the music, "there will be consequences."

They stared at each other until Shaun pulled away and took a step back. He rubbed the heels of his palms over his closed eyes. "Fuck. I'm sorry. I don't know what the hell I was thinking."

Lore didn't reply.

Shaun stood there with his eyes closed for a few minutes while he waited for the second shot of adrenaline to wear off. He could hear Lore talking to the bartender, but he couldn't make out the words so he just concentrated on taking slow, deep breaths. By the time he opened his eyes again, his hands were shaking.

"Here." Lore pushed a shot glass full of glowing purple liquid in Shaun's direction.

"What's that?" Shaun asked, but before Lore could answer him, he downed the shot in one go. It burned like real alcohol—strong alcohol, at that—and left an aftertaste in his mouth that shifted from licorice to mint.

Shaun toyed with the glass for a moment, then looked up at Lore, who motioned for Shaun to join him at the bar. They claimed two stools near the far end of the counter, and a few seconds later, Shaun was glad he was sitting down because the effects of the alcohol slammed into him without any warning whatsoever.

"Holy fuck," Shaun said as he swayed and grabbed at the edge of the bar to keep himself upright. "God damn, why didn't you warn me that shit was this strong?"

"Because it wouldn't have made any difference," Lore replied before ordering two glasses of water and another shot for Shaun.

They sat in silence for awhile. The first shot left Shaun feeling warm and lightheaded, and he eyed the second shot, wondering if it would turn off whatever was left of his higher cognitive functions. Lore sat beside him, staring off into space and drumming his fingers on the bar.

Finally, Lore said, "You've never seen someone die before."

"No," Shaun muttered. "Never chased a potential serial killer or been interrogated by a mob boss before, either."

"Was this your first time seeing a dead body?"

Something ugly twisted in Shaun's gut, and his jaw tightened. "No."

"What was it like?"

"What?" Shaun turned to glare at Lore.

Lore stared back. Innocent curiosity looked out of place on him. "What was it like to see a dead body for the first time? How old were you?"

Shaun felt sick. For the most part, he considered himself an open book, but trust Lore to hit on the one area of his past that he considered most private. "I can't deal with this right now," he snapped before downing his second shot and sliding off the stool to push his way into the crowd.

By the time he reached the middle of the dance floor, the alcohol had taken hold of his senses; it made the world spin, but it also calmed the roiling in stomach and soothed his nerves. Shaun never got this tipsy from just two shots, and he suddenly understood why Lore had been ordering water.

Someone grabbed him by the arm, and Shaun turned to find a pair of elven twins smiling at him. They reminded him of the person he'd seen earlier, before the car bomb, but these were definitely women. They tugged him into an awkward hug so he had an arm around each of them, then grabbed his hips to keep him moving in time with the music. In a matter of minutes, Shaun was dancing with his eyes closed, concentrating on the heat from the crowd and the vibrations of the bass thundering through his body. The girls were pressed against him, warm and breathing and fragile, and he took every opportunity he could to touch them.

Half an hour later, they were piled atop one other on a loveseat in one of the club's seating areas.

The twin to Shaun's left—Sierra, or Sienna, or something like that—was nibbling at his earlobe and rubbing his inner thigh, and the other girl, Ivy, was busy exploring his mouth with her tongue.

There was a little voice in the back of his head telling him that he should probably pull away and go home to sleep it off, but that voice was drowned out by the pounding music and the rush of alcohol in his veins.

"Have you ever had twins before?" Sierra-or-Sienna purred into his ear.

Shaun nodded, and Ivy laughed into his mouth. "Mm, then you'll know just what to do with us."

Shaun flashed her a smile and bit her bottom lip. While they kissed, Sierra's hand slid higher on Shaun's leg. He was already hard (he'd been inappropriately excited to discover that girls still did it for him) and Sierra's fingers traced the outline of his cock through his pants. When she rubbed the tip with her thumb, Shaun gasped and Ivy pulled away from the kiss to bite the side of his neck.

"You know, I ah—" Shaun gasped and spread his legs a little wider "—I probably shouldn't be doing this right now."

"We won't tell if you won't," Sierra whispered.

Shaun was about to protest again when Ivy's hand joined Sierra's between his legs, and they worked in unison to get his pants open. A shiver rippled through him when he realized they were about to pull his cock out right there in the middle of the club. Fooling around in public had always been one of his fantasies, but he hadn't had many partners who'd been willing to go through with it. When the twins got his jeans undone and freed his prick, Shaun groaned and turned his head to shove his tongue into Sierra's mouth.

"Mm, I knew you'd have a nice cock," Ivy hummed into Shaun's ear. "It's so hard you must be uncomfortable. Should I lick it better?"

Shaun didn't reply out loud; he tangled his fingers in her hair and tried to push her head down into his lap. It wasn't like him to be so insistent, but between the alcohol skittering through his blood and the fact that they were in public, everything felt too urgent for him to help himself. Thankfully, she didn't seem to mind; she let out a quiet huff of laughter and looked at him, eyes twinkling, before lowering her head and flicking her tongue against the head of his cock. The dainty licks sent shivers rippling through Shaun's body, and he had to stop kissing Sierra for a moment because he was afraid of accidentally biting her.

"You know what I want?" Sierra whispered against his lips. "I want to watch you stroke your thick, gorgeous cock while my sister licks your balls and you play with my nipples. Can you do that for me?"

Shaun was too out of breath to reply out loud, so he just nodded. Ivy pulled away and nuzzled his inner thigh with her nose, and he reached down to wrap his fingers around his cock. The shaft was slick with her saliva. As soon as he began stroking himself, Ivy dragged her tongue over his balls and he groaned.

Meanwhile, Sierra climbed astride him and slid the straps of her dress down her shoulders. Her breasts were small but perfectly shaped, and her light pink nipples contrasted nicely with her pale skin. Shaun ducked his head a little to nuzzle one of her nipples with his lips. It hardened almost immediately and he sucked it into his mouth before grazing it with his teeth. Sierra let out a soft little mewling sound and squeezed his shoulder, which just encouraged him to bite down a little harder.

"Let me fuck you," Shaun whispered. Part of him knew it was probably a bad idea—he was supposed to be working, and Lore was sure to come looking for him eventually—but he was aching, and he needed a little more stimulation than Ivy's tongue on his balls and the warmth of his own hand. When Sierra shifted in his lap, he lifted his hips and rubbed the head of his prick against the back of her thigh.

Sierra purred and wriggled so that the tip of his cock rubbed against the wetness between her legs. "Is that what you want?"

"Yeah," Shaun groaned. He shivered when Ivy's tongue slid from the base of his prick, over his fingers, and across the head of his cock before disappearing completely. A few seconds later, Sierra let out a surprised yelp. It took Shaun a moment to catch on, but when he realized that Ivy was fucking Sierra with her tongue, he had to squeeze the base of his cock to stave off his orgasm. Sierra was clutching at his shoulders and rocking against him, and Shaun leaned up to kiss her, hoping it would distract him from the ache between his legs. This kiss was more forceful than the one before it, and he lost himself in it until Sierra pulled away with a whimper. Shaun opened his eyes to watch her face, but what he saw just over her shoulder made him freeze.

Lore was leaning against the wall a few feet away, watching them.

Shaun jerked in surprise and instinctively tried to push the twins away, but Ivy chose that moment to knock his hand away and wrap her mouth around his cock. Shaun let out an undignified whimper and grabbed at her hair, but it was too late. His orgasm was so powerful it left him breathless, and he realized too late that he was staring into Lore's eyes as his cock emptied itself down Ivy's throat.

Shaun panicked. "St-stop," he gasped as he shoved a little more insistently at the two girls. They both lifted their heads to blink at him, obviously confused and a little annoyed. Shaun licked his lips and tried to explain, "I really do, ah—I need to go—"

"At least half the people in this club should be doing something else right now," Sierra cooed at him. Her cheeks were flushed and her lips were swollen, and it would have been easy for Shaun to stay right where he was and do whatever she asked. She stroked his jaw with her fingertips, pressed her pert little breasts against his chest, and leaned in to whisper against his ear, "Just stay put and let us get you hard again so we can take turns riding you. I'll let you watch my sister lick your come out of me."

Shaun almost relented, but when he saw Lore turn away and disappear into the crowd, embarrassment and common sense finally won out against his libido.

"Shit," Shaun cursed as he disentangled himself from the twins and fumbled with his zipper. "I'm really sorry—really, really sorry. You have no idea how sorry I am. But I can't do this right now."

When Shaun pushed to his feet, the girls curled around each other on the couch and stared up at him with matching pouts. If the situation had been just a little bit different, he would have literally cut off his own foot for a chance to spend the night with them. But he wasn't so drunk that he didn't realize what a bad idea that would be, and he'd already fucked up more than enough for one night.

"Are you sure you don't want to stay?" Ivy asked him.

Shaun shook his head, which made the world spin around him and caused him to sway on his feet. Once he'd regained his balance, he said, "No— no, I'm not sure at all, but I've still gotta go. I'm really sorry."

The twins' expressions changed like someone had flipped a switch; they rolled their eyes and stood, then shoved past him. Ivy muttered something under her breath that sounded a lot like 'cock tease' and Sierra glared at him over her shoulder. Shaun watched them go with a wistful sigh, then rubbed both hands over his face in a vain attempt to sober up.

When he was feeling a little more steady on his feet, he set off in the direction Lore had gone. After fifteen minutes of searching the club and the street outside, he gave up. It was probably for the best that he couldn't find Lore anyway; Shaun was far too drunk to have a meaningful conversation.

Shaun staggered down the street to the public phone box. A short queue had formed, and he went to stand in line with his hands in his pockets and his eyes closed. To his embarrassment, he almost dozed off standing up until someone nudged him from behind and told him to, "keep the line moving, asshole." Shaun opened his eyes and muttered an apology before moving forward. When it was his turn, something made him pause and glance down the street at the building where the suspect had been watching from the rooftop.

Lore was standing on the front steps of the building with his hands in his pockets. It was impossible to see his expression from that distance, but he was looking directly at Shaun.

"Hey, moron, are you gonna just stand there all night? Get a fuckin' move on, will ya?"

"Sorry," Shaun mumbled again. As he stepped into the phone booth, he lifted a hand and waved.

Lore didn't wave back.

Sobriety hit Shaun like a cement block as soon as he logged out. For a few seconds, he lay there inside the cocoon of his tank, squinting at the glowing screen above him and trying to reorient himself. Then, he dragged both hands over his face, sighed, and muttered, "Shit."

Chapter Five

Shaun woke the next morning to the smell of smoke.

He leaped out of bed and dashed down the hallway, expecting to find his apartment engulfed in flames. What he found instead was even more alarming: the door to the balcony was open, and the wind was blowing the smoke from a nearby brush fire into the apartment.

Shaun closed the door and turned the deadbolt, then stood there with his heart hammering in his chest. The door had been locked just seven hours ago; he kept the doorknob locked at all times, and he checked it every night before going to bed. It was possible that he'd forgotten to turn the deadbolt and the wind had forced the door open, but something about that theory didn't sit well with him.

There was no one in the living room, but he hadn't checked the kitchen or the bathroom, and he'd bolted from the bedroom too quickly to take stock of his surroundings. Part of him felt foolish for even entertaining the thought—he lived on the fourth floor, and climbing up to his balcony without being seen would take serious skill—but he wasn't going to relax until he was sure he was alone in the apartment. The kitchen and bathroom were empty, so he headed down the hall toward the bedroom and stopped just outside the door to listen. All he could hear was the faint buzzing of his neighbor's alarm clock.

Shaun eased the bedroom door open and wished, not for the first time, that the department had issued him a gun. The room looked exactly as it always had, rumpled sheets and laundry pile and all, but that didn't stop him from checking under the bed and in the closet like a paranoid child. There was no one there.

"Jesus," Shaun muttered as he sat down onto the edge of his bed and rubbed both hands over his face. His heart was still racing, and he tried to coax it into slowing by taking deep breaths through his nose.

While he waited for the adrenaline to wear off, he let his gaze wander to the framed picture on his nightstand. The girl in the photograph stared back at him, mouth smiling but eyes solemn. Shaun wondered what it would have taken to make her laugh.

The sound of his cell phone vibrating on the nightstand startled him out of his thoughts. He reached over to grab it. There were two text messages waiting for him: one from Hudson ('new victim will give details later') and an anonymous message that contained nothing but a Simulnet address. Shaun groaned. He'd been so distracted by his panic that he'd almost forgotten what had happened the night before, but now he was wondering if he'd ever be able to look Lore in the eye again.

The investigation couldn't stop just because of his lackluster decision-making skills, though, so he pushed to his feet and went to make breakfast. While he waited for his coffee to finish brewing, he wandered into the living room to check the back door. It was locked. Shaun sighed and pressed his forehead against the glass, and stared out at the dirty stucco and peeling billboards of the San Fernando Valley. Smoke was billowing up from behind the hills to the north

Los Angeles was a creature unto its own. There wasn't a city on Earth that could match its glittering filth. It was a living, breathing paradox: proud and self-conscious, hateful and compassionate. Shaun loved and despised it for the same reasons he loved and despised himself, and sometimes when he was alone, with no one to protect or entertain, he wished the flames would come and swallow the city whole.

Brighton Hill was one of Simulnet's largest entertainment districts. The city was owned by a Fortune 500 development company that used it as a testing ground for new technology. Visitors were treated

to zero-g nightclubs, fully immersive movies, the most cutting-edge programs on the market. The buildings in Brighton Hill were sleek and curvy, like overgrown sports cars, and the streets were impossibly clean.

Shaun had always felt uneasy in Brighton Hill. Its artificial sterility reminded him that nothing he saw inside Simulnet was real.

As soon as he emerged from the public transport chamber—this time in the form of a white, cylindrical booth—Shaun's phone beeped. It was another text message, this time with a set of coordinates. Shaun heaved a sigh and plugged the numbers into his phone's GPS program.

The map on his screen led him to a large shopping mall in the south end of town. Shaun experienced a little twinge of doubt as he pushed through the mirrored front doors and weaved his way through the building's lower level. Vendor carts were scattered throughout the mall, selling everything from mobile phones to exotic pets. Shaun dodged a woman who was selling tickets to a fantasy-themed retreat ("Experience real magic! Let us augment your avatar with spell casting abilities and teach you the ways of sorcery!") and took an elevator up to the second floor where an androgynous holograph was pacing circles around a display model personal jet and explaining its features to no one in particular.

When Shaun finally reached his destination and found himself standing in the accessories section of a chain department store, he voiced his bewilderment aloud: "What the fuck?"

Lore was leaning against a glass display counter near the far wall, tapping his foot and looking out of place in his dusty blazer and tattered scarves. When he glanced in Shaun's direction, Shaun's confusion was replaced with a vague sense of dread. There was nothing accusatory in Lore's expression, but there was a new awareness in his eyes that hadn't been there before. Surely, they weren't going to talk about what had happened the night before; surely they were both grown-up enough to understand that some things shouldn't be discussed.

"So uh…" Shaun tucked his hands into his pockets. His fingers brushed the silver anchor Lore had given him, and he closed his hand around it as he moved closer and leaned his hip against the counter. When Lore glanced over at him, he offered Lore a lopsided grin. "I didn't know you were into designer handbags."

Lore raised an eyebrow at him.

"I mean, it's cool if that's your thing." Shaun shrugged. "I'm just not sure you'd make a good-looking woman. No offense or any-thing."

Lore stared at him, then looked away and pretended to study the wristwatches that were on display beneath the glass. "I'm not interested in dressing as a woman, but if I was, you'd hardly be in any position to judge me for it, considering your choice in partners last night."

"God damn it, I knew you were going to bring that up—wait, what?" Shaun eyed Lore. "What do you mean, my choice in partners?"

"The twins, they were both men."

"Uhm no, they weren't," Shaun insisted, despite a little twinge of doubt. Anything was possible inside Simulnet. "I got up close and personal with them, you know; I think I would've noticed if they'd been guys."

Lore shook his head. "They didn't look male, but they were."

"Look, I've made out with guys before, okay? Believe me, I can tell the difference." Shaun huffed and tried to ignore the embarrassed flush tickling the tips of his ears. He'd never exactly been secretive about his love life, but he hadn't intended to tell Lore that much about his sexual past—or anything about his sexual past, really. To deflect attention away from himself, he asked, "What put it in your head that they were guys, anyway?"

"They're traps, men who use female avatars to lure straight men into having sex with them." Lore sounded distracted, like he'd lost interest in the conversation. "Those two in particular are notorious in Okui. Of course, you had no way of knowing that."

"Yeah, thanks, that makes me feel much better." Shaun groaned and rubbed a hand over his face. "Fuck, were they really guys?"

Lore nodded.

"Fuck." Shaun sighed.

"If you're planning to have a sexual identity crisis, please wait until we've left the store."

Shaun rolled his eyes. "Thanks for the sympathy. And no, I'm not having a sexual identity crisis, I just feel a little... I don't know, creeped out I guess. Not—" he held up a finger "—because they were guys. It's just... I didn't know, y'know?"

"They presented you with a fantasy that looked and felt real."

"But they lied," Shaun countered. "It's not like they walked up to me and said, 'Hey, we know we look like super hot elves, but we're actually wrinkly old men in real life. Wanna fuck us anyway?'"

"Men and women lie to each other all the time for the sake of luring each other into bed."

Shaun wasn't deterred. "Lying about what you do for a living or whether or not you've had a boob job isn't the same as lying about your gender. I can't believe we're even having this argument. Are you seriously telling me you're okay with people doing that kind of shit?"

"No." Lore turned to look at Shaun. He scanned Shaun's face as if scrutinizing every little nuance of his expression, and Shaun fought the urge to turn away. "But if we're going to make any progress in this investigation, you need to forgo the notion that a person's appearance defines who they are."

Shaun opened his mouth to reply, but he was interrupted by the sound of someone clearing their throat. There was a pretty, Latina woman standing behind the counter, smiling at them. Once she had their attention, she said, "I'm sorry for interrupting, but I found the information you were looking for, Mister Reston."

"Wonderful," Lore replied with a smile so dazzling it could star in its own Vegas floor show.

The girl behind the counter beamed. "You're in luck; I found records of a purchase that was made using your girlfriend's user ID. Sarah came in three weeks ago to buy a piece of limited edition jewelry." She tapped a well-manicured fingernail against the counter. The glass seemed to fog over before displaying a set of thumbnail images. She touched one of them, which expanded to show a full-sized photograph of a silver cuff bracelet studded with purple gemstones. "This is our International Women's Day bracelet. Does this look like the one she lost?"

"That's the one," said Lore. "I don't suppose you've got any more?"

"Well, they were a limited run, even here in Simulnet, but I'd be happy to check and see if we have any more in stock."

"Please."

"It's so sweet of you to try and replace it for her. She's a very lucky woman." The salesgirl reached over to touch Lore's elbow, then disappeared off to parts unknown.

Meanwhile, Shaun turned to Lore and demanded, "What the hell was that about?"

"I spoke to some of the staff at Platinum last night while you were occupied."

"And?"

"One of the bouncers remembered seeing Ruby with a blonde woman who matches Sarah's description. They came into the club together on the night before Sarah died." Lore tapped his fingers against the glass while he spoke. "He said the blonde woman seemed out of place there, and that she and Ruby had an argument an hour or so after they arrived. Ruby left the club angry, but the other woman stayed."

"Did she leave with anyone?"

"He didn't see her leave."

"Okay, so we know Sarah and Ruby might have known each other," Shaun said. "What's with the bracelet?"

Lore was using both hands to tap on the counter now, as if he was typing on an invisible keyboard. "The bouncer noticed that Sarah was wearing one because he'd just bought one for his wife."

"I see," Shaun said, then nudged Lore's elbow and muttered, "You're ah... typing, I think."

Lore paused, then folded his arms atop the counter and leaned against it. After a moment, Shaun did the same thing. They were standing close enough to each other that their shoulders touched.

To Shaun's surprise, Lore didn't shy away from the contact.

"So," Shaun began.

Lore hummed.

"I'm sorry for going off on you yesterday—in the bar, you know, after the bomb and everything." Shaun glanced at Lore from the corner of his eye. "It would've been nice to know you had my back, though." He tried to keep the bitterness out of his voice, but he didn't quite succeed. After he'd logged off and had some time to think, he'd realized just how much danger he'd been in the night before. First there had been the car bombing, then chasing a murder suspect without backup, and finally being kidnapped. He'd survived the ordeal, of course, but that didn't mean he'd always be so lucky. "I don't suppose you'd be willing to give me your number so I can get in touch with you if I need to? The anonymous text messages are cute and all, but..."

Lore didn't reply; he took his phone out of his pocket and started pressing buttons.

Shaun watched, awed that anyone could be so dismissive over something so important. He was about to comment on Lore's lack of sympathy when his phone vibrated in his pocket. He hoped it would be a message from Hudson, but it turned out to be a blank text message from an unfamiliar number. Shaun stared at his phone, then looked up at Lore. "Are you serious? All I had to do was ask?"

"More or less."

"You're really fucking confusing, you know that? Really, really confusing."

"I know," Lore said, and went back to tapping his fingers against the glass.

Fifteen minutes later, they left the mall with a hundred dollar bracelet and solid evidence that Sarah was the blonde woman who'd been seen with Ruby. Once they were outside, Lore handed the wrapped box to Shaun.

"What am I supposed to do with this?" Shaun tried to hand the box back to Lore.

Lore waved him off.

"Fine." Shaun sighed. He was starting to learn that there was no point in trying to make Lore do anything he didn't want to do. Besides, he figured the bracelet might come in handy the next time he needed to apologize to Kim for something. "Can we at least stop at a mailbox so I can mail it to my apartment? I'd rather not lug it around for the rest of the day."

"If Sarah and Ruby were friends, Ruby may have visited Oubliette as well."

"Mailbox?"

Lore was staring off into space and tugging absently at the frayed edge of one of his scarves. "The club's logs would contain her user ID, which could be used to find her real name."

"Can we have one conversation at a time, please?" Shaun pleaded.

Lore's faraway expression sharpened to one of annoyance. "You don't need my permission to mail something."

"I wasn't asking—never mind." Shaun shook his head, then turned on his heel and walked away without looking back to see if Lore was keeping up. There was a mailbox three blocks down. Shaun dumped the box containing the bracelet inside, entered the address of his apartment, and sent the bracelet on its way. When he was done, he turned around and promptly tried to crawl backward out of his skin. Lore standing right behind him. "Jesus, man, would you stop that? You're gonna give me a fucking stroke."

"Being startled doesn't induce strokes." Lore's expression said, quite plainly, that he couldn't understand how anyone could be so stupid and yet still function as a human being.

"It's a figure of—you know what? Never mind. Again. Let's just go to Oubliette."

Lore nodded, then turned and strode away, leaving Shaun to catch up as usual.

Ruby wasn't a regular at Oubliette. There was no mention of her in the club's logs, and no one they spoke to remembered seeing her there. Shaun and Lore stuck around long enough to pretend they were interested in the flogging demonstration, then left again.

"Well, that was a bust." Shaun sighed as they stepped out into the mid-afternoon sunlight. He was tired and frustrated, and he had no idea where to go next. "So what now?"

"Have you heard from Hudson?" Lore asked.

Shaun shook his head. "No, I was trying to decide whether or not I should send her another text. She said she'd get in touch when she had more info, though, so I figured I should leave her alone until then."

Lore nodded, and shielded his eyes against the sunlight as he looked up at the sky.

"Isn't there any other way of getting a hold of Ruby's user ID?" Shaun asked. "I mean, Platinum should have it if she was working there, right?"

"She was paid cash."

"Of course." Shaun sighed again and shoved his hands into his pockets. "And I guess you didn't get anything else out of her co-workers? No addresses or anything?"

"No, none of them know her in real life, and she never mentioned owning any Simulnet property."

"Fuck. This is like trying to track down a ghost."

"Indeed."

Shaun resisted the temptation to point out that Lore wasn't much better, and just tipped his head back and closed his eyes, enjoying the warmth of the simulated sunlight on his face. He knew there was really no such thing as a cold trail, that it was just a matter of knowing where to start looking again, but that didn't make him feel much better. He was used to being able to find the answers, but this wasn't a problem he could run through a search engine. After a few minutes of pondering and coming up with very little in the way of ideas, he opened his eyes and said, "Well, I guess maybe we could duck into a couple of the places around Platinum? I mean, if she was a regular at the ramen shop, maybe she was a regular at some of the other restaurants and stuff too."

They made their way toward the club, stopping here and there to ask about Ruby. Shaun knew that eventually, people were going to figure out that he and Lore weren't who they claimed to be, and when that happened, they would probably end up on the receiving end of some questioning themselves. For now, though, no one seemed suspicious. Unfortunately, they weren't very helpful, either. Ruby was a regular at some of the local restaurants and convenience stores, but no one seemed to know how to find her. For a social butterfly, Ruby was surprisingly secretive.

Eventually, after almost four hours of talking to people, Shaun couldn't take the frustration anymore. He stopped and plopped down on the curb with his head in his hands. After a few minutes, Lore sat down beside him.

"I don't understand," Shaun said without looking up, "how so many people knew her, and not a single fucking one of them knows where she might be."

Lore was silent except for the faint tapping of his toe against the concrete.

"No user ID, no last name, no address..." Shaun tugged his fingers through his hair. "I can't believe that even her fucking employer has no info on her. I mean, what kind of business owner doesn't keep employee records? It fucking figures she'd be working under the table."

Lore made a vague humming sound that Shaun decided to take as acknowledgment.

"My fucking life," said Shaun, "is turning into a fucking nightmare."

This investigation was turning out to be one of the hardest things he'd ever done, and he was starting to worry that maybe he wasn't cut out for this line of work after all. The anxiety that came with that thought was almost bad enough to make him want to give up altogether. Life was too short to keep doing something at which he was destined to fail.

Shaun finally lifted his head and stared across the street. Two white paper lanterns swayed in the breeze outside the entrance of a massage parlor. "God, what I wouldn't give for a drink and a shoulder rub right now."

A long silence passed before Lore pushed to his feet without warning and shoved his hands into his pockets. He stood there for a moment, then looked back over his shoulder at Shaun. "Are you coming?"

"Coming where?" Shaun threw his hands into the air in frustration. "There's nowhere else to look, Lore. We've been looking all damn day and we haven't found a single fucking thing."

Lore sighed and inclined his head toward the other side of the street.

"What?" Shaun frowned and shook his head. Then it dawned on him, and his eyes widened. "Wait, are you suggesting what I think you're suggesting?"

"Probably."

Shaun was bemused. "If I go over there with you, you're not gonna complain later about me being irresponsible, are you?"

"What's irresponsible is to languish here in your own self-doubt and self-pity, running yourself in exhausting mental circles that will do nothing but prevent you from thinking clearly when the situation calls for it. This will take an hour, which is an hour that you would probably otherwise spend sitting here, feeling sorry for yourself. Now, stand up and follow me before I change my mind and leave you to your one-man tragedy act."

By the time Lore was finished speaking, Shaun's eyes were as wide as saucers.

"Stop staring," Lore said.

Shaun stared up at him, then offered a weak grin. "You were sitting here this whole time, coming up with that speech, weren't you?"

If Lore had been the type of person to roll his eyes, Shaun had no doubt he would have.

❧

The interior of the massage parlor looked nothing like Shaun expected. The reception area was clean and bright, and the front desk was staffed with two pretty girls in neatly pressed uniforms. Shaun was disappointed.

"This place reminds me of the spa my ex-girlfriend used to drag me to," Shaun muttered to Lore while they waited. "Basically, I'd get a massage and then hang around for three hours while she blew a thousand bucks to take a mud bath. Mind you, this was the same chick who got pissed off at me for splashing around in puddles when it rained."

He might have imagined it, but Shaun thought he saw the corners of Lore's lips twitch.

Eventually, they were led to a small room with two massage tables and instructed to undress. The attendant left before Shaun could protest, and as soon as the door was closed, Lore began unwinding the scarves from around his neck. Shaun was surprised that Lore would not only be agreeable to the idea of undressing in front of him, but that he'd go about it with such disturbing nonchalance.

Shaun wasn't nearly as mature about the situation. "Wait, wait, wait!"

Lore paused and gave him a look. "What?"

"I just..." Shaun replied. "You know."

The expression on Lore's face said that he didn't, actually, and that he probably didn't care to either.

Shaun shifted his weight from one foot to the other and tried to come up with a protest that wouldn't make him sound childish or homophobic. When he couldn't think of anything, he sighed and flapped his hand dismissively. "Never mind."

The truth was, Shaun didn't know why he felt so awkward. He'd always been comfortable with his body, and he was usually comfortable with looking at other people's, but the fact that it was

Lore made him feel inexplicably shy. Still, he wasn't going to embarrass himself by admitting his discomfort out loud, so he just took a deep breath and tugged his shirt up over his head.

Shaun noticed from the corner of his eye that Lore had started undressing again, and to his credit, he managed to hold out for almost thirty seconds before sneaking a peak. Seeing Lore's bare neck for the first time shouldn't have felt so voyeuristic, yet as he eyed the tattoo that covered the side of Lore's neck and disappeared beneath the collar of his shirt, Shaun felt the sudden need to blush. Thankfully, Lore didn't seem to notice.

When Lore started to unbutton his shirt, Shaun looked away and didn't turn around again until they were both naked except for the towels around their waists. To Shaun's surprise, half of Lore's body was covered in tattoos. A black dragon wrapped up over his shoulder, down his back, and around his ribcage on the opposite side, and the kanji Shaun had glimpsed when they'd first met ran all the way up his forearm. They were beautiful tattoos, and Shaun wondered why Lore went to so much trouble to hide them.

"Staring."

"Sorry!" Shaun offered Lore a bashful grin, then climbed onto one of the tables and settled on his stomach with his cheek resting on his folded arms. Lore took the same pose on the other table and turned his head so that he and Shaun were looking at each other.

"D'you like my towel?" Shaun asked. "Does it make my butt look big?"

"Yes."

Shaun let out a surprised laugh—he hadn't expected Lore to respond to the joke—then sobered a bit and asked, "Do you think we'll find her in time? Ruby, I mean."

"I don't know."

Shaun nodded. Most people would have added something to their reply to make him feel better, even if it was just, 'I hope so.' Lore wasn't most people, though, and the fact that he hadn't offered any bullshit reassurance was comforting. It meant that one of them, at least, was able to view the situation objectively, without clouding the facts with false hope. Still, Shaun shouldn't help but to wonder what had happened to make Lore so detached from his emotions.

"You know," Shaun said, "I still don't know anything about you. I know Hudson trusts you, but I don't know why, and I get that you're a hacker, but I don't know how you got started. It'd be nice to know something else, even if it's something you don't think is important."

Lore was quiet for a moment, as if he didn't plan to answer, but then he frowned and said, "I don't like eggplant."

The look on his face made it seem like he was divulging the secrets of the universe. Shaun almost laughed, but he knew that would probably damage the fragile bond he was trying to build between them, so he settled for a grin and replied, "I don't like eggplants either. Actually, I don't think I trust people who do like eggplants."

Lore stared at him for a moment before offering him a faint, blink-and-you'll-miss-it smile.

Meanwhile, Shaun's stomach flipped in a way it hadn't done since the first time he'd seen his kindergarten sweetheart, Marcie Green.

Like an act of divine intervention, their massage therapists chose that moment to enter the room. Shaun was relieved to have an excuse to stay quiet while analyzing his reaction to seeing Lore smile at him. He turned his head away and buried his face in his arms as one of the girls began kneading his shoulders.

For the first few minutes of the massage, Shaun's mind was a state of chaos. Thoughts came to him in fits and starts, jerking him from one idea to the next so rapidly it made him want to press his hands over his ears as if that would somehow quiet his mind. Eventually, though, everything began to slow down as his muscles gradually relaxed and his breathing evened out. By the time his massage therapist's hands made their way to his lower back, Shaun was a dead weight on the table and his mind had begun to drift, first to the investigation, then to his sister, and finally to Lore.

Shaun had never met someone as unreadable as Lore, and he

wondered if that was why he was so fascinated. They'd been working together for three days, and he still hadn't figured out where Lore's accent was from, what he actually did for a living, or even what his real name was. Lore was a complete enigma—a frustrating, stubborn enigma—and yet, as irritating as that was, it just made Shaun want to get to know him even more.

By the time his massage therapist asked him to roll over, Shaun was so relaxed he could barely make his muscles move. He eventually managed to flop over onto his back, though, and repositioned the towel around his hips. A few minutes later, he heard Lore turn over as well, and Shaun glanced at the other table without thinking.

Lore was watching him. The intensity of his gaze was startling.

Shaun's heart was doing somersaults in his chest, and he was relieved when Lore finally broke eye contact. The reprieve didn't last for very long, though, because instead of looking away, Lore let his gaze wander down Shaun's body. Shaun tensed. The way Lore was looking at him was so uncharacteristically forward that he wondered if Lore even realized what he was doing. Lore was examining him, memorizing him. It made Shaun want to flee the room, but he didn't; he took a deep breath and stayed where he was, although he couldn't bring himself to watch Lore's face anymore. He looked away, trying to find something else to stare at, and his gaze darted to Lore's crotch.

Lore was hard. His erection was covered by the towel, but he was still noticeably, unmistakably hard.

The realization tore through Shaun like lightning. He had no idea whether or not Lore's arousal had anything to do with him, but it didn't matter because his body reacted all the same: his toes curled, and his cock twitched, and the muscles in his thighs tensed. He couldn't remember the last time he'd gotten this turned on this quickly.

To his eternal shame, Lore seemed to notice his reaction. His gazed settled on Shaun's face again and stayed there, watching him as if he could see inside Shaun's mind and was busy picking apart every single one of his secrets. Shaun opened his mouth to remind Lore of the 'no staring' rule, but all he could manage was a weak-sounding, "I uhm—"

The two massage therapists carried on without comment.

Shaun closed his eyes and lay there in silence, concentrating on the sound of his own breathing and trying to ignore his hardening cock. Eventually, though, curiosity triumphed over self-preservation, and he opened his eyes again.

Lore was still watching him, but there was nothing clinical about it. His lips were parted and his lashes were lowered, and he was scanning Shaun's face; his gaze flitted here and there, back and forth between Shaun's eyes, then to his mouth. They were four feet away from each other, but Lore may as well have been dragging his fingernails down Shaun's stomach for the way Shaun's body was reacting to him.

The minutes seemed to crawl by. The tension between them grew with each second that passed, until the air in the room felt heavy with it. Shaun's entire body was tingling, and his cock was embarrassingly hard, and he was fighting the urge to reach over and grab at Lore. He was weighing his options—flee the room before he could embarrass himself, or cut the massage session short and risk shaming himself by making a serious pass at Lore—when the unbearable silence was broken by the sound of his phone ringing.

"That's my phone!" Shaun exclaimed as he sat bolt upright, startling his massage therapist so badly that she leaped away from him. He almost lost his towel in his haste to scramble off the table and get to his phone. After fumbling with his jeans for a second, he managed to retrieve his phone from the pocket. He didn't bother to check the caller ID before answering. "Hello?"

"I need to talk to you." Hudson's voice sounded gruffer than usual, and Shaun promptly forgot all about the sexual tension in the room. "Meet me at your apartment in ten."

Shaun cradled his phone between his shoulder and his cheek as he tugged on his pants. "Glad you called, 'cause I need to talk to you too. We're trying to find a girl who might have—"

"Not over the phone."

"Oh, right, sorry," Shaun said. "Lemme just get my avatar back to my apartment here and log out."

They hung up without saying good-bye. Shaun held his phone between his teeth while he buttoned and zipped his jeans, then shoved it into his pocket. After grabbing his shirt off the floor, he turned to Lore, the awkwardness between them momentarily forgotten, and said, "Sorry, I've gotta run. Hudson needs to see me."

"I gathered." Lore sat up and swung his legs over the edge of the table.

"I'll text you as soon as I know what's up," Shaun promised. "If you find anything in the meantime, let me know?"

Lore nodded.

Shaun hurried out of the room, then paused before turning and poking his head back inside. Lore had already slid off the table, and he stood there eying Shaun while holding the towel closed around his waist. Shaun offered him a hesitant smile and gestured to the room in general. "Thanks, by the way. Y'know, for all this. It helped."

Lore didn't smile, exactly, but his expression softened and he replied, "You're welcome."

Chapter Six

Shaun woke to the sound of someone knocking on his apartment door. He scrambled out the tank, dripping float solution all over the carpet, and grabbed the terrycloth robe he'd draped over the top of the tank. His knees felt weak, and he leaned against the side of the tank to steady himself. The knocking continued and he called out, "I hear you! I'm coming, just gimme a second."

Once he felt like he could walk without falling over, he went to answer the door. Hudson looked as put-together as usual in her crisp white shirt and neatly pressed trousers, but she also looked exhausted. There were dark circles under her eyes and her shoulders were slumped. Shaun ushered her into the apartment, then shut the door behind her and followed her into the living room.

"That doesn't exist," Hudson said as she dropped a manila folder on the coffee table. Then she sank down into an armchair, closed her eyes, and rubbed her temples with her fingertips. "If you've got coffee and whiskey to put in it, I'll personally see to it that you get a raise after all this shit is over."

"Coming right up," Shaun replied. He went into the kitchen and came back ten minutes later with a cup of coffee in each hand and a bottle of whiskey tucked under his arm.

Hudson had the folder open on the table, and she was leaning over it. When Shaun came into the room, she looked up and accepted the cup of coffee he handed her. "You're a fucking saint, Mason."

Shaun plopped down on the couch and reached for the folder. Clipped to the inside cover was a coroner's photo of a middle-aged man with a dark hair and a long beard. He looked peaceful. Shaun had to force himself to look at it

"James Gillard," Hudson said. "He died in a cybercafe in Santa

Monica around the same time as the explosion you reported. Lore lifted his user ID from the car that was bombed."

"Wait, Lore picked up an ID from the car? He never mentioned anything about an ID." Shaun frowned. "Besides, he wasn't even there when the explosion happened; he was in the bar the whole time."

Hudson pressed her lips together in a thin line. "I don't give a shit if he was in Antarctica when it happened. All that matters is that he made the match."

The fact that Lore hadn't told him any of this made Shaun's jaw tighten, but he kept quiet and turned his attention back to the report. "This says he died of a seizure?"

"With no history of epilepsy."

"Same as the others, then." Shaun sighed and pushed the folder away, then rubbed the heels of his palms against his eyes and said, "I think I saw the killer."

Hudson paused with her coffee mug lifted halfway to her lips. "Excuse me?"

"On a rooftop after the explosion. He was watching to see what would happen, I think. I chased him, but I—he got away."

"He got away," Hudson repeated. Her eyes were narrowed and the wrinkles between her eyebrows deepened.

Shaun could tell she suspected something, but if he told her about the kidnapping, he'd have to tell her about Katou, and he wasn't about to admit that he'd accepted money from a third party.

Thankfully, Hudson didn't push for details about how the suspect had gotten away. Instead, she asked, "Do you remember what his avatar looked like?"

Shaun shook his head. "No, that's the weirdest thing about him: I've gone over it in my head a few times, and I just can't remember what he looks like. I mean he was standing this close to me at one point, and I still can't tell you anything about him except that he was white and he was wearing a hooded sweatshirt."

"Don't beat yourself up about it too much, kiddo. It's not like you've got a ton of fieldwork experience, and hell, even some of my most experienced detectives forget the details sometimes. Adrenaline can make you—"

"No," Shaun interrupted. "No, it wasn't the adrenaline. There was something—I don't know, something wrong with the avatar he was using. It was like looking at fifty different people all at once. I can't explain it."

"Interesting," Hudson replied thoughtfully. "And you said Lore wasn't with you at the time?"

"Well, I figured he was in the bar the whole time, but I guess he might have been checking out the car. But no, he wasn't with me when I was chasing the guy."

"So much for secondary witnesses," Hudson said as she put her cup down and pushed to her feet.

"Hey, uhm, I have a question." Shaun stood to follow Hudson to the door. "Who is Lore? I mean, what does he do? Getting him to talk about himself is impossible. I only just got him to tell me he hates eggplant."

Hudson gave him a wry smile. "All I can tell you is that I trust him, Mason. I wouldn't have introduced you to him if I didn't. You'll have to figure the rest out on your own."

Shaun saw Hudson out, then shuffled back into the living room, rubbing his eyes. It occurred to him that he'd neither eaten nor used the bathroom yet that day, so he ambled down the hallway toward his bedroom and flipped on the light switch in the master bath. The first thing he saw was the knife.

A butcher knife with a blade the length of his forearm had been taken out of the block in his kitchen and put on the counter beside the bathroom sink. There was no note and no trace of the person who'd left it, but the knife itself was a clear enough message on his own.

Shaun checked the rest of the apartment, went back into the living room, and called Hudson.

❧

Palace Inn didn't even try to live up to its name. It was a flea motel in North Hollywood with pink stucco walls and carpets that smelled like they'd been rescued from a frat house. Shaun's room was on the fourth floor, with a view of an alleyway through the greasy windows. It didn't matter. The sheets were clean enough, the room had a Simulnet hook-up, and it was safer than Shaun's apartment at the moment.

"Mason, I can get you a nicer place," Hudson said as she surveyed the room with obvious skepticism.

Shaun waved her off. "It's not a big deal. It's not like I'm moving in permanently or anything."

"At least let me get you some guard detail," Hudson insisted. "No one needs to know you're working the case. All they need to know is that someone broke into your apartment and threatened you. We take care of our own, you know."

"You don't think anyone's going to start asking why I was targeted?" Shaun pointed out. He finished connecting his tank to the Simulnet jack, then straightened and rubbed his hands on the fronts of his jeans. He flashed Hudson a grin, but even he could tell it was weak.

Hudson's lips were pressed together in a thin line. She didn't even need to say anything to make her annoyance palpable. Shaun couldn't decide whether it was a shame or a tragedy that she'd never had kids.

"Look, there are flood lights right out there—" he jerked his thumb toward the window facing the alleyway "—and the door has four locks on it. I'll be okay, I promise."

Hudson finally conceded, though she didn't look happy about it, and cast one last, disapproving glare over her shoulder when Shaun showed her out. As soon as she was gone, Shaun sighed and bolted the door behind her, then leaned back against it with a heavy sigh. Things were starting to get a little too realistic for his liking.

❧

Shaun sent Lore six text messages in the next three hours, but he didn't receive a reply to any of them. He wondered if that meant Lore actually slept sometimes, or if Lore was purposely avoiding him.

Shaun wandered the nighttime streets of Okui with his hands in his pockets, trying to calm his racing mind and hoping that, by some miracle, he'd have an epiphany that would put him back on the right trail. Without realizing it, he made his way to Platinum—or more specifically, the sidewalk across the street from Platinum. All evidence of the car bomb had been neatly cleaned away, but Shaun's mind flashed back to what it had looked like in the direct aftermath, with the broken glass and twisted metal, and the sight of a blackened, oozing body in the driver's seat. Shaun closed his eyes and tried to block the memory, but it didn't work. Someone had gone to a lot of trouble to make the explosion look as realistic as possible, and it had stuck with Shaun. It would always stick with him.

"Katou's men got it cleaned up in a matter of minutes."

Shaun opened his eyes and spun around, startled, to find Blake standing a few feet behind him. Blake's white-blond hair was loose around his shoulders, and he was wearing a plain black coat and dark-colored trousers. He tipped his head to one side and offered Shaun a lazy half-smile. "I didn't mean to startle you."

"It's fine. Don't worry about it. My part—uhm, my friend does it to me all the time."

"Speaking of your friend..." Blake trailed off and cast a meaningful glance around, as if looking for Lore.

Shaun shrugged. "Probably sleeping. Hell if I know." The way Blake was looking at him was starting to make him uncomfortable, as if Blake knew something he shouldn't and was amused by it. Shaun wondered if word had finally spread around Okui that he and Lore had been snooping. It was bound to happen eventually, no matter how careful they'd been.

"Would you like to take a walk with me?" Blake asked.

Shaun glanced down at the empty pavement where the burning car had been just the day before. He couldn't get the image of the body out of his head.

"Let me rephrase: it would be in your best interests to take a walk with me," Blake insisted, and then added, very softly, "Shaun."

Every part of Shaun's body seemed to seize up at once, and for a second, he couldn't even draw a deep enough breath to speak. Then, in barely more than a whisper, he asked, "How do you know my name?"

"I promise to tell you everything, but not here," Blake murmured. The purr was gone from his tone, and his expression was serious. "I know I'm asking you for a leap of faith, but I need for you to follow me. Please."

Shaun hesitated. He knew it was probably a bad idea, but he desperately hoped that whatever Blake had to tell him could put him and Lore back on the right path. After a few seconds of silence, he put his hand in his pocket to double-check that he had his phone. His fingers encountered the anchor Lore had given him, and the feeling of the warm metal under his fingertips was oddly comforting.

"Shall we?" Blake prompted.

Shaun nodded.

Blake made a pleased sound and gestured for Shaun to follow him as he turned and led the way through the darkened city streets.

Chapter Seven

The ramen shop was dark when they arrived. Blake led the way inside, but Shaun hesitated in the doorway, holding the beads aside and peering into the restaurant. He half expected men with guns to jump out and grab him at any second.

Blake paused and turned to look back at him. "You can pat me down if you like," he drawled, but the smile on his face looked forced. "Just to make sure there are no weapons, of course."

Shaun felt a ridiculous little twitch of interest, but he shook his head.

Blake chuckled. "No? What a pity."

After a few more seconds of hesitating in the doorway, Shaun followed Blake into the restaurant and toward the back room. His pulse was racing and his palms were sweating, and he felt woefully unprepared to face whatever was on the other side of that door. Just a week ago, he would have gone without batting an eyelash, but after everything that had happened, he was actually afraid of walking into something completely unknown.

Blake paused at the door to the back room and turned to look at Shaun with such a serious expression on his face that he almost looked like a different person. In fact, there was something vaguely familiar about him when he wasn't smirking and purring, Shaun thought, though he couldn't put his finger on what it was or who Blake reminded him of. "Before I let you in, I need to know that what happens behind this door stays behind this door. Of course I expect you to share the information with Lore, but it's best for all parties involved if it doesn't go any further than that."

"Sure, no problem." Shaun tried to sound composed, but his voice came out strained.

Blake nodded and opened the door, then ushered Shaun inside. The back room, as it turned out, was a tiny living space, barely larger than Shaun's living room. There was a small futon against one wall, a large television against the other, and a beaded, floor-to-ceiling curtain that acted as a room divider. Shaun could see the silhouette of someone sitting on a bed on the other side of the curtain.

"Go in," Blake murmured as he pushed the curtain aside and gave Shaun a gentle push into the makeshift bedroom. The beads clattered shut behind him, but Shaun hardly noticed because he was too busy staring down at the woman huddled on the bed.

"Ruby?"

Ruby looked terrible. Her short, blue hair was in disarray, and she had her knees drawn up to her chest with her arms wrapped around them. She was petite anyway, but the way she was curled in on herself made her seem even smaller. There was a wary look in her eyes when she glanced up at Shaun and asked, "Where's Lore?"

Shaun was taken aback. "You know Lore?"

"I'm not talking to you unless he's here. Please don't take it personally." Ruby's voice was quiet, but firm.

"I don't know where Lore is right now," Shaun admitted. "But look, I promise that anything you tell me—"

"Sorry, but no," Ruby interrupted. Her gaze was clear and unwavering, but there was a haunted look about her that hadn't been there in the photo Shaun had seen. He wondered how anyone could look so strong and so fragile at the same time.

"All right," Shaun conceded. "All right, I'll try to find Lore."

Ruby nodded and uncurled one of her slender arms from around her knees. She reached over to open the nightstand drawer, and hunted around inside it until she came up with a piece of paper and a pen. She scribbled a Simulnet address on the slip of paper and handed it to Shaun. "Give this to Lore, please. He'll know what to do with it."

Shaun took the paper and glanced at it, then folded it and tucked it into his pocket. Then, sensing an opportunity to dig out another scrap of information about Lore, he asked, "Will you at least tell me how you and Lore know each other?"

"Lore doesn't know me, not yet." Ruby lowered her chin to her knees and stared at the far wall.

Shaun waited, hoping she would elaborate, but Ruby remained silent until Blake pushed the beaded curtain aside and gestured for Shaun to come with him. "I'll see you out."

"But what about her? Will she be okay?" Shaun asked as the curtain fell shut behind him. He glanced over his shoulder at Ruby's huddled silhouette.

"Yes," Blake replied as he took Shaun by the elbow and led him out of the room.

Neither of them spoke a word until they were outside and Blake was locking the door of the restaurant behind them. Shaun stuffed his hands into his pockets and rocked back and forth on his heels a few times. "If you knew where she was, why didn't you tell me when I was here for lunch?"

"Darling, although you positively exude good intentions, I wasn't willing to potentially endanger a good friend before properly doing my research," Blake replied. Once he was finished closing up, he slipped one hand into the pocket of his coat and wrapped the other around Shaun's arm. His grip wasn't forceful or controlling, just companionable. He flashed Shaun a smile and said, "Now then, that's the last we'll speak of her for the time being. Let's talk about something more interesting, shall we?"

Shaun got the hint: Blake didn't want to talk about Ruby where passer-by could overhear. He nodded his assent and asked, "Well, what can you tell me?"

"Oh, lots of things," Blake replied airily, then cast a sly glance at Shaun from the corner of his eye. It was a little alarming, actually, how effortlessly he could switch between seriousness and flirtation. "A drink might loosen my tongue a little."

"Hold on," Shaun muttered, as he dug his phone out of his pocket and sent another text message to Lore: 'found a breadcrumb. need to talk 2 u. txt me when u wake up.' Once he'd sent the message, he tucked his phone away and explained. "Sorry, just needed to check in with my partner."

"There's that word again," Blake said with a teasing smile. "Don't you mean 'friend'?"

"Whatever." Shaun shrugged, and wondered why he felt like blushing. "So uh, how about that drink?"

Fifteen minutes later, they were tucked away in the back corner of a rundown bar. Shaun wasn't sure where they were in relation to Oubliette or Platinum, but at the moment, he didn't care. Blake was being charming and informative, and had bought him a drink that tasted vaguely of cinnamon.

"So you guys have been friends for awhile, then?" Shaun asked as he swirled his drink around in his glass.

"For six blissful years," Blake drawled. "I met her when I was a bartender at Platinum. It was an absolutely wretched job, which is why I quit shortly after I was hired. Ruby brought a little spot of happiness to my nights there, though."

"Why'd you hate it so much?"

Blake waved his hand dismissively. "Oh, you know, the usual problems I suspect any bartender has: rowdy patrons and bad tips. Of course, Platinum being the sort of place it is, I was also forced to deal with grabby drunks. I'll grant you that Kim Lee isn't exactly refined, but at least it's mine to manage as I please."

"Oh, I didn't realize you owned it. Do you live there, too? When you're logged in, I mean." Shaun slouched in his seat so that his knee bumped Blake's underneath the table. It had been awhile since he'd seriously flirted with another man—at least intentionally—but Blake was attractive and obviously interested, and even though it might end up being a very bad idea later, Shaun was starting to think it might be worth it.

"I live everywhere, darling," Blake replied with a mischievous little smile. He slipped a hand underneath the table and let it rest on Shaun's leg, stroking the inseam of Shaun's jeans with his thumb. "I'd be happy to take you on a tour of my properties, if you're interested."

The warmth of Blake's hand seemed to travel up Shaun's thigh to his groin, and he shifted a little as his cock took notice of the physical contact. Before he could reply, though, his phone buzzed in his pocket and he automatically reached for it, hoping it might be Lore. When he saw that it was a text message from Kim, he frowned.

"Lore?" Blake looked amused. "Feel free to invite him here, though I hope he's not the jealous type. I've made too much progress to want to stop flirting with you now."

"No, it's not him," Shaun muttered. He paused to read the text message ('You lied to me you dick. Call me asap.') then sighed and rubbed his eyes.

"What is it, love?" Blake asked, his forehead creased with concern.

"Nothing, it's fine, it's just my sister," Shaun replied as he grudgingly pushed to his feet. "I need to call her and do some damage control, though. Thanks for the drinks."

Blake waved his hand dismissively, then smiled up at Shaun and said, "Believe me when I say it was my pleasure."

Shaun offered him a wink and a grin, then turned to leave the bar. When he reached the door, though, he paused and looked over his shoulder. Blake was staring off into the distance and toying with his drink, and he looked nothing like anyone Shaun could remember meeting before, yet there was still something so familiar about him it gave Shaun chills.

Kim answered on the second ring, and in lieu of greeting, she snapped, "You lied to me."

"About what?" Shaun asked. He tried to keep his tone neutral, but Kim had always had a way of riling him up.

"You're not on a project."

Shaun glanced both ways before darting across the street from the bar. There was a public transport chamber at the end of the block, and he headed toward it. "What do you mean I'm not on a project?"

"Don't play stupid with me. I tried calling you at work and your boss told me you're on vacation, and I know you're not home because I tried calling you there too. So where the fuck are you?"

Shaun resisted the urge to curse under his breath. He hadn't counted on Kim trying to call him at work since she usually just rang him on his mobile. "Listen, Kim, it's a long story, okay?"

"I've got all day," Kim replied tersely.

Shaun stopped next to the transport chamber, sighed, and rubbed his forehead. On one hand, he knew he could trust Kim to keep her mouth shut, but on the other, he'd made a promise to Hudson. Finally, he settled for telling her a half truth. "Okay, look, I didn't lie, all right? I really am working an investigation. It's just— well, it's not really legal. It's on Simulnet, and technically, the LAPD doesn't have jurisdiction, so I'm not really supposed to be poking around."

"Uh-huh." Kim didn't sound convinced. "And is there any particular reason why you decided to go all maverick?"

"I—" Shaun hesitated and chewed on his bottom lip, then lowered his voice and said, "You know all those accidents that have been happening? People dying in their tanks?"

"Yeah," Kim replied slowly. Judging from the tone of her voice, Shaun had piqued her interest. "I remember you telling me you thought there was something weird about them. Is that what this is about? Did you find something out?"

"You could say that, yeah," Shaun muttered as he glanced around to make sure there was no one nearby who could overhear him. "Look, I can't give you the details right now. I shouldn't even have told you what I'm doing, so you've gotta promise me you'll keep it quiet."

Kim huffed. "Who the hell would I tell?"

"I mean it, Kim," Shaun said. "If anyone found out about this, losing my job would be the least of my worries."

"Shaun, chill out. I'm not five; I'm not going to tattle. You still haven't told me where you are, though."

"A hotel. The line at my house has been down for a couple of days, and I didn't want to wait for the repair guy to come." Shaun hated lying to Kim, but he knew that if he told her about the break-in, she'd be on the first plane back from France to try and take care of him.

Thankfully, Kim seemed to buy the excuse, because all she said was, "Fine. Just—god, you're such an idiot sometimes. Just promise you'll be careful, okay? I'm not visiting you in jail if you fuck this up."

"Yeah," Shaun muttered. "Yeah, I promise."

Chapter Eight

Lore didn't reply to Shaun's text messages until nearly five hours later, and when he did, it was with nothing more than a Simulnet address. Shaun had taken the radio silence as an opportunity to have a nap, and he was awakened by the feeling of his mobile phone vibrating underneath his pillow. It took him a few seconds to figure out whether he was in the real world or still logged in to Simulnet, and then another few to remember why he wasn't in his own bedroom. Once he'd oriented himself, he picked up his phone and scowled at the message. He was exhausted and in no mood to play nice, so he replied with, 'where the hell have u been?'

Predictably, he didn't get a response.

Shaun showered and ducked out for a quick breakfast at the cafe around the corner. The air was heavy with smoke from the fires, but he sat outside anyway, eating and watching the tourists flock back and forth across the boulevard. He'd been enthralled by Hollywood once upon a time, half in love with its blinking neon. Now when he looked at it, all he could see was dirty cement and overfilled garbage cans. The neighborhood felt tired and faded, a withered old magician standing on a street corner in a tattered tuxedo. Shaun was starting to understand why some people lost years of their lives to Simulnet; the real world could never measure up.

Back at the hotel, he closed the curtains and locked the door, then disrobed and climbed into his tank. Fifteen minutes later, he was emerging from a block of white marble and onto an island no larger than his living room. The miniscule landmass was covered in spongy green moss and surrounded by a vast ocean that stretched out, uninterrupted, in every direction. The water reflected the slate blue sky, and it was so still it looked like glass.

Shaun stood there, transfixed by the scenery, until he was shaken back to reality by a deep, echoing rumble. At first, it sounded like distant thunder, but when the ground began to shake, he stumbled backward and flattened himself against the side of the marble chamber. All around him, the sea rippled and shimmered, and bubbled as if some gargantuan beast was rising from its depths.

The top of the gate emerged first, with water running in rivulets down its black marble frame as it eased itself into place. Then came the gate itself: a tangle of impossible shapes—Shaun recognized a Penrose triangle and a Necker cube—wrought in black iron. The gate was easily a hundred feet wide and twice that in height, and Shaun stared up at it with his neck craned and his eyes wide. Eventually, it came to a stop, and an enormous covered bridge rose out of the sea behind it, building itself from the bottom up with creaking slowness.

Shaun stayed where he was, with his back pressed against the cold marble, until a loud thunk from inside the chamber startled him and he leaped away. As he watched, the seam of the door began to fade until he was staring at a perfectly smooth cube with no visible way back inside the chamber. Shaun frowned and ran his hand over the marble, and tried to ignore the little spark of panic that skittered through him when he realized he was trapped.

A few seconds later, the gate screeched and began to open. It gave way a few inches at a time until the gap was large enough for Shaun to walk through. Shaun hesitated, then swallowed his anxiety and climbed a short flight of stairs that led up to the covered bridge.

The bridge was at least half a mile long and had been built as an arch, making it impossible for Shaun to see what lay on the other side until he'd cleared the peak of the arch and started making his way back down. His destination came into view a piece at a time: the stairs that led down from the end of the bridge, a tiny patch of bright green grass, and finally a curved, white wall with a tiny black door. It wasn't until Shaun had emerged from underneath the bridge's overhang that he realized the curved wall was the side of an impossibly tall spire. It was barely as wide as a regular house, yet it was easily taller than the Al Burj. There were no moorings that Shaun could see, nothing to keep it toppling to one side or the other. A tower of that height could never have existed in real life; physics would never allow for it.

"Come inside."

"Shit !" Shaun stumbled backward and almost sent himself sprawling when he tripped over his own feet. Lore was standing in the doorway, watching him, and Shaun scowled. "How many goddamn times do I have to tell you not to sneak up on me like that?"

"All I did was open the door," Lore pointed out, obviously unimpressed by Shaun's blustering. "You're easily startled for someone who wants to work in Homicide."

"And you're pretty mouthy for a guy who's been ignoring my texts for the last twelve hours," Shaun retorted. Of course his brain chose that moment to suggest that maybe Lore had been ignoring his texts because he felt awkward about what had happened at the massage parlor. Thinking about it made Shaun blush, but he glared even harder to make up for it. "Where the hell have you been?"

"Here."

"Doing what?"

Lore didn't reply; he just turned around and disappeared into the spire, apparently expecting Shaun to follow him inside.

"Would you quit doing that, too? I'm not your fucking puppy dog. I'm not just gonna trot along behind you and—oh fuck it." Shaun sighed and rubbed both hands over his face, then followed Lore inside. He knew he should probably tell Lore about Ruby and the break-in at his apartment—in fact, he was pretty sure those should have been the first things out of his mouth—but for now he wanted to hold on to the childish satisfaction that for once, he was the one withholding information. Besides, he was still trying to figure out how to look Lore in the eye without remembering the tension that had stretched between them last time they saw each other.

They made their way up a spiral staircase to an open, circular room that occupied the full circumference of the tower. There was a large bed on one side of the room, heaped in furs and flanked by two elaborately carved nightstands. Directly across from the sleeping area was a tidy little kitchenette. The focus of the room, though, was the enormous table in the center of the floor, piled to overflowing with computer equipment, some of which Shaun didn't even recognize. In the middle of the table was an array of twelve monitors, all of them flickering with scrolling data. Lore stood in front of them with his hands in his pockets, and Shaun drifted closer under the pretense of getting a better look.

Shaun had never felt completely at ease in Lore's presence, but it was even worse now, after what had happened between them. In addition to being annoyed at Lore's lack of social skills and bemused by his seeming omniscience, Shaun could feel the slow burn of attraction, the kind that made him want to stand too close and find excuses for them to touch. He knew what an awful idea it was to harbor those kinds of feelings toward Lore, but he'd never quite gotten the hang of switching himself off.

Lore, meanwhile, didn't even seem to notice, which annoyed Shaun even more.

"What're you compiling?" Shaun gestured to one of the screens, trying to distract himself from the tangle of emotions whirling in his brain. He didn't recognize the programming language, but he could tell that Lore's computers were hard at work turning lines of code into a functioning program.

"A surveillance program. I've been working on cracking the passwords for the private addresses Sarah visited before she died. Once we have access, remote surveillance would be a better than going there ourselves."

"Remote surveillance, huh? Are you sure you're not CIA or NSA or something?"

"I never said."

"No, I guess you didn't," Shaun gritted out, unamused by Lore's evasiveness. "Is that how you know Hudson? Or is this another one of those questions you're not gonna answer?"

Lore eyed Shaun. "If I was federal, I wouldn't be at liberty to talk about it."

"I don't know why I even bother asking you questions," Shaun replied. He glared and crossed his arms as if he could somehow defend himself from his own rising impatience.

"Tell me why you're in a bad mood," said Lore.

"None of your business." Shaun knew he was being surly, but he wasn't in the mood to have a heart-to-heart with a man who seemed to neither understand nor want to understand basic human interactions. Besides, he was tired of telling Lore everything and getting nothing in return. He doubted that turning the tables would have any effect whatsoever, but it was making him feel marginally better.

Lore didn't seem inclined to back down. "You make it my business when you decide to take your bad mood out on me, and when your childish moping begins to interfere with work. Now, tell me what happened, then get over it."

"That's not how it works." Shaun scowled at Lore, who glared right back. The silence stretched out to the point of being uncomfortable, until Shaun eventually heaved a sigh and said, "I'm just really fucking sick of you never telling me anything. You disappear without telling me where you are, you don't return calls or texts—you didn't even tell me about the user ID you picked up off the car from the bombing. Meanwhile, I feel like a total jackass because I tell you everything, because that's what partners are supposed to do." Shaun sighed again and pressed the heels of his palms against his eyes. "Fuck, I sound like my ex-girlfriend."

"Julie?"

"Yeah," Shaun muttered. "She used to bitch at me like this all the time and I never understood until now. Maybe I owe her an apology after all."

"Why did you break up?"

Shaun narrowed his eyes. He doubted Lore was asking because he actually cared, but he was willing to play along. "Does it matter?"

"It matters to you."

Shaun rolled his eyes. "She wanted to get married. I didn't. She thinks I'm childish and irresponsible."

"You are."

"Oh, thanks," Shaun replied sarcastically. "Has anyone ever told you how good you are at comforting people?"

Lore looked away and went on as if Shaun hadn't even spoken. "You're also good at your job, you have a strong code of ethics, you're intelligent despite your refusal to show it, and I can imagine you'd be what most people would regard as a good friend."

Shaun's eyes were wide by the time Lore finished, and for a few seconds, he was at a complete loss for how to respond. Then, when his brain finally caught up with the situation, he shoved his hands into his pockets, looked down at his feet to conceal his blush, and muttered, "Thanks."

There was another long, drawn-out pause before Lore said, in a softer tone than Shaun would have thought him capable of, "I know about the break-in."

"You do?" Shaun jerked his head up to stare at Lore, though he didn't know why these little revelations surprised him anymore. "Did Hudson tell you or something?"

"Or something," Lore agreed. He actually looked guilty—not much, but enough that Shaun picked up on it.

For once, though, Shaun decided not to press the issue. Lore wasn't likely to give him an explanation anyway, and he didn't feel like arguing about it.

"Do you feel better now?" Lore asked after a brief pause. To Shaun's surprise, he actually sounded like he cared.

Shaun nodded. "Yeah, actually. Not one hundred percent, but yeah." He glanced at Lore, then looked away and muttered, "Sorry—you know, for being a dick."

"It's fine," Lore replied. He was looking at the monitors, but judging by the expression on his face, he wasn't really seeing them; he seemed lost in thought, and for once, he wasn't fidgeting or tapping. This was the most relaxed Shaun had ever seen him, but even when he was at ease, he carried a sense of guarded melancholy.

"Hey, uhm," Shaun began.

Lore glanced at him.

"What—you know, did something—" Shaun broke off. He couldn't think of a way to ask something as personal as 'what happened to you' without sounding insulting. "Never mind."

"All right," Lore said with a slight frown. Then he seemed to snap out of the contemplative mood he'd fallen into and said, "What was the breadcrumb?"

"Huh?" Shaun was completely bewildered.

"In one of your text messages, you said you had found a breadcrumb."

"Oh!" Shaun replied with a self-deprecating laugh. He'd gotten so wrapped up in thinking about Lore that he'd forgotten all about the meeting with Ruby and Blake. He dug the slip of paper that Ruby had given him out of his pocket and handed it to Lore. "Ruby gave that to me and told me to give it to you. She said you'd know what to do with it."

"Ruby?" Lore looked up from the paper and narrowed his eyes at Shaun.

Shaun recounted the events from the night before—Blake finding him outside of Platinum and taking him back to the restaurant to meet with Ruby—and explained that Ruby had refused to talk to him without Lore there.

Lore listened to the story with a frown, then nodded and gestured with the paper in his hand. "It may take awhile to crack the password for this address. Make yourself at home in the meantime."

"Password? How do you know there's a password?" Shaun asked.

Lore just gave him a look that Shaun interpreted as, 'You are so thick I can't even be bothered to dignify your questions with a response.'

Shaun rolled his eyes, but Lore's attention had already strayed back to the array of monitors on the table. A few seconds later, he was hunched over the keyboard, typing furiously without even bothering to sit down. Shaun watched him for a second, then sighed and went to drag a chair over to the table from the kitchen.

Lore didn't seem to notice when Shaun put the chair down behind him, so Shaun gave the chair a shove so that the edge of the seat hit the backs of Lore's knees.

Lore sat.

"You realize how ridiculous you are, right?" Shaun complained to the back of Lore's head.

Lore didn't reply.

"You're really, really ridiculous," Shaun informed him. Again, he received no response, but for the first time, Lore's silence made him want to laugh instead of tear his hair out. Shaun wondered if that was some sort of sign that his mental health was starting to degrade.

Shaun watched Lore work for a few minutes, then wandered around the room. He drifted over to the bookshelf near the door and ran his finger along the spines of the books. They were all in different languages: French, German, Spanish, Russian, Chinese, and a few more that Shaun didn't even recognize. The handful of English titles he could find were all absurd: The Bachelor's Guide to Cooking With Legumes, A Practical Introduction to Scandinavian Beekeeping, The Buccaneer's Handbook...

"Do you actually read these?" Shaun asked as he pulled 'Cooking With Legumes' off the shelf.

"Mm," Lore replied.

Shaun put the book down and stuffed his hands into his pockets. He walked the length of the bookshelf, then ambled over to a window to peer out of it----and found himself staring down at a two thousand foot drop.

"What the fuck?" Shaun squeaked and scrambled backward until he collided with Lore's desk. One of the monitors toppled and Lore looked up at him with an annoyed scowl, but Shaun hardly noticed. They'd only climbed a few dozen stairs on their way up, yet the room they were in was at the top of the spire.

"Now who's ridiculous?" Lore said. "What's ridiculous is being afraid of heights in a world where people throw themselves off of skyscrapers for fun."

Shaun swallowed the lump in his throat, then caught his breath and glared at Lore. "First off, for your information, I'm not afraid of heights. But I sure as fuck don't remember climbing all the way the hell up here—and before you give me another lecture about shit not being what it seems, and crazy ass Simulnet architecture and all that—"

"The stairs shift," Lore said. His voice was quiet and he wasn't looking at Shaun, and if Shaun didn't know any better, he'd think Lore sounded shy.

Shaun frowned. "What do you mean, they shift?"

"When I was working on building the tower, I tried making this room mobile, like an elevator, but it took too much system memory. It was easier to just leave it at the top of the tower and then lengthen or shorten the staircase as needed. The staircase is usually short, like it was when we came up here, but the tower's security system will automatically extend the staircase to the full height of the tower if any intruders manage to make it past the gate and over the bridge."

"Whoa, wait a second... are you telling me you built this place?"

"Yes."

"Are you serious? Jesus, it must have taken you months."

"Eleven days."

Shaun felt like the wind had been knocked out of him. "Eleven days? You've got to be fucking with me. There's no way you built all this in eleven days. I know you think I'm and idiot when it comes to Simulnet, but even I know the only way a place like this could've been put together in less than three months would be if you had a whole team of programmers working on it 'round the clock."

Lore looked like a sullen little kid who'd just watched someone crumple up a finger painting they'd spent hours working on.

"Shit, you're serious, aren't you?" Shaun was stunned.

Lore looked away. "I get bored."

"You get bored," Shaun repeated. "You get bored? Do you understand how many people would kill to be able to do something like this? I don't even understand how it's even physically possible.

You'd have to, I don't know, type like a million words per second or something."

Lore blinked at him for a moment, then flashed Shaun a brief but dazzling smile and ducked his head. He huffed and darted a glance at Shaun from the corner of his eye. "I take shortcuts."

Shaun's heart was beating out of control, and he was pretty sure a swarm of butterflies had suddenly taken up residence in his stomach. For the first time, he felt like he actually understood something about Lore, and he wanted to capitalize on it as much as possible, so he grinned and said, "Shortcuts? More like you'd have to bend time and space or something. Seriously, eleven days? That's amazing."

Lore smiled again, like he couldn't quite help himself. "Now you're being absurd."

"Just now?" Shaun beamed. "I thought I was always absurd."

"Are you finished interrupting me?" Lore sighed, but he still looked incredibly pleased with himself.

"Nah," Shaun replied with a smirk and a dismissive wave. "But feel free to go back to what you were doing anyway."

Lore was typing again before the words had even left Shaun's mouth.

While Lore worked, Shaun continued his self-guided tour, stopping every few seconds to glance over at Lore. It took a lot of self-control not to cross the line between curiosity and snooping. The 'bedroom' felt off limits, even though it was just ten feet from the door, so he ventured into the kitchen area instead. A set of copper pots hung over the stove, and there were a dozen cookbooks on a shelf above the sink, all of them dog-eared and stained. Lore didn't seem the type to make elaborate meals for himself or to entertain others, but Shaun could imagine him methodically making his way through each cookbook, trying each recipe just for the sake of assuaging his curiosity. The thought made Shaun smile.

"Are you hungry?"

This time, Shaun barely even twitched; he just glanced over his shoulder at Lore, who was standing right behind him, and said, "Nah, but thanks. Any luck with the password?"

Lore shook his head. "Not yet. I have a script running now, trying to crack it."

"Ah."

They lapsed into another long, awkward silence, standing side-by-side in front of the sink. Shaun kept his hands in his pockets and stared up at the cookbooks, and tried to ignore the fact that he could feel Lore watching him. Just once, Shaun thought, it would be nice if Lore was the socially adept one who could navigate them through an uncomfortable situation.

"So uhm," Shaun said as he rocked back on his heels, "should we go check out one of the other clubs, d'you think? While we wait, I mean."

"The private addresses are our best lead right now."

"Right," Shaun muttered.

Lored turned and walked away to plop down cross-legged on the floor, facing one of the windows. He didn't speak and he didn't fidget; he just sat there with his hands on his knees, staring off into the distance. It was unnerving to see him so still.

Shaun felt like an intruder, suddenly. He stood there in the kitchen, chewing his bottom lip and wondering if he should make an excuse and leave.

"You can sit with me," Lore said without looking at him, then added almost hesitantly, "unless you have somewhere you need to be."

"No," Shaun replied, probably a little too quickly. "No, I don't have anywhere to be." He walked closer and sank down onto the floor beside Lore with his knees pulled up to his chest and his arms wrapped around them. They sat close to each other, but without touching, and Shaun was so distracted by Lore's nearness that he didn't even realize Lore was talking to him at first.

"—Los Angeles."

"Huh?" Shaun jerked to attention. "Sorry, I must've been zoned out. What was that?"

Lore eyed him for a moment, then went back to staring out the window. "I said tell me about Los Angeles."

"L.A.?" Shaun squinted at Lore's profile. "But you're in L.A., aren't you? I mean, unless you're crossing over from another cluster..."

"No, I'm in L.A. I just haven't had a chance to see the city," Lore replied softly. There was something vulnerable about him, in the set of his shoulders and the tone of his voice, and it threw Shaun off guard. He wondered if this was what it felt like to have Lore's trust, and if so, what he could do to keep it.

"Well," Shaun began, "most of it is pretty much what you'd expect, I guess... lots of palm trees, lots of sunlight, lots of taco stands and graffiti. There's other stuff here, though, like uhm—oh, have you been up to the Buddhist temple in Hacienda Heights?"

Lore shook his head.

"You'd like it," Shaun said, then frowned and said, "maybe."

Lore's mouth tightened like he wanted to smile but wouldn't let himself. "It really does bother you that you don't know anything about me, doesn't it?"

"Yeah," Shaun muttered. "I mean, I guess I'm sort of learning to accept it, but that doesn't mean I like it."

Lore's brows drew together, and he looked out the window at the endless sea. After a few seconds, he said, "My father was half Japanese and my mother was Indian."

Shaun's eyes widened and he curled his fingers into the fabric of his jeans. He couldn't remember ever being this excited to hear someone talk about their family before. A million different questions sprang to mind, but he kept his mouth shut, worried that if he started asking, he wouldn't be able to stop.

"My parents died when I was three," Lore went on.

"I'm sorry," Shaun said.

Lore made a dismissive sound in the back of his throat. "I don't remember them."

"Still, that must've been really hard, growing up without your parents."

"You adapt. That's what human beings are best at: adaptability. That's why people are such good liars. We have to be, to survive."

"Not everyone's a good liar. My sister used to make fun of me all the time when we were kids because I was so bad at it I ended up getting myself into even worse trouble than if I'd just kept my mouth shut."

"A good liar would probably tell a story like that."

Shaun frowned. "Are you calling me a liar?"

"I'm saying that everyone lies, whether it's about something as important as stealing money, or about something they think is harmless, like how much they weigh. Everyone misrepresents themselves, every day. Sometimes it's to keep themselves out of trouble, but most of the time it's because we can't stand for the people around us to know the truth. If we can make ourselves look better than we really are, even if it's a lie, other people will like us more, and in turn, we'll like ourselves."

Shaun watched Lore while he talked—watched the lines between his eyebrows deepen, watched the corners of his lips turn down, saw the way his hands tightened on his knees—and thought that maybe, just maybe, he was starting to understand.

"Do you think—?" Lore began, then made an irritated sound and shook his head.

"I think," Shaun said, drawing the words out, considering what he wanted to say next, "that you're really frustrating sometimes, and you're also really fascinating, and I'm glad Hudson introduced us to each other."

Lore flicked a glance at Shaun, and Shaun was struck with the sudden urge to lean over and kiss him. Before Shaun could say anything, though, Lore whispered something that sounded like it might be a curse in another language, then shoved to his feet and walked over to the table to peer down at his monitors.

"And that's that, I guess." Shaun sighed and flopped backwards to stretch out on the floor and stare up at the ceiling. He could hear Lore typing away behind him, and he closed his eyes and imagined that the clicking of Lore's keyboard contained some strange Morse Code that would tell him what the hell Lore was thinking.

"We have it."

"We have what?" Shaun had been half-dozing on Lore's floor, and he opened his eyes to find Lore hovering over him with an impatient look on his face.

"The password for the address Ruby gave us."

"Oh—oh, right," Shaun replied with an embarrassed laugh. He climbed to his feet and dusted the back of his pants off, then followed Lore over to the makeshift desk and leaned in to peer over his shoulder. When Lore tensed and turned his head toward Shaun, Shaun was suddenly aware of how close he was standing. His stomach fluttered, but he didn't move away this time; he cleared his throat and said, "Didn't take long for you to crack the password. Is that normal? For it to be so easy, I mean? Didn't you say you'd been working on the other passwords all night?"

"Mm." Lore nodded, and Shaun thought his voice sounded a little softer than usual when he said, "But the guest password for Ruby's property is linked to my public encryption key. If I'd thought of that sooner, it would only have taken me a few seconds to gain access."

Public encryption keys worked the same way inside Simulnet as they did in the real world. The keys were like passwords that were billions of characters long. Each user had a pair of keys linked to their ID: one key that was kept private and another that was handed out to anyone who needed to send sensitive information to the key's owner. Once a file was encrypted using the public key, it could only be decrypted using the private key. It was like having a mailbox with two locked doors: one door that would let friends and family deposit letters and packages into the mailbox, and one door that would let the owner retrieve the mailbox's contents.

Encryption keys were used for email and file transfers, but they were also used for authorizing access to buildings inside Simulnet. Shaun had added Kim's public key to his apartment's database of authorized visitors so that she could come and go from his apartment as she pleased. Anyone else would need to drop by while he was home, or they wouldn't be allowed inside.

Guest passwords were different. They were usually used for parties, where the host could set up a temporary password to be given to his or her guests, and then remove all the other access controls to the property. That way, the only people who could get into the party would be people who knew the password. Guest passwords could also be used in addition to public encryption keys. Because public keys were linked to a person's user ID, they wouldn't do any good if that user's account was hijacked. A hacker would only need to sign onto Simulnet using someone else's account, and they'd automatically gain access to any properties that listed the victim as an authorized visitor. Guest passwords weren't associated with particular user ID's, however—they were memorized by the users themselves—so even if a user's Simulnet account was stolen, the thief wouldn't know any of the guest passwords the user had been given.

From what Shaun gathered, Ruby had not only added Lore's public encryption key to the list of authorized visitors, she had also used his public key as the guest password to the property. Because the public key was so enormous, it would take password-cracking scripts thousands of years to guess it, but for Lore or anyone who had his public key, it would take only seconds. It was an elegant solution. There was just one thing that struck Shaun as odd.

"Hey..." Shaun squinted at the back of Lore's head. "I'm pretty sure Ruby said you guys don't know each other, so how'd she get your public key?"

"Because it's public, Mason," Lore replied with a sigh.

"Yeah, I know that, but where'd she get it from? Is there some kind of public key directory, or—?" Shaun leaned in closer to try and get a look at the screen, but Lore chose that moment to straighten up. The back of Lore's head collided with Shaun's chin, and Shaun let out a pained grunt when his teeth clacked together. He took a step back and winced as he clapped a hand over his mouth, and reached out to steady himself by grabbing hold of Lore's arm.

"Are you okay?" Lore asked. He actually looked concerned.

Shaun let out another muffled grunt against his palm, then pulled his hand away from his mouth to rub at his jaw. "Yeah, I think so."

"You shouldn't have been standing so close." Lore gave him an irritated look, then shrugged Shaun's hand off of his arm and brushed past him.

Shaun rolled his eyes. "Thanks for the two seconds of concern."

Lore grabbed his coat off a hook near the door and slipped it on, then gestured for Shaun to follow him over to a wardrobe in the bedroom area. Shaun hadn't noticed before, but there was a rectangular-shaped piece of glass set into the wardrobe's wooden door, and it lit up at Lore's touch.

"Wait, you've got a transport chamber up here?" Shaun asked. "Why'd you make me come through the front, then?"

"This is outgoing only."

"Oh. Well, okay, I guess that makes sense. No point in traipsing all the way back out there if you don't have to. Still, this place would be a pain in the ass to come home to drunk. I'd probably end up falling off the bridge or something." Shaun chuckled to himself as Lore opened the wardrobe doors. The inside of the cabinet looked exactly like any other wardrobe Shaun had ever seen, and he sighed as Lore ushered him inside. "Couldn't you have at least made it bigger? Seriously, you can make a staircase that gets longer or shorter at the push of a button, but you couldn't have added a few inches of headroom in here?"

Lore didn't reply; he climbed into the wardrobe with Shaun and closed the door behind him.

It was pitch black inside the cabinet with the doors closed, and they were forced to stand so close to each other that Shaun could feel Lore's breath on his cheek. Shaun shivered and licked his lips, and had to resist the urge to lean closer so that he and Lore were touching. In an attempt to break the tension, more for himself than anything, he smirked into the darkness and said, "If we end up in Narnia, I'm gonna be pissed."

There was a long moment of complete silence before Lore let out a quiet huff of laughter.

The sound made Shaun feel warm all over, and he was glad it was dark so Lore couldn't see his idiotic grin. He was still smiling when something beeped above their heads and Lore opened the wardrobe door.

Dim, greyish light spilled into the cabinet, and Shaun blinked as he followed Lore out of the wardrobe and onto a foggy cobblestone street. Barely-visible sunlight filtered in through the mist, but most of the light came from two flickering gas lamps situated on either side of a wrought iron gate directly in front of them. Shaun couldn't see anything else through the fog, but he could hear the rattle of carriages and the clomping of horse hooves behind him.

"What city are we in?" Shaun asked, sticking close to Lore so they wouldn't lose each other in the mist.

Lore shook his head. "It's a privately hosted address. What you're hearing is just for effect, to give the illusion that we're standing on a city street. I guarantee that if you turn and walk into the fog, you'll wind up right back here."

"So the fog is just there to keep us from staring off into blank space? Sort of like the ocean at your place?" Shaun guessed.

Lore nodded. "Exactly."

"Neat," Shaun said, and meant it. He knew that most Simulnet cities simply erected a city wall to act as a boundary, but he'd always wondered how small, privately-hosted properties handled it. Now he had his answer.

Lore went up to the gate and inspected it. The guest password had allowed them to travel to the property to begin with, but it was Lore's public key that would get them inside. Lore put his hand on the lion's head in the center of the gate and gave it a little push. The gate swung open.

"After you," Shaun muttered.

Lore led the way up a stone path to a brick townhouse. There was a light on in one of the front windows, but Shaun couldn't see anything past the heavy curtains. They climbed the stairs to the little wooden porch, and Lore rapped on the front door with his knuckles. A few seconds later, Shaun heard footsteps on the other side of the door, and the light coming through the peephole disappeared as whoever was on the other side looked out at them.

Ruby's voice called out to them, "Where did we meet, Shaun?"

"Kim Lee Ramen," Shaun replied.

There was a pause while Ruby unlocked what sounded like half a dozen bolts, and the door opened to reveal Ruby standing in the front hall in a pair of ripped tights, an oversized grey sweatshirt, and a pair of bright pink socks. She looked more relaxed than she had at the restaurant, but still wary and exhausted. She ushered them inside, then peered out into the fog before shutting and locking the door behind them.

"This way," Ruby said. She raked her fingers through her spiky blue hair and led them into the front parlor. The room looked like something out of a Charles Dickens novel, complete with patterned wallpaper and velvet-upholstered loveseats.

"Whose house is this?" Shaun asked as he perched on the edge of a brocade-covered chair. When Ruby gave him a surprised look, he explained, "You don't really strike me as the tea-and-doilies type, so either you've got a hidden soft spot for Victorian England or this isn't your house."

Ruby sank down into one of the loveseats and pulled her knees up to her chest. "It's Blake's. He's been letting me use it whenever I'm logged in. We thought it was safer than staying at my apartment."

"That's probably true," Shaun said.

Lore had been wandering around the room with his hands in his pockets. To the casual observer, he would probably have seemed bored and restless, but Shaun was beginning to pick up on Lore's body language, and he could tell that Lore was feeling impatient.

"So, now that Lore is here, what did you want to talk to us about?" Shaun asked.

Ruby's arms tightened around her knees, and she glanced at

Lore before saying, "I know you were looking for me. It's about Sarah Poulsen, isn't it?"

Shaun glanced at Lore, who looked as pleased as he felt. They'd been on the right track after all. "You knew Sarah?"

"We were—" Ruby broke off and swallowed, then took a deep breath and said, "Sarah was my girlfriend."

"You two were involved?"

Ruby nodded, and her gaze darted to Lore again. "We've been seeing each other for almost two years. Sarah had a boyfriend, but she wasn't happy with him. She always swore he'd never hit her, but she was still afraid to leave him. I've been helping her figure out how to get away."

"Did she say why she was scared to leave?"

"He was really jealous. I don't think she told me everything he did, but I know he was constantly grilling her on where she'd been when she was logged in and who she'd been hanging out with. I think she was afraid he'd hurt whoever he thought she'd been spending time with."

Shaun frowned and rubbed a thumb over his bottom lip. "Do you think he knew she was hanging out in Okui?"

"No." Ruby looked troubled. "That's the thing, Sarah never came to Okui, not until the last week or two before she—before the accident. Okui wasn't her kind of place. She wasn't big on partying or anything like that. That's one of the reasons I liked her, actually: she was so different from most of the people I hang out with."

Shaun looked up at Lore, who had stopped pacing and was now watching them with a focused expression on his face.

"Sarah visited Okui several times before she died," Lore said. "You argued with her in Platinum. What was she doing there?"

"I don't know." Ruby seemed determined to look anywhere but at Lore's face. "I know this sounds strange, but I'm not even sure it was really her. It was like she'd turned into a completely different person."

"Explain." Lore sat down in the chair next to Shaun's, directly across from Ruby, and leaned forward with his elbows on his knees.

Shaun had never seen him so intense before, which was saying something, and he actually pitied Ruby for a second, that she'd be on the receiving end of his stare.

"Well" Ruby said, staring at Lore's hands, "I was working a late shift at the bar. Sarah and I hadn't planned to meet up that night, but she called me and asked if she could see me. She was acting weird, even on the phone, but I thought maybe she and Keith had been fighting again. Anyway, I told her where I was and then asked my boss if I could take some time to talk with her."

"And she'd never come to visit you at work before?" Shaun asked.

Ruby shook her head. "No, never. I mean, she knew where I worked but she never came there. Like I said, Okui just wasn't her kind of place. The only time she ever came to Okui before then, at least that I knew about, was when a bunch of us were protesting outside a club over on the west side. That's how I met her."

"What kind of club was it?" Shaun asked.

"It was this place called Shame," Ruby replied. "It's shut down now, but it used to be a fetish club that catered to guys who liked to humliate women, and I mean really humiliate. There are lots of clubs like that in Okui, but this one was really out there."

"How so?"

"Lots of rape fantasies and torture scenes, and just really gross, demeaning stuff. Technically, they weren't breaking any rules, though, so Katou wouldn't shut them down. A group of us got together and figured maybe if we made enough noise, the owners would tone things down a little or just leave town altogether."

Shaun nodded.

"Go back to when Sarah came to visit you at Platinum," Lore prompted.

"Ah, right, sorry." Ruby ran her fingers through her hair before continuing. "So, Sarah showed up about fifteen minutes after she called, and I knew something was wrong pretty much right away. She wasn't acting like herself at all."

"How?" Lore demanded. "We need specifics."

"I don't know, she was just... more aggressive, I guess. Sarah was always really outgoing around new people, but once you got to know her, she was actually pretty self-conscious, almost submissive. Keith took advantage of that, I think; he convinced her she'd never be able to make it without him. Anyway, she usually let me take the lead in pretty much everything. That night, though... I don't know, even the way she kissed me was different. It was like she was mad at me or something, but she wouldn't tell me why. Like I said, it was like she'd turned into a different person."

"Like she'd turned into a different person, or like she was a different person?" Lore asked.

"I don't know," Ruby said. "I've thought about it over and over, and I just don't know."

Lore leaned forward a little further and held Ruby's gaze. "Think about it some more: do you or do you not believe that someone else could have been using her avatar?"

Ruby's brow furrowed, and her jaw clenched, and she lifted her head to glare directly into Lore's eyes. Shaun couldn't tell if she was intimidated, irritated, frustrated, or all of the above. Finally, she said, "Look, I get what you're saying, but if it was someone else in Sarah's avatar, why would they have come to see me? I mean, wouldn't most hackers—oh god." Ruby's eyes widened and she made a quiet, choked sound. "Keith."

"Sarah's boyfriend?" Shaun asked.

Ruby nodded and looked at him with a horrified expression. "That would explain everything. If Keith found out about me and Sarah somehow, and logged in to find out who I was... oh god, I didn't even try to pretend like nothing was going on between us. I didn't think to. No wonder he got so angry."

Lore was tapping his foot on the floor and drumming his fingers on the armrest of his chair. "What did you fight about?"

"She— he—whoever it was in Sarah's avatar, they got really aggressive after a few drinks and pulled me out on the dance floor. They got really grabby while we were out there, tried to pull my top down and shove their hands down my pants. Eventually, I told her—or him, or whoever it was—to stop, and they said something about me being a whore, and whores don't get to choose where they get fucked. So I left. I didn't even call my boss to let him know I was going, I was so angry. I really thought she'd call me the next day and apologize, but then I heard—" Ruby broke off and closed her eyes, and lowered her head so that her forehead was pressed to her knees.

Shaun resisted the urge to pet her hair and comfort her. "Why'd you go into hiding? Why didn't you go to the police?"

"Which police?" Ruby's voice was muffled. "When I heard about it on the news, they still hadn't figured out who'd be investigating. And besides, I'm not stupid. I was Sarah's lover on the side, and a whole club full of people saw us fighting on the night before she died. Even if I'd gone straight to the police, I would have been their first suspect."

Lore's cell phone interrupted the conversation. He pulled it out of his pocket to check it, then frowned and said, "excuse me," before striding out of the room and down the hall, toward the back of the house.

Once he was gone, Shaun turned his attention back to Ruby, who had finally lifted her head from her knees. Her eyes were red, like she was about to cry but was forcing herself not to, and Shaun again had to resist the urge to move over to the couch and wrap his arms around her. Instead, he just reached over and took one of her hands to give it a squeeze. "What made you decide you could trust us? I mean, for all you know, we could've been trying to track you down to arrest you, or worse."

Ruby shook her head and offered Shaun a humorless smile. "I don't trust you, Shaun. I trust Lore."

"I thought you said you didn't know him?"

"No, I said he doesn't know me. I know him, though. Everyone knows Lore."

Shaun thought about the girls who had been whispering about Lore at Oubliette, and all the other people who seemed to have been eying him whenever they were out in public. "What do you mean everyone knows Lore?"

"Are you serious?" Ruby was obviously surprised. "But Lore is a legend."

Shaun shrugged. "I'm not exactly a Simulnet regular. I'd never even heard of him until about a week ago."

Ruby would probably have looked less astonished if he'd told her he didn't know who The Beatles were. She shook her head at him and said, "I can't believe you don't know about Lore. I mean, I guess I can understand you not knowing about him when you first got here, but you're telling me you've been hanging out with him for a week now, and no one's said anything to you?"

"Well, people stare at us sometimes," Shaun admitted. "But he's never told me why, and whenever I ask, no one wants to talk about it."

Ruby's lips tightened and she frowned as if she was debating with herself, then she sat forward and replied in a quieter tone, "Lots of people are afraid of him, so if you're hanging out with him, chances are pretty good they're afraid of you too."

"Afraid of him? Why?" Shaun felt the hairs on the back of his neck stand on end.

Ruby glanced at the door of the room, then licked her lips and whispered, "There are rumors about him, about what he can do. The first story I ever heard about him—I'd been working at Platinum for a couple weeks, I guess, and I overheard one of the customers telling my co-worker that he'd seen Lore out in the east end. He said Lore had been standing there on the sidewalk one second, then just disappeared right into thin air, just like that." Ruby snapped her fingers.

Shaun frowned. "But people do that all the time when they log out. I mean, I get why it would freak someone out if they'd never seen it happen before, but..."

"That's what I said, too," Ruby whispered. "But the guy insisted Lore hadn't logged out, that he'd teleported."

"Teleported," Shaun repeated. The eerie, tingling sensation that at the back of his neck spread through his body. He knew, logically, that it was impossible to teleport without a chamber, that the brain wasn't designed to accept instantaneous travel, and yet all he could think about was the day he'd met Lore, when Lore had seemed to simply appear in the chair across from him at the cafe.

"They told me a bunch of other stories about him, too. My co-worker, Jadin, said she'd heard that Lore was born already connected to Simulnet."

Shaun actually laughed out loud at that, though it came out sounding nervous. "I hate to crush anyone's dreams, but that's not possible."

"I know," Ruby replied, but Shaun could see a little spark of doubt in her eyes. "I've also heard that he's some kind of advanced A.I. program or something, that he's not even human at all."

That wouldn't be all that surprising, thought Shaun. "Where did all these rumors start?"

"I don't know. I don't think anyone does." Ruby shrugged. "But I believe he can do things with Simulnet code that no one else can. I don't know how or why, but I know there's something special about him. That's why I wanted his help."

"But you said people are scared of him," Shaun pointed out. "So why do you trust him so much?"

Ruby stared at Shaun for a moment, then glanced at the door again before leaning forward and whispering, so quietly that Shaun had to strain to hear her, "There was this club in Okui a couple of years ago... it didn't even have a name, it was just this big black building in the middle of the city. Usually Katou would've shut it down because it violated Terms of Service."

Shaun knew there were only a handful of things that would violate Okui's Terms of Service—pedophilia being the main culprit—so he didn't bother to ask what kind of club it had been. "Why didn't Katou close the place down?"

"He couldn't get rid of it," said Ruby. "The club owner had figured out a way to modify Okui's code or something so Katou couldn't even delete the plot of land the club was on. None of this was public knowledge, of course.

"Katou didn't want to admit that someone had hacked Okui's servers," Shaun guessed.

Ruby nodded. "Exactly, but word travels pretty quickly in Okui, so of course all of us regulars knew about it in a matter of days. Anyway, a group of us got together to see if we could figure out some kind of solution. You know, Okui is kind of a haven for weirdos, but even the freaks don't want that kind of thing going on in their neighborhood."

"I can't imagine many people would."

Ruby opened her mouth to reply, but a door creaked somewhere in the back of the house and they both went quiet. Then, after a few minutes of silence, Ruby glanced at Shaun, who let out a soft chuckle. Ruby gave him a wan smile in return, then went on in a whisper, "Long story short, someone mentioned we should try and track Lore down to ask for his help. I'm pretty sure they meant it as a joke, because as far as I know, no one actually knows how to find him, and if they do, they're not sharing. So anyway, we all just sort of laughed it off, right? Well, the next morning, when I got to work, everyone was talking about a fire that had happened the night before."

A shiver rippled down Shaun's spine. "The club?"

Ruby nodded. "No one would admit that they were there when it happened, of course, but word got around anyway that right before the explosion, everyone in the club got knocked offline so the building was empty when the fire started. Nothing like that had ever happened in Simulnet before. We never figured out how he did it, but we knew it had to have been Lore. There's no one else who could have—"

The door to the sitting room opened and Ruby abruptly stopped talking as Lore strode into the room.

"Everything okay?" Shaun asked to cover up the awkward silence.

Lore looked at Shaun as if he'd just sprouted wings, and said nothing as he reclaimed his seat in the chair across from Ruby. "I'm attaching a tracker to your avatar. It will alert me whenever someone logs on using your user ID. While you're logged on, it will also tell me your avatar's location and monitor your vitals." He still had his phone out, and he began typing something on its keypad. "I'll need your user ID and the serial number for your avatar."

Ruby nodded and rattled off the number.

While Lore added the tracker to Ruby's avatar, Shaun watched Lore from the corner of his eye. Shaun usually felt fumbling and inadequate in Lore's presence, but now, after seeing the things Lore had created and hearing the stories Ruby had told him, he'd be lying if he said he wasn't a little in awe. Part of him wanted to pass the rumors off as urban legends, but knowing he might have witnessed some of Lore's abilities firsthand...

"Shaun."

Shaun jerked to attention to find Lore staring at him expectantly. "Sorry, what?"

"We're leaving."

"Oh, sorry." Shaun pushed to his feet, embarrassed to have been caught daydreaming. When Ruby stood, Shaun stuck his hand out just as she moved in to hug him. A few seconds of awkward position-changing followed, with Ruby switching to a handshake and Shaun switching to a hug, before they both gave up with awkward laughs. Shaun scratched at the back of his neck and said, "Uhm, so, are you gonna be okay alone?"

"Yeah," Ruby replied, then glanced at the door where Lore was standing, watching them with an inscrutable expression. "I'm going to log out, and I don't think I'll have to worry about anyone bothering me in real life."

Shaun nodded and gave Ruby a quick hug before following Lore out of the house and into the fog. Once the door had closed behind them, Shaun looked at Lore, who was staring straight ahead as if lost in thought. "So what do you think? Maybe I should pay the boyfriend a visit?"

Lore nodded, obviously distracted by something, and murmured, "I have some work to do, too."

Shaun followed Lore down the path and through the gate, and tried to ignore the odd fluttering in the pit of his stomach.

❧

Keith Carter was a muscular man in his late twenties, with a blond buzz cut and a scar on his jaw. He could have been attractive in a hard-edged way, but his shirt was stained and there was dirt underneath his fingernails, and the stubble on his face made him look unkempt rather than rugged.

With some help from Lore, whose many talents apparently also included cell phone tracking, Shaun found Keith in a North Hollywood strip club, situated between a dollar store and a pho restaurant. There were only a handful of customers in the club, which wasn't that surprising considering it was four in the afternoon on a weekday. Shaun sat at the bar, four stools down from Keith, sipping his beer and watching Keith in the greasy mirror behind the rows of bottles. From the looks of him, Keith had spent at least a couple of days supplementing alcohol for sleep, which meant it probably wouldn't take much to get him talking. Still, Shaun didn't want to come on too strong. Getting spotted for poking around in Simulnet had taught him a few things about subtlety.

As it turned out, Shaun didn't have to open conversation on his own. Not long after he arrived, the bartender went to refill Keith's drink and remarked, "Fourth day in a row."

"S'that it?" Keith slurred into his glass. "Feels like a fuckin' eternity."

"You should go home and get some sleep." The bartender eyed Keith as if trying to decide between kicking him out to let him sleep it off elsewhere or making a profit by letting him stay.

"Can't sleep," Keith mumbled. "Can't do anythin' without the goddamn cops breathin' down my neck."

Shaun seized the opportunity to jump in. "Fuckin' cops, man. What've they got their panties in a twist about now?"

Keith looked up from his glass. His eyes were glazed and he swayed a little on his stool. He stared at Shaun for a minute, as if trying to decide whether or not Shaun could be trusted, then said, "Girlfriend died about a week ago. Guess who they think did it."

"Ouch, man. Sorry to hear that." Shaun turned a little,

pretending to watch the girls on the stage behind them. "They let you out on bail or what?"

Keith shook his head. "Nah, they've got their heads up their asses. Can't decide whether it's the local pigs or the feds who're gonna handle shit, so no one's doin' anything. Meantime, I've got a dead girlfriend and whoever did it is probably halfway to fuckin' Mexico."

Shaun nodded and tried to look sympathetic. "How'd she die?"

"Y'know all those people who've been dying in SR tanks? Sarah was one of 'em." There was a pained expression on Keith's face: his eyebrows were drawn together and he stared down into his glass before taking another swig.

One of the dancers chose that moment to catch Shaun's eye and make her way over to him. After convincing her that he really didn't need a lap dance, even if she was willing to give him 'something extra' for a few dollars more, Shaun turned his attention back to Keith, who was slumped over his glass with his eyes closed. Shaun frowned. "Hey man, are you okay?"

"What d'you think?" Keith mumbled without opening his eyes. "Cops think I killed my fuckin' girlfriend, man. And get this." He straightened up and blinked at Shaun, his eyes unfocused. "The night before she died? Found out she'd been cheatin' on me. Bet the cops know it, too. How's that for shit fuckin' luck?"

"Yeah, that's some pretty shitty luck, right there. How'd you find out she was cheating?"

"Been suspicious for awhile now, so I set up a logger on our Simulnet line—nothin' fancy, just something I downloaded that'd let me keep track of where she was going and who she was calling. Night before she died, I logged in on her avatar and called up this number that kept showing up in the logs. Turns out it was the girl she'd been cheating on me with."

Shaun thought about Ruby's comment that Sarah hadn't seemed like herself, and Lore's suspicion that it had been Keith using Sarah's avatar. "So you had access to her account?"

"Yeah, had it for awhile," Keith said with a shrug. "I know s'not the most legal thing in the world but I got curious, y'know, so I signed on a couple times as Sarah."

Shaun nodded and tried to keep his expression neutral. "So what was it like? Being in a girl's avatar, I mean."

"Honestly?" Keith muttered as he lifted his head and stared at Shaun, then flashed him a humorless smile. "I had the time of my fuckin' life."

"The killer is targeting men who use female avatars."

"Shaun?" said Hudson. "Where are you?"

"On the freeway, driving back to the hotel," replied Shaun. "I just talked to Keith. Don't worry, he doesn't know who I am. Even if he did, he was so drunk he would've forgotten what happened five minutes after I walked out the door."

"Hold on," said Hudson. Her end of the line went muffled like she'd put her hand over the mouthpiece of her phone. Shaun could hear her talking to someone in the background, though he couldn't make out the words. A minute or so later, Hudson came back on the line. "Explain, but make it quick. I've got an office full of feds breathing down my neck."

"Okay," said Shaun, "so only two of the victims have been female, right? And we know at least two of the male victims had been using female avatars. Well, guess what? I just talked to Sarah's boyfriend, and he admitted he'd been using Sarah's avatar before she died."

"For what?"

"Well, some of the addresses in Sarah's activity logs didn't seem like the kinds of places she'd hang out in, so me and Lore checked them out. We managed to track down this girl, Ruby, who Sarah had been seeing on the side. She told us Sarah had been trying to figure out how to leave her boyfriend for a long time, and the last time they saw each other, Sarah was acting really weird. It was actually Lore who came up with the idea that maybe Sarah's boyfriend had been using her avatar."

"So you think the boyfriend was the target, not Sarah?"

"Yeah, I think so."

"You don't think he's a good suspect, himself?"

"No." Shaun shook his head even though Hudson couldn't see him. "The guy's sleazy as fuck, and I can understand why Sarah wanted to get away from him, but he seemed pretty broken up over her. I don't think he killed her."

"What about the other female victim? Why did the killer target her?"

"I haven't figured that out, yet," said Shaun.

"Well, it's still a pretty solid theory, and it's a fuck of a lot better than anything my team has come up with. See if you can track down the Simulnet identities of the other victims, especially the men. Find out what kind of avatars they used and the kinds of places they hung out. If we can prove that the male victims used female avatars, that gives us a pattern."

"Will do," said Shaun. They hung up, and he scrolled through the list of contacts in his phone until he found Kim's name. He knew there was a chance she wouldn't answer—he wasn't sure what time it was in France, but he knew it must be late—but he had the sudden urge to hear her voice. Her voicemail picked up after seven rings, and he hesitated before saying, "Hey, it's me. I just wanted to talk. Y'know, about whatever. I love you."

Shaun hung up and tossed his phone into the passenger seat. The traffic in front of him slowed to a crawl, and he sighed.

The headlights from oncoming traffic formed eight neat lines against the backdrop of a dusty California sunset. The Santa Ana winds whipped through the palm trees and kicked up dirt that swirled in eddies across the shoulder of the highway. In a few hours, the glow from the fires would be visible over the mountains.

Shaun rubbed his forehead; he could feel a headache coming on. There was a knot in his throat, and a rush of adrenaline made his muscles tense. His chest felt tight, and he forced himself to keep breathing through his nose. Shaun was bewildered; he hadn't had a panic attack in years.

Someone behind him honked, and Shaun gave a violent start.

Traffic had started moving again. He waved a hand at the person behind him, then merged over until he could pull off onto the side of the road. Once he'd put the car in park, he slouched and rubbed both shaking hands over his face.

He needed to talk to someone. He needed to ramble about the case to someone who'd listen without judging, without having to worry about giving too many details. He debated with himself for awhile, then reached for his cell phone.

Lore answered on the fourth ring. "What?"

"Hi," said Shaun, and then paused, suddenly unsure of himself.

Apparently, he let the silence drag on for too long, because after a few seconds ticked by, Lore said, "Well?"

"I talked to Hudson," said Shaun. He didn't know what else to say. Lore didn't like chit-chat, but Shaun couldn't bring himself to admit that he'd just had a panic attack and needed someone to talk to.

"Okay."

"She wants us to find out if any of the other male victims used female avatars."

"I'm already working on that."

"I know," said Shaun. There was another long silence before he cleared his throat and asked, "So uhm, are you online or offline right now?"

"You called me on my Simulnet number."

"Yeah, I know, but I didn't know if you had your Simulnet number linked to your real life number." Shaun tried to sound non-chalant, but he couldn't quite disguise how flustered he was feeling. "I just asked 'cause, uhm... Well, I was thinking maybe we could meet for drinks. Y'know, we could go over case stuff or—I don't know, maybe just talk or whatever."

"Mason, are you asking me—"

"I have to go," Shaun interrupted. The anxiety he'd been feeling had erupted into a full-blown meltdown as soon as he realized what he was doing. Before Lore could reply, Shaun hung up and stared down at his phone in horror. He half expected it to ring at any moment, but it stayed silent.

"Fuck," Shaun whispered to himself, then rubbed the heel of his palm against his forehead and muttered again, "Fuck, fuck, fuck."

Chapter Nine

Kim Lee Ramen was deserted. Most of the lights inside were off, and the sign on the door said, "CLOSED," but Shaun could see Blake through the front window, leaning against the counter with a coffee mug in one hand and a tablet in the other. He looked up when Shaun rapped on the door, then frowned and put his mug and tablet down to come unlock the door. "Darling, is everything alright? You look dreadful."

Shaun hesitated just inside the doorway, scratching at the back of his neck and looking everywhere except at Blake.

"Has something happened?" asked Blake. He reached out and gave Shaun's arm a squeeze. He was wearing bits and pieces of his white suit—trousers, shirt, and vest—but he was barefoot, and his hair was loose around his shoulders. In the dim light of the restaurant, he looked much more approachable than Shaun remembered.

"Yeah," said Shaun. It came out rough, and he wanted to elaborate—he wanted to tell Blake everything, just to have someone to talk to—but his sense of responsibility kept him quiet.

"Shaun."

Blake's expression broke something inside Shaun, and before he could even think about what he was doing, he was grabbing the front of Blake's shirt and hauling him into a kiss. Blake let out a surprised grunt and tried to pull away, but Shaun buried his fingers in Blake's hair to keep him in place.

"Shaun," said Blake, "as flattering as this is, I don't think—"

"Shhh," whispered Shaun. "Shut up. Just keep kissing me."

"Are you sure?"

"Don't," Shaun interrupted. "Please don't ask me if I'm sure. Don't ask me anything. Please."

Blake didn't reply; he just nodded and let Shaun walk him

backwards through the restaurant. He pulled Shaun into the back room by the front of his shirt, then kicked the door closed and pressed Shaun up against it for another kiss. Blake approached kissing with a languid intensity that made Shaun's toes curl. One of Blake's hands was still gripping his shirt, and the other found its way into his hair. Shaun sighed and slumped against the wall, tipping his hips forward to rub against Blake through their clothes.

The angles were different. Shaun had forgotten what it felt like to have another man's chest pressed to his, or another man's cock rubbing his thigh, but it didn't matter. Blake's lips were soft, and the noises he was making had Shaun hard in a matter of seconds.

"This way," whispered Blake. He pulled away and walked backwards towards the bed. His lips were swollen and his cheeks were flushed, and there was a hungry gleam in his eyes.

Shaun trailed after him in a daze, stumbling through the beaded curtain and then shoving Blake backwards onto the bed. Shaun followed him down, planting one knee between his legs and his elbows on either side of Blake's head. He ducked his head for a kiss, which Blake returned for a few seconds before using the weight of his body to flip them over. Shaun frowned when he suddenly found himself on his back with Blake hovering over him.

"Don't worry, sugarplum, I'm not going to stop," Blake purred with a lazy smile that showed off his pointed canines. He slipped a hand underneath Shaun's shirt to stroke his belly. "What I am going to do, though, is take my time. I hope you don't mind."

Shaun sucked in a breath when Blake found one of his nipples and pinched it. Blake made a pleased sound in the back of his throat and repeated the gesture, a little harder this time. He used his other hand to shove the hem of Shaun's shirt up to his chin, which Shaun took as a hint. He sat up just far enough to pull his shirt the rest of the way off, then tossed it in the vague direction of the floor before threading his fingers into Blake's hair.

"Tell me darling, what made you crawl over to the queer side, hm? You can be honest: it was my charm, wasn't it?" Blake smirked and dragged his tongue down the center of Shaun's chest, all the way down to right above his belt buckle.

Shaun let out a breathless chuckle, but he wasn't sure he wanted to talk about it after all—not Lore, not the case, not any of it—so he nodded and muttered in as dry a tone as he could, "Yeah, it was all you. You're just so hot I couldn't help myself."

"Flattery will get you everywhere," said Blake. He was smiling, but it was obvious that he was still curious. Thankfully, though, he seemed more interested in unbuckling Shaun's belt than in asking any more questions.

Shaun reached down to help, but Blake batted his hand away and finished tugging his jeans open with agonizing slowness. By the time Blake was dragging his pants off, Shaun was breathing harder just from watching. When Shaun was in nothing but his boxer briefs, Blake sat back on his heels and stared at him, raking his gaze over the length of Shaun's body. The curious gleam in his eyes reminded Shaun too much of Lore, so he sat up and pulled him down for another kiss.

"You're not naked enough," Shaun muttered. He broke the kiss to concentrate on tugging the front of Blake's vest open.

Blake laughed into Shaun's mouth and helped to push the vest off his shoulders, then pushed Shaun's hands away and started unbuttoning his shirt. "Are you always this impatient?"

"Are you always this much of a tease?"

Blake smiled. "Always, darling."

Once they were both naked, Shaun rolled them over again so he could stretch out along the length of Blake's body. This time, Blake didn't protest; he wrapped a leg around Shaun's hips and arched off the mattress so his belly rubbed against Shaun's cock. Shaun cursed under his breath and bit down on Blake's jaw.

He was a little surprised by the intensity of his own reactions. He'd gotten off with other men before, a handful of times in college, but it had never affected him like this. His cock was smearing pre-come all over Blake's skin every time Blake moved against him, and he was making soft growling noises against Blake's mouth. He curled his fingers into the sheets on either side of Blake's head, trying to suppress the urge to scratch, and bite, and tug.

He managed to hold back until Blake lifted his head to whisper in Shaun's ear, "I'm not fragile. I won't break unless you want me to."

Shaun growled and hauled Blake's ass into his lap. Blake laughed and squirmed so that Shaun's cock rubbed directly over his hole. They kissed again, hot and urgent, and when Blake slid a finger between their mouths, Shaun laved it with his tongue. Blake pulled his finger away a few seconds later, then worked his hand down between their bodies. Shaun was too far gone at first to realize what Blake was doing, but when he felt Blake's knuckles graze his cock, he shuddered and clutched Blake's shoulder hard enough to leave bruises.

"Wanna fuck me?" whispered Blake. He sounded out of breath already, and Shaun felt another tug of want in his balls.

Shaun nodded and pulled back so he could reach between Blake's legs. Blake was working himself open with his fingers, and Shaun pressed his forehead against Blake's with a groan. "God, you have no fucking idea."

"How do you want me?" asked Blake. He let his knuckles graze Shaun's cock again as he worked a second finger into his body. "On my knees with my legs spread and my ass in the air, or do you want me to ride your beautiful cock until we both come so hard we can't breathe afterward?"

"No, I want you like this," Shaun whispered, staring down into Blake's eyes. "I want to see your face."

Blake smirked up at him. "You're something of a romantic, aren't you?"

Shaun couldn't bring himself to tell the truth—that he was afraid he'd start thinking of Lore again if he couldn't see Blake's face—so he just ducked his head and sucked at the hollow of Blake's throat. Blake made a purring sound that vibrated against his lips, then wrapped a hand around his prick. Shaun groaned through his nose and pulled back to stare down at Blake, then slowly canted his hips forward until the head of his cock was pressed against Blake's hole.

"Slowly," Blake whispered as he wrapped his legs around Shaun's waist.

Shaun nodded and let Blake hold his cock steady as he pushed his hips forward. The head of his prick nudged against the resistant muscle for a a second before Blake relaxed beneath him and his cock sank into the tight heat of Blake's body. Shaun closed his eyes and exhaled slowly, determined to keep himself in check at least until Blake had adjusted. Waiting was agony, though, and shivers rippled through his body as his cock sank inch-by-inch into Blake's ass.

Once the length of his prick was buried to the hilt, Shaun opened his eyes to watch Blake's face. Blake's usually pale cheeks were red, and his eyes were half-closed. His white hair was splayed out on the pillow around his head, and Shaun stroked it with his fingertips. He'd been worried that being there, in the moment, might be a problem—that it would be hard for him to concentrate on Blake instead of thinking of Lore—but as luck would have it, concentrating on Blake took not a lot of effort at all.

"You're so fucking sexy," whispered Shaun.

"Mm, you think so, do you?" purred Blake. He smirked and licked Shaun's lips, then said, "So quit talking and fuck me."

Shaun didn't need any more encouragement than that; he pulled his hips back, nice and slow until he felt Blake's muscles start to quiver, then slammed back inside. The lack of proper lube made the friction on his cock a hundred times more intense, and he growled when he felt Blake clamping down on the girth of his prick. He grabbed Blake's hip to hold him still, and fucked him hard enough to make the headboard of the tiny bed slam against the wall.

The sex was mind-blowing. Blake moved underneath Shaun in just the right ways to make Shaun's blood burn, and from all the growling Blake was doing, the feeling was apparently mutual. They didn't say a word, but they didn't really need to; they both seemed to know what the other needed.

Shaun kept the pace hard and steady until Blake was gasping for breath and working a hand down between them to stroke himself. When Shaun sat back on his heels so he could watch, the angle deepened and they both moaned. Shaun pulled Blake's legs up over his shoulders and lifted Blake's ass up off the bed. That seemed to be all Blake needed, because just a few seconds later, his eyes fluttered closed and he grabbed at the sheets with his free hand as a shudder raked through his body and his cock jerked in his fist. The clenching of his muscles pushed Shaun over the edge as well, and he turned his head to bite the side of Blake's leg as he came with a rumbling growl.

As soon as the last of his orgasm was wrung out of him, Shaun slumped forward, catching himself on his elbows to keep himself from crushing Blake, and pressed their lips together in an almost chaste kiss. Blake groaned tiredly through his nose, then pulled back to look up at Shaun with a satisfied smile.

"Did it work?" Blake asked, stroking Shaun's spine with his fingertips.

Shaun closed his eyes. "Mm? Did what work?"

"I'll take that as a yes."

Twenty minutes later, Shaun was sprawled on his back across Blake's bed, smoking a cigarette and staring at the ceiling. He could hear the shower still running, and he considered taking Blake up on the offer to join, if only to distract himself. As soon as Blake had gone into the bathroom, Shaun's brain had kicked in again (albeit at a slower pace than when he'd first arrived), and he was right back where he'd started: analyzing the case, analyzing Ruby, analyzing Keith, analyzing Lore...

The water shut off, and a minute later, Blake emerged from the bathroom, toweling his hair dry. When he saw Shaun lying there on his bed, he paused and sighed. "Well, that certainly didn't last long. I must be getting rusty."

"Hm?" Shaun roused himself and looked up at Blake. "What didn't last long?"

"Helping you forget whatever you came here to forget," Blake said as he walked over and sat on the edge of the bed. He plucked the cigarette from Shaun's fingertips and took a drag, then exhaled towards the ceiling and asked, "Is it Lore?"

Shaun just sighed and crossed his arms behind his head.

Blake stubbed the cigarette out, then reached over to push the hair away from Shaun's forehead. The gesture reminded Shaun of his mother. That thought probably should have been horrifying, but it wasn't. It was comforting.

After a brief silence, Blake said, "For what it's worth, I don't get the feeling he's the type to be interested in anyone."

Shaun wanted to deny that what he was feeling had anything to do with Lore, but he figured Blake would probably see right through him. He heaved another sigh and flopped over onto his stomach to bury his face in the pillow.

The bed shifted as Blake stretched out beside him, close enough that Shaun could feel his body heat.

"I don't know what the fuck I'm doing," Shaun mumbled into the pillow. "I'm supposed to be tracking down Sarah's killer, and I'm trying, I really am, but there's so much other shit happening. My head feels too full. Feels like my brains are gonna leak out of my ears."

Blake's hand was a comforting weight on his lower back. "That would be a pity. These sheets were expensive."

Shaun snorted, then turned his head so he could peer up at Blake out of one eye.

"You can talk to me if you need to," said Blake. The teasing purr was gone from his voice, and for once, he looked completely serious. "You don't have to tell me specifics. In fact, it's probably safer for both of us if you didn't. But it might not be the worst idea in the world for you to get some things off your chest, even if it's only in the vaguest of terms."

Shaun considered for a moment, then rolled onto his side so he was facing Blake. Their noses were almost touching. Shaun wondered how it was possible for him to feel such a strong connection to someone he'd known for just a few a days. After chewing on his bottom lip for a few seconds, he took a deep breath and said, "The other day, outside of Platinum, after the car bomb went off? That was only the second time in my whole life I've ever seen a dead body. I know it was fake, but..."

Blake frowned and nodded.

"The summer I was twelve, my sister and I went to stay with my uncle in San Diego." Shaun hadn't told this story in years, and now he remembered why: just thinking about it made his chest tighten and his throat close up. He looked away for a second to study the pattern of hair leading from just underneath Blake's navel to down between his legs, then took a deep breath and continued. "The back of my uncle's house faced a canyon. All the neighborhood kids used to go down there and ride their dirt bikes or whatever. So one day, my sister convinced me to go down there with her because she wanted to meet up with some guy she had a crush on, but she didn't want to go alone. She was actually pretty shy until we were in high school. Course, you wouldn't know it now from talking to her. Anyway, we got about halfway down into the canyon when I saw this garbage bag all wrapped up in duct tape. At first I thought it was a Christmas tree or something that someone had dumped, but something made me decide to go check it out."

Blake had been listening with his brows furrowed, but then horrified comprehension dawned on his face, and his eyes widened.

"She was thirteen," said Shaun, "just a couple months older than me and my sister. They never found the person who killed her."

Blake was quiet for awhile. He didn't try to comfort Shaun, and he didn't ask any of the questions Shaun had expected him to. Usually when people heard the story, the first thing they asked was whether that was why Shaun had decided to become a cop, and the second question was whether or not Shaun had ever tried to find the killer. Shaun had always declined to answer.

When Blake finally spoke again, it was to say, "It seems cruel, doesn't it? That we're evolved enough to be aware of our own impending death, but we're not evolved enough to postpone it."

"Yeah," said Shaun. "Yeah, exactly." He stared into Blake's eyes for a moment, then smiled and said, "Y'know, you're pretty fucking awesome. Anyone ever tell you that?"

"All the time." Blake smirked. "But it's always nice to hear it again."

Chapter Ten

Shaun was whistling when he stepped out of the telechamber and into the coffee shop where he'd first met Lore. The cafe was empty, but he could see Lore sitting at a table outside, hunched over his laptop and jogging his leg up and down. Shaun rolled his eyes and stepped up to the counter to greet the elven barista with a lopsided grin. "Just a coffee, please."

Once he had his coffee, Shaun made his way outside and ambled over to the table where Lore was sitting.

Lore's hands paused over his keyboard, and he looked up at Shaun without raising his head. When Shaun grinned at him, his eyes narrowed. "You're in a good mood."

"Yep," Shaun agreed as he plopped down in the chair across from Lore. He still wasn't feeling a hundred percent like his usual self, but talking to Blake had helped. They'd parted ways as friends (though not without hinting they'd be up for another round if the mood struck), and Shaun had logged out and gone straight to sleep. He'd only managed a couple of hours before he'd been woken up by a text message from Lore, but it was the best sleep he'd gotten in over a week.

Lore's mouth tightened, but although it was pretty obvious he wanted to know why Shaun was in a good mood, he didn't ask, and Shaun didn't answer. After a few seconds of silence, Lore turned his attention back to his laptop and said, "I've cracked the passwords to two of the private addresses Sarah visited."

"Keith, you mean," said Shaun. "He already told me what they were. Private sex clubs, right? He said he got an invitation from a guy he met at Der Kamf, but he didn't know what the places were until he got there."

Lore nodded. "According to the logs, he wasn't at either location for very long. He stayed at one for twenty minutes, and the other for only six."

"Still worth checking out. Mind if I finish this before we go, though?" Shaun held up his cup of coffee.

"You have time. I've gotten us invitation codes, but I still need to add our public keys to the list of authorized users."

Shaun froze with his cup lifted halfway to his lips. "Not our real public keys, I hope?"

"Of course not." Lore sounded insulted, but then he paused and glanced up at Shaun. "Weren't you complaining less than a week ago about violating terms of service?"

Shaun shrugged and offered him a grin. "Things change."

Lore gave him a disbelieving look and went back to typing.

Shaun sipped his coffee while he waited and watched the people passing by on the sidewalk. A group of petite girls with iridescent skin walked past, chattering to each other in what sounded like Japanese, but then they switched to Spanish, then German, and finally to English. Shaun listened to them, and once they were out of earshot, he sighed and propped his chin on his fist. "Man, I wish I knew another language. I can speak a little Spanish, enough to order a beer or whatever, but I wish someone had taught me French or something when I was little. Seems like everyone speaks more languages than I do."

"I speak nineteen," Lore replied distractedly.

Shaun snorted. "Bullshit. No one speaks nineteen languages."

"I do."

"No you don't." Shaun rolled his eyes, then flapped his hand in the general direction of Lore's laptop. "Stop trying to impress me and just do your stuff."

"My stuff?" Lore's fingers paused on the keyboard, and he glanced up at Shaun with one eyebrow quirked. "Use your big boy words, Mason."

"Shut up," muttered Shaun.

Lore went back to typing, but his barely-there smirk made Shaun smile. The feeling didn't last long, though, because it was followed shortly thereafter by a deep, inexplicable guilt, similar to what he'd felt the one and only time he'd cheated on his college girlfriend. He tried to ignore it, knowing it was irrational, but eventually he couldn't stand it anymore.

"I slept with Blake," he blurted.

Lore paused again, but he didn't look up.

"Blake, from the ramen shop," Shaun clarified. His heart was racing, and he could feel the blush on his cheeks.

"I know who Blake is," said Lore. There was an edge to his voice that Shaun probably wouldn't have noticed if he hadn't spent the last week analyzing Lore's every move. "Does this affect the investigation in any way?"

Shaun swallowed and shook his head. "No, I don't think so."

"Then why are you telling me?"

"I don't know," Shaun admitted. There was a long silence, and he could tell that Lore expected a better answer, but he couldn't think of an explanation that wouldn't make him sound childish or insane, or both. "Never mind."

Lore said nothing, but he resumed typing with a little more force than was probably necessary.

Shaun watched him with a frown and tried to decide whether Lore's reaction should leave him feeling worried or hopeful.

Thirty minutes later, they were standing in front of a public telechamber in Stackston. They were wearing the same suits they'd worn to Oubliette, but Shaun was pretty sure Lore hadn't looked this good last time. He didn't even realize he was staring until Lore stepped into the phone booth and turned to give Shaun a look.

"Sorry," Shaun muttered as he stepped into the chamber and stood next to Lore. The interior of the booth was small, but they were able to fit inside it without touching. Shaun could tell that Lore was still irritated with him, so the last thing he wanted to do was invade Lore's personal space.

They waited in silence until the light above the door turned from red to green. Lore immediately wrenched the door open as if he couldn't stand to be trapped inside with Shaun for a moment longer. Shaun swallowed his own annoyance and followed Lore out of the booth.

They made their way up a flagstone path that led to an enormous, Greek Revival mansion. There were people milling about on the porch, talking and drinking cocktails. A few of them glanced in Shaun and Lore's direction, but for the most part, no one seemed to pay them any mind. That was a relief. Shaun had been worried that they'd stand out in the invitation-only club.

Two androgynous, humanoid creatures were guarding the front door. They were covered in black, shining scales, and had large, dark eyes that followed Shaun and Lore as they came up the front steps. Their waist-length hair was in dreadlocks, flecked here and there with iridescent beads.

"Names," the creatures hissed in unison.

"Stephen Malone and Lee Reynolds," Lore announced.

The creatures eyed them for a moment, then nodded. The large double doors swung open, revealing a set of heavy black drapes, which Lore pushed aside before stepping over the threshold and into the house. Shaun followed, and came to an abrupt halt beside Lore, staring at the scene before them.

"You said Keith was only here for twenty minutes?" Shaun asked under his breath.

Lore nodded.

"I can't imagine why," said Shaun.

The room looked a lot like Oubliette at first glance: well-lit and crowded with people in all states of undress. But that was where the similarities ended. Unlike Oubliette, the people who were standing around chatting were almost exclusively men, while the women in the room were chained up, gagged, or locked in cages. None of the women looked happy to be there.

Shaun's skin was crawling.

"Go mingle," murmured Lore.

"Mingle?" said Shaun incredulously, then grabbed a hold of Lore's sleeve. "Wait, where the hell are you going?" A group of men who'd been chatting nearby apparently overheard his outburst, because they looked over in his direction. Shaun lowered his voice to an irritated whisper and said, "You are not ditching me again, not here."

"I doubt you'll have any trouble entertaining yourself while I'm gone," Lore snapped and jerked his sleeve out of Shaun's grasp. After glaring at Shaun for a moment, he turned and strode away, leaving Shaun to stare incredulously at his back.

A few seconds later, Shaun realized that the men who'd been glancing his way before were now openly watching him and Lore. Shaun mentally shook himself and offered them a tight-lipped smile. "Guess he's still pissed at me for not taking out the trash."

The men chuckled politely and went back to their conversation, and Shaun turned away to scan the crowd. There was a rectangular bar in the center of the room, and he made his way toward it, wondering whether he should stick with water or order something a little stronger. Alcohol might help him deal with what was going on around him.

The bartender was an Amazon of a woman, with enormous breasts and wide hips. Her nipples were visible through the sheer fabric of her bikini top, and when she bent over to retrieve something from the bottom shelf, her skirt rode up to reveal that she was wearing a black, rubber harness instead of underwear. She spotted Shaun when he sat down on one of the barstools, and she made her way over without a smile.

"I'll just have water, please," Shaun told her.

The bartender bowed her head, then went off to get his drink.

Shaun kept his back to the room while he waited, though he could still see what was happening on the other side of the bar. A blonde woman in a skimpy red dress was draped over a table on her back. Her skirt had been pushed up to her waist and her top was pulled down to expose her breasts. Eight men were standing around the table, all of them with their cocks out. One of the men was holding the woman's wrists and another was holding her ankles. The other six were masturbating over her body while she struggled and pleaded with them to let her go. Shaun knew it had to be consensual—if it wasn't, all the woman would have to do was log off—but the sight still made his stomach churn.

Apparently, his revulsion showed on his face, because someone sat down on the stool next to him and said, "You don't approve."

Shaun jerked in surprise and glanced over to find a familiar, dark-haired man smiling at him. It took him a few seconds, but then he remembered where they'd seen each other: Oubliette. Nick had been one of the two men Shaun had been watching on his first night at the club. He was even more beautiful up close, with bright green eyes and delicate cheekbones that made him almost feminine. The way he smiled reminded Shaun of Blake's teasing little smirks, but there was something more predatory about the way Nick was eying him. Shaun felt the same tug of attraction that he'd felt at Oubliette, only this time, he didn't try to ignore it.

"A lot of people have that reaction their first time here," said Nick.

The bartender came back with Shaun's water and a drink for Nick. Shaun wondered if Nick had ordered without Shaun realizing it, or if he came to this club often enough that the bartender already knew his order. He decided not to push his luck by asking.

Nick eyed Shaun over the rim of his glass, and asked, "Why are you still here if you find it so distasteful?"

"No, no, it's not that. I've just never been anywhere like this before. I guess it's taking me a while to take it all in."

"Would you like a tour, then?"

Shaun wanted to say no, but he knew that if he did, he'd just end up sitting at the bar alone until Lore came back. Besides, he could do worse than spending time with a man as attractive as Nick. He took a sip of his water, then put his glass down and slid off his stool.

"So you're new to the lifestyle?" asked Nick as he led Shaun through the crowd.

"The lifestyle?"

Nick smirked and gestured to the room in general.

"Oh—oh, right." Shaun chuckled uncomfortably. He considered

lying, but he wasn't sure he'd be able to bluff his way through a conversation about S&M so he said, "Yeah, I guess you could say that. I mean, I've always been curious, but I've never had the guts to do anything about it."

"Really? You don't strike me as the type to be easily intimidated." Nick arched an eyebrow, a hint of a smile playing on his lips. "Especially not with the company you keep."

Shaun felt a twinge of worry, but he kept his expression neutral. "What do you mean?"

"I saw you when you came in." Nick led Shaun in a wide circle around a woman who was chained to a large, metal cross. He paused to run a hand up her leg, and Shaun's stomach lurched when the woman whimpered behind the patch of duct tape over her mouth. "That's Lore you're with, isn't it? He was with you at Oubliette too."

Shaun wasn't sure how to respond to that, so he just shrugged.

"I take it he doesn't mind sharing?"

"Oh, we're not—y'know, we're not involved or anything."

Nick was still rubbing the chained woman's leg, but he didn't seem particularly interested in her; his movements were distracted, and he was staring at Sean. "But you'd like to be."

"He's just a friend," said Shaun, forcing himself to hold Nick's gaze.

"I see," replied Nick with a vague smile. Apparently he decided it wasn't worth pushing the issue, because he took his hand away from the woman's leg and gestured for Shaun to follow him again. "If you're available, then I won't waste your time by beating around the bush." He stopped near a set of French doors and turned to eye Shaun in a way that left no doubt as to what he was about to ask. "Would you like to come into one of the back rooms with me?"

Shaun ignored the warning bells that went off in his head and offered Nick the lopsided grin he used to use as a kid to get himself out of trouble. "Depends on what you plan to do to me back there."

"We can keep it vanilla if you'd like." Nick smirked and walked backwards a few steps, then reached back to open the French doors.

Shaun followed Nick into a long, dimly lit hallway lined with doors. On the walls between each of the doors were reproductions of famous paintings that had been animated so that the characters in them were perverted versions of themselves: Botticelli's Venus dropped the lock of hair that had been protecting her modesty and slid two fingers between her legs, and Rembrandt's David and Jonathan shared a kiss with visible tongues and roaming hands.

Nick stopped at a door near the end of the hall and ushered Shaun into a suite that looked like it been copied straight out of the pages of a glossy travel magazine. Shaun didn't get much time to admire the plush carpeting and sleek leather couches, though, because as soon as the door was closed, Nick was behind him, slipping both arms around his waist and nuzzling his ear.

"You don't mind if we get straight to business, do you?" whispered Nick. "I figure if we both know why we're in here, there's no point in going through the drinks-and-conversation routine."

Less than ten minutes later, they were sitting across from each other on matching couches with their trousers shoved down to mid-thigh and their hands around their cocks. It had taken Shaun a few minutes to get hard—he was nervous, and he wasn't used to people being so straightforward and abrupt about sex—but now that he'd gotten himself stiff, the way Nick was looking at him was keeping him that way.

"What do you think about?" asked Nick as he stroked himself. He paused with his fingers just beneath the head of his cock and gave the shaft a squeeze. A bead of precome formed at the tip, and he smeared his thumb through it.

"All sorts of things," replied Shaun, his gaze fixed on Nick's hand. He knew that Nick was looking for something more specific, but talking about his fantasies with a stranger felt dangerously intimate.

"Do you think about men or women?"

"Both," Shaun admitted.

Nick slid further down in his chair so he could spread his legs. He let his head fall back against the couch, baring his throat. His skin was completely unblemished except for a tiny scar just below his jaw. "I think about men," he said. "I think about getting fucked. I look at men on the streets and I wonder how big their cocks are, and how they'd feel inside me. I think about what I'd do to get them to spread me open and fuck me with their tongues. I like it rough and dirty. I like pain."

Shaun swallowed and didn't reply. He mirrored the movements of Nick's hand, squeezing himself under the head of his cock and sometimes pushing the tip of his thumb into the slit.

"Do you ever think about getting fucked?" asked Nick, then let out a shivery laugh and said, "No, you don't, do you? You're always the one doing the fucking, aren't you?"

"Yeah... yeah, I'm always doing the fucking."

"Have you thought about fucking him?" Nick's voice dropped to a whisper, like he was sharing a secret. "Do you think he'd let you if you asked, or do you think he'd make you beg first? Beg for a chance to fuck his uptight, snotty little ass."

It took a second for Shaun to figure out who Nick was talking about, and when he did, his cock jerked in his fist. He wanted to deny it, but he knew there was no point. Nick already knew what he wanted, and there was no one else there to overhear his guilty confessions.

"What would you give him? Hm? What would you do for the chance to get him into your bed?"

"Anything," Shaun gasped. Admitting it out loud made his stomach clench and his cheeks flush, but he held Nick's gaze.

"Anything?" Nick sounded slightly out of breath. "Would you get on your knees for him? Let him grab your hair and fuck your mouth until he came down your throat?"

Shaun's fingers tightened around his cock and his eyes fluttered half-closed. "Yeah."

"Do you think about that? Do you think about sucking him off? Maybe you jerk off sometimes and lick your fingers afterward, and imagine it's his come on your tongue."

"Why are you so interested in what—ah—in what I think about

him?" asked Shaun. Heat was spreading through his body, making his toes curl and the tips of his ears burn, but he wasn't so far gone that he didn't find it strange that Nick was so focused on Lore.

"Because I'm interested in you and what goes on in your head," replied Nick. "Anyone can stick their cock in a hole; mental fucking takes skill."

"You do this a lot?" Shaun was panting, and his cock was throbbing in his hand, and he knew that if Nick didn't shut up soon, he was going to come.

"Enough to know which buttons to push, and right now every single one of yours is wired to Lore."

Shaun didn't even try to argue. He let his head fall back and stared at Nick from beneath his lashes, and slid his free hand between his legs to squeeze his balls.

"Are you thinking about him now?" Nick's voice was strained, and his prick was leaking precome all over his fingers and the shaft. "Are you thinking about fucking him? About holding him on your cock so he can feel every inch of it before you fuck his hot little ass until he's screaming your name?"

The thought of Lore screaming anyone's name was ridiculous, but Shaun's body didn't seem to care. His hips bucked and his balls tightened, and he bit down on his lip to stifle a moan.

"You know he'll never give it up, though. Not willingly. You'll have to surprise him," said Nick. "Do you know where he lives? You should find him and sneak in when he's sleeping..."

Shaun froze with his hand still on his cock. His body protested the sudden lack of stimulation, but he ignored it.

"You could tie him down while he's asleep, maybe stuff a gag in his mouth to keep him quiet. With the right drugs, you could make him do anything you wanted. All it would take is one quick jab in the arm—"

"That's not what I want."

"Don't kid yourself, Stephen. That's what every man wants." Nick stopped moving his hand as well, and he stared at Shaun from beneath his lashes. "That's what sex is: control."

"Really? 'Cause I was kinda under the impression it was just what people did when they liked each other." Shaun felt out of breath and shaky, and his prick was twitching impatiently in his hand, but he forced himself to let go and pull his trousers up. "I think I should get going."

Nick made a face at him, like he was frustrated by Shaun's naivety. "You can't be serious. It's a fantasy. It's not like I'm suggesting—"

"You're suggesting rape," Shaun interrupted as he pushed to his feet. He knew he was probably overreacting, but he couldn't help it. The mere suggestion that he'd want to do something like that to someone was enough to make him angry, but the fact that Nick had dragged Lore into the equation had him so furious his hands were shaking.

Nick said nothing as Shaun glared down at him and then turned to leave. When Shaun got to the door, though, Nick called after him, "I have to admit, it's refreshing to meet a man your age who still romanticizes sex. I didn't take you for the type."

Shaun wished he had some kind of sarcastic response, but he was still too angry to think of anything other than, "Have a nice night."

A group of men who were chatting to one another in the hallway gave Shaun curious looks as he stormed out of the room and slammed the door behind him. He ignored them and made his way out into the main room where he stopped and scanned the crowd. Lore was lounging against the bar, sipping a glass of soda water and looking attractively detached as usual.

Shaun went over to him and took the glass from Lore's hand. He took a sip of water, then plunked the glass down onto the counter. "If you're finished with whatever you needed to do, we're leaving."

To his amazement, Lore didn't protest. He stared at Shaun for a moment with a strange, hesitant expression on his face as if he wanted to say something but decided against it, then nodded and gestured for Shaun to lead the way.

Neither of them said a word as they made their way outside. They stopped at a public chamber in Okui first, then traveled from there to Lore's property—or at least, to what Shaun had thought was Lore's property.

"Where are we?" Shaun forgot his anger as he and Lore stepped out onto a small, arched bridge shrouded in heavy mist. Water lilies dotted the water beneath the bridge, and there was a large Quan Yin statue standing on a rock in the middle of the stream.

"I got bored," said Lore as he led the way across the bridge. The mist parted around a large building with a raised porch and a flared roof. It reminded Shaun of a Buddhist temple he and Kim had visited during their senior year vacation in Hawaii.

"You got bored?" said Shaun. He tipped his head back to gaze up at the building. "Y'know, normal people just read a book or take up knitting or something."

When he looked down again, Lore was standing on the porch, watching him with the same odd expression as back at the club.

Shaun wanted to ask if Lore was still angry, but he couldn't quite summon the courage, so he just offered Lore a faint smile and stepped up onto the porch. They stood there, looking at each other, and for the first time since they'd met, Shaun didn't feel uncomfortable being the object of Lore's scrutiny. In fact, he realized, he actually enjoyed the attention; he liked the thought that Lore found him interesting even if it was only in the most clinical of ways.

"Did he hurt you?" asked Lore after a long silence.

The question caught Shaun off guard, and he frowned. He hadn't realized that Lore had seen him go into the back room, but now that he knew, he was just glad Lore hadn't been there to overhear the conversation. "No, he didn't do anything, he was just weird. I mean, you know, he'd have to be weird to be hanging out in a place like that, but I thought I could handle it long enough to see if I could get any information out of him. Turns out I was wrong."

"I see," replied Lore without inflection, then glanced down at

Shaun's feet and said, "Take your shoes off before you come inside." With that, he turned, slipped his own shoes off by the door, and disappeared into the temple.

Shaun watched him go, then let out a soft chuckle.

The inside of the temple was surprisingly modern compared to the exterior. The floors were bare wood and there was an open hearth in the center of the main room, but the fire pit was ringed by comfortable-looking couches piled with throw pillows. One wall was dominated by a large statue of Buddha, and a door on the wall opposite the statue led to a bedroom; Shaun caught a glimpse of Lore's fur-covered bed through the open door.

Lore stood beside one of the couches, fidgeting with the frayed ends of his scarves. He looked uncomfortable, almost like he was waiting for Shaun's approval, although that was ridiculous. Shaun couldn't imagine Lore seeking anyone's approval for anything

"This is really nice," said Shaun as he drifted around the room. "What happened to all the security stuff, though? The giant gates and the expanding staircase?"

"We didn't trigger the security system."

"Got it." Shaun stopped by a side table and gestured to a silver tray that was crowded with liquor bottles and two glasses. "Expecting company?"

Lore gave him a look. "You complained about the lack of hospitality last time."

"Oh. Right." Shaun blushed. "I didn't mean—y'know, I was just kidding around, but thanks." He poured himself a glass of whiskey and took a sip, then licked his lips and asked, "So what was it you ran off to do back there? More visitor logs?"

Lore shook his head. "Places like that don't keep logs. That's part of the appeal for their clientele. I was examining the architecture."

"The architecture? I'm guessing that means you were checking out the source code, unless you've got a secret Greek Revival fetish you're not telling me about." Shaun offered Lore a lopsided grin and flopped down onto one of the couches.

To his surprise, Lore gave him one of those rare, blink-and-you'll-miss-it smiles, then sat down on the opposite end of the couch. Never one to let himself get too comfortable, he perched at the very edge of the cushion with his elbows on his knees, and explained, "The way a program is written, whether it's simple like the glass you're drinking out of or something more complex like flight-enabled avatars, can tell you things about the person who created it. No two people write code in exactly the same way."

Shaun was listening to what Lore was saying, but he was much more interested in watching. Most of the time when Shaun asked for explanations, Lore replied with either impatience or outright disdain. Sometimes, though, like now, Lore gave the explanation with an almost childlike enthusiasm. His eyes brightened and he made quick, graceful gestures with his hands.

"The more experienced the programmer," said Lore, "the more unique their code. Programmers develop their own style over time, just like musicians and artists. It's like a signature, but more elaborate."

"And what about the place we were just at? What could you tell about the guy who built it?"

"The code was elegant. Precise. The person who wrote it is probably obsessive, maybe even controlling, which isn't surprising considering the club's theme. If we can find out who created the club, we've also found the owner."

"You're thinking whoever built the club also runs it?"

Lore nodded.

"And I'm guessing you already tried to find out who the address for the club is registered to?"

"A user ID linked to a bogus real world identity. There aren't many people who would want their real names associated with a place like that."

"Well, it was worth a shot, I guess." Shaun considered their predicament for a moment, then said, "I still think it's a stretch to say that whoever created the club owns it. I mean, couldn't the owner have just hired the job out to someone?"

"No, the builder put too much of himself into creating these programs to just collect a fee and walk away. If he isn't the owner of the club, then he's at least a regular."

"And you can tell all this just from looking at the code?" Shaun raised both eyebrows. He'd never put much stock in things like handwriting analysis, and this seemed like a similar kind of pseudoscience. Still, Lore seemed convinced that he knew what he was talking about, and he had a way of saying things that could make even the most ardent nonbeliever question themselves.

"Yes." Lore's bright blue eyes were staring directly into Shaun's. "Mason, believe me: whoever wrote this code is an emotionally-invested control freak; he'd want to stay near the programs he writes... admire them, take care of them, make sure no one tries to modify the code."

Shaun examined Lore's face, the careful lack of expression juxtaposed with the faint tightening of his jaw, and realized that Lore was speaking from experience. "Fine," he said, "so even if the person who built the club is also the owner, I don't get how that brings us any closer to finding Sarah's killer. I mean, Keith went all over the place in her avatar, not just those private addresses."

"Because I have part of the code from the car bomb."

Shaun's whole body froze; his lungs seemed to stop moving and his stomach felt heavy. "What?"

"While you were meeting with Katou, I was able to get a look at some of the source code from the car bomb," said Lore. "I've never seen anything like it. It created itself as it ran, then deleted itself as soon as it ended its run."

"Wait, stop, back up." Shaun held up a hand and glared at Lore. "Go back to the part where you've had the code all this time and you're just now telling me about it."

Lore frowned at Shaun like he genuinely had no idea what the problem could be.

Shaun's jaw clenched. "This is the kind of shit you're supposed to tell me."

"Would it have made a difference?"

Shaun gaped. "What the hell do you mean, 'would it have made a difference'?"

"If you had known I had it, would it have helped you or the investigation in any way?"

Shaun opened his mouth to reply that of course it would have made a difference, but then he realized that it probably wouldn't have. He knew his way around standard code in the real world, but he was completely inexperienced with Simulnet code, and he wouldn't have been able to offer any kind of help with it whatsoever. But even so, that wasn't Lore's call to make, and Shaun was tired of feeling like a tag-along little kid. "That's not the point," he said. "The point is that we're partners and you're supposed to tell me this kind of shit, whether I can do anything to help you or not. No withholding information."

"I see," said Lore. His tone was annoyed, but to Shaun's surprise, he didn't argue. In fact, he said, "No withholding information, then."

"Good," said Shaun.

"All right," said Lore.

"Fine."

Lore gave Shaun a pointed stare.

Shaun heaved a sigh. "Okay, so you've got the code from the car bomb. Now what? You compare it to the code from the club?"

"Yes. If they look like they've been written by the same person, we can assume that our killer is the club's builder and therefore spends a lot of time at that address. Then, if I can create a program that will analyze avatars and look for similarities between their code and the killer's code..."

"Then all we have to do is take that program to the club and have it scan the crowd," said Shaun. "Of course, I guess there's a chance he could've bought his avatar from someone else, but he's probably too vain for that, right?"

The look Lore gave him—amused and a little proud, like he was a toddler who'd just learned to tie his own shoelaces—should have been irritating. It wasn't.

Shaun smiled, and he was trying to work up the courage to suggest they celebrate their breakthrough with dinner and drinks when his phone buzzed in his pocket. The number was blocked, and he considered not taking the call until Lore made an impatient gesture and said, "It could be important."

Shaun sighed answered the call. "Hello?"

"Mason?" Katou's voice was barely recognizable; it was distorted and there was a strange echo to it that made him sound like he was calling from the bottom of a well. Shaun couldn't make out what Katou said next, but it sounded panicked.

"Mister Katou?"

Katou said something else that Shaun couldn't distinguish, then very clearly said, "Trapped."

Chapter Eleven

From the street, the administration building looked the same as it had every other time Shaun had seen it: a crumbling old town-house with blue steps. Once he and Lore were inside, though, it was obvious that something was wrong. When Shaun had been there before, the building's interior had been a maze of rooms and corridors. Now, it was a clean, sparsely furnished house, and no matter how many times they checked and re-checked each room, they couldn't find Katou.

"Maybe he's just not here," Shaun suggested for what was probably the eighth time. They were standing in the living room, having just completed another search of the house.

"He's here," said Lore. He glanced up from his phone long enough to give Shaun a look, then went back to typing. "An entire section of the building's source code is encrypted."

"It might just be part of the security system," said Shaun. "Y'know, maybe the house changes to look normal when no one's in here, then turns back into a maze when Katou is around?"

Lore paused and glanced up at Shaun through his lashes. Judging from the expression on his face, he hadn't considered that possibility. "That's possible, yes," he admitted, "but that doesn't change the fact that Katou is here somewhere."

"But how do you know?" asked Shaun. He knew he was pushing the matter, but he was tired of having to drag explanations out of Lore.

"I just do," Lore snapped. He was glaring, but he seemed more defensive than angry, which made Shaun even more curious.

Lore obviously had no intention of explaining anything, though, so Shaun gave up with a sigh and stuffed his hands into his pockets. He hated standing around, feeling useless, so after a few minutes, he announced, "I'm gonna look around outside."

Lore nodded distractedly.

Shaun rolled his eyes and headed for the front door. When he got there, though, the handle refused to turn. Shaun frowned and tried it again, without success. "Uh, Lore?" he called. "You didn't happen to spot anything in the code that would keep the door from opening, did you?"

There was a pause, and then Lore appeared in the doorway of the living room. "What?"

"The door is stuck." Shaun gave the handle a yank to demonstrate. "It's not moving."

Lore eyed him for a moment before crossing the front hall and trying the door himself. It didn't budge. He took a step back and stared at it, eyes narrowed as if he could somehow intimidate it into opening.

"Security?" Shaun guessed. "Maybe it's supposed to keep trespassers trapped until someone can get here and deal with them?"

Lore shook his head. "No, I just looked at the building's security system. There's nothing in it that should trigger a lock-down."

"Let's try the back door," Shaun suggested.

Lore looked doubtful, but he followed Shaun through the house anyway. When they got to the tiny kitchen in the rear of the house, they found the back door locked as well.

"Damn it." Shaun slammed the heel of his palm against the door, right above the handle. The apprehension he'd felt at finding the front door stuck was slowly turning into full-blown anxiety, which got worse and worse as he tried each of the windows in the kitchen and found those locked as well.

Lore still had his phone out, holding it with both hands, but he wasn't typing anything. He was staring at the screen, but he didn't look like he was actually reading it; there was a faraway look in his eyes, like he was lost in thought.

Shaun decided not to disturb him, and instead concentrated his efforts on finding a way out of the house. He found a dishtowel in one of the kitchen drawers and wrapped it around his fist before punching the glass in one of the windows. The glass didn't even rattle.

"Stop," Lore murmured when Shaun started hunting through cabinets for something heavy to use on the window. "You're still trying to apply real world physics to Simulnet. The glass isn't going to break no matter what we do to it."

"Have you got a better idea?" Shaun snapped.

"We shouldn't have come inside," said Lore. He was staring at his phone again with his brow furrowed. "You were right, the house does change when it's unoccupied, but it's not supposed to lock down."

Any other time, Shaun might have felt smug from hearing the words 'you were right' come out of Lore's mouth. Right now, though, he was more concerned with the implications of what Lore was saying: they were trapped. His heart clawed its way up into his throat. "We're in the encrypted section, aren't we?"

Lore nodded. "I think so, yes."

They were trapped. A shot of adrenaline ripped through Shaun's body, but he took a deep, steadying breath and said, "But that's okay, though, right? I mean, all you have to do is decrypt this section of the house's source code and we can get out of here. No problem. You do this kind of shit all the time."

The expression on Lore's face wasn't encouraging. He frowned at his phone and didn't reply.

"Fuck," Shaun muttered and raked a hand through his hair. "You think it's a glitch or what?"

"I don't know," said Lore without looking up.

"Shit, what if—Lore, what if it's him? What if he—I don't know, what if he kidnapped Katou or something and made him call us down here?"

Lore's fingers paused momentarily on the keypad of his phone. "That's already crossed my mind. So has the fact that Katou himself doesn't seem to be on your list of suspects. You have too much faith in people."

Shaun dragged both hands over his face and held them against his mouth for a minute while he watched Lore go back to typing. After an anxious silence, he asked, "Should I call Hudson?"

"Something is interfering with the signal; I can't ping my computers at home." Lore's eyes were moving as he read whatever was on the screen of his phone, but then he paused and looked up at Shaun. "But you can log out and call her."

Shaun blinked, then let out a shaky laugh. Logging out hadn't even crossed his mind. He pulled his phone out of his pocket and navigated to the account control screen, then pressed the logout button. Nothing happened. He tried again. Nothing.

"Mason?"

"I can't log out." Shaun fought to keep his voice steady.

"What do you mean, you can't log out?" Lore leaned in to peer over Shaun's shoulder, then reached out and tapped on the screen of Shaun's phone. When nothing happened, his expression turned worried.

Shaun wet his lips and asked, "Do you think whatever is keeping us from making phone calls is also blocking the logout signal?"

"Yes."

"So we really are trapped?" Shaun asked, even though he already knew the answer.

Lore stared at him for a moment, then looked away and replied very quietly, "Yes."

"Right," Shaun muttered. He wondered why he felt so shaky, why the thought of being trapped there was affecting him so badly. Compared to some of the other things he'd been through, this was nothing.

Then he glanced at Lore, realized how close they were standing to each other, and suddenly it dawned on him that it wasn't himself he was worried about.

"Hey," said Shaun. When Lore looked up at him, he forced a smile. "I guess it could be worse, right? At least the place isn't filled with snakes or sea urchins or something."

Lore raised an eyebrow, but the corners of his lips were twitching. "Sea urchins, Mason?"

"They're evil," replied Shaun in the most serious tone he could manage.

Lore's smile widened, then faded almost as quickly as it had appeared, but his expression stayed soft. His gaze was just as intense as always, but for once, his weren't narrowed with impatience. His features were relaxed, his lips were parted, and he looked more human than Shaun would have ever thought him capable of being.

"Who are you?" whispered Shaun. His pulse was throbbing, and his fingers were itching to reach out and tug at Lore's hair.

"Shaun." Lore looked conflicted, like he wanted to say something but he wasn't sure if he should.

Shaun had no idea what was happening between them, and part of him knew that they should both be concentrating on finding a way out of the house, not standing there in the kitchen and staring at each other. He couldn't seem to make himself pull away, though, not when the air between them was so thick with tension he felt short of breath. He felt himself leaning closer—not close enough to touch, and definitely not close enough to kiss, but close enough to watch Lore's pupils dilate. It was a tiny detail, one that Shaun would never have thought of if he'd been asked to create an avatar, but it made Lore seem more real to him than ever.

"What are you doing, Shaun?" asked Lore. His tone was cautious, but he didn't pull away.

"Probably something stupid," whispered Shaun. "Something stupid and impulsive, and—"

A jolt shuddered through the house, like the building had just been picked up and dropped. It was strong enough to rattle the windows and make the lights flicker. Shaun's first thought, after living in Los Angeles for so long, was that it was an earthquake, and he reacted on instinct: he grabbed Lore and dragged him into the doorway just before a second shockwave hit.

"What the fuck is that?" Shaun had to yell to be heard over the racket. He expected it to stop after a few seconds, but it didn't.

Lore shook his head and braced a hand on the door frame as he stared up at the kitchen ceiling. A large crack was splintering its way across the plaster, and the middle of the ceiling was starting to droop. "This isn't supposed to be happening; it's not built into any of the house's code."

"Then what the fuck is doing it?"

The kitchen ceiling gave way. Shaun and Lore raised their arms to shield themselves as the overhead beams broke and crashed through the crumbling plaster, that sending up a cloud of dust. In a normal earthquake, Shaun would have gotten them both outside, but this wasn't a normal earthquake and there was nothing either of them could do to protect themselves except to huddle together in the doorway.

"There's an encrypted data stream coming into the house," shouted Lore. That faraway look was back in his eyes, like he was staring at something Shaun couldn't see. "Someone is using a modified version of the car bomb program."

Shaun had no idea how Lore knew that, but he didn't get a chance to ask. Another jolt almost knocked him off his feet, and he reached out to grab hold of Lore, trying to keep his balance. Lore stumbled and clutched at the doorframe, but it was too late. They tumbled to the floor together, and seconds later, the doorway they'd been standing in began to splinter around its frame. The entire wall seemed to drop six inches, and bits of plaster rained down on them as they struggled back to their feet. They managed to stand and duck out of the room into the hallway just before the doorframe collapsed completely, sealing the kitchen off from the rest of the house with a pile of splintered wood and broken plaster.

"We've got to get out of here before the whole thing comes down," said Shaun as he grabbed Lore's arm and pulled him down the hallway toward the front door. He had no idea what would happen to them if they didn't make it out of the house in time, but he didn't want to find out.

The front door was still locked, but that didn't stop Shaun from tugging at it just to make sure. When that didn't work, he stumbled into the front parlor and looked around, trying to find an alternate escape route. He glanced back to ask Lore to help him and found Lore still standing in the hallway, staring up at the window above the front door with the same focused expression he'd worn in the kitchen.

"Hey, I could use a little help here," Shaun called, exasperated.

"Not now," Lore snapped. The house rumbled, as if responding to his annoyance.

"What the fuck, dude? What part of 'we need to find a way out of here' don't you understand?"

"I'm working on it. Be quiet and let me concentrate."

"You're working on it? Looks to me like you're just standing there and—" The ground lurched beneath Shaun's feet, and he grabbed at the back of a chair to keep himself upright. Once he regained his balance, he opened his mouth to continue, but he was caught off guard by the sight of Lore standing with his eyes closed and both hands pressed against the front door. It was hard to tell for sure, but it looked like the front hall had stopped shaking. The hair on the back of Shaun's neck stood on end.

'Lore is a legend,' Ruby had said. 'There are rumors about him, about what he can do... he can do things with Simulnet code that no one else can.'

As Shaun watched, the house seemed to slowly respond to Lore's touch. The area that had stopped rocking grew wider and wider, encompassing the front hall and working its way outward until it reached the parlor where Shaun was standing. Shaun had been struggling so hard to keep himself upright that when the floor beneath his feet suddenly stilled, he swayed like a drunkard.

Silence crept through the house. Shaun listened to the muffled rattling of the kitchen windows give way to sudden quiet. Eventually, the only thing he could hear was the sound of creaking wood and his own labored breathing.

Lore stayed by the door with his palms still pressed against the wood, then slowly exhaled and let his hands fall to his sides. He opened his eyes and turned his head to look at Shaun. "We might not have much time before it starts again."

"How did you do that?" whispered Shaun. His heart was pounding, his chest felt tight, and he wasn't convinced it was just because of the earthquake.

"That's not important right now," said Lore. He looked away

and pulled his phone out of his pocket, but Shaun stalked over to him and snatched it out of his hands. Lore didn't try to take it back, but he did scowl. "We don't have time for games, Mason."

"I'm not the one playing games. Tell me how you made it stop."

Lore made an exasperated sound and threw his hands in the air. It was the first time Shaun had ever seen him look truly close to losing his temper. In a sharp, biting tone, he replied, "I re-routed the flow of data to another address, then reversed it back to the sender. They would have been forced to either log off or—"

"That's not what I meant and you know it," said Shaun. He was still holding Lore's phone, and he held it up between them. "How the fuck did you do that without this?"

"Mason."

"Lore." Shaun glared. He knew Lore was right, that it was more important for them to escape than for him to get his questions answered, but he was having a hard time letting go. Eventually, though, after a few seconds had passed and Lore had done nothing but scowl at him, common sense got the better of him and he thrust the phone back in Lore's direction.

Lore took the phone without even so much as a 'thank you' and set to work.

Shaun glared at the side of Lore's head, but when Lore didn't look up again, Shaun eventually gave up. He turned away, shoved his hands into his pockets, and began pacing, first over to the fireplace, then over to the window where he paused and stared out at the street. There were people passing on the sidewalk outside, and he tapped on the window, trying to get their attention, but to no avail. He wondered if they'd even be able to see him if they looked in his direction.

He was still standing there, staring out at the street, when a low, rumbling sound made the house shiver. Shaun immediately grabbed hold of the window ledge, waiting for the rocking to start, but the vibration stayed at a steady hum. He glanced at Lore, who seemed unfazed, and asked, "What the fuck is that?"

"Decryption. It should only take a few minutes."

"Good, so that gives you some time to tell me what the fuck is going on with you."

Lore's eyes narrowed. "It's none of your business, Mason. I'm none of your business."

That hurt more than Shaun would have expected, and at first, he didn't even know how to respond, but then he shoved his hands back into his pockets and glared at Lore. "You're my business as long as you're my partner. After that, I don't give a shit what happens to you."

And just like that, Lore's expression went blank.

"Shit," said Shaun. "Shit, I'm sorry, I didn't mean that."

Lore stared at him for a moment, then turned away and went back into the hall.

"Seriously, I didn't mean that," said Shaun. He followed Lore out of the room and put a hand on his shoulder, then snatched it away when Lore stiffened. "I'm just—I just get so fucking frustrated because you never tell me anything. How am I supposed to help you with anything if you never explain things to me?"

"I explain when explaining will make a difference," said Lore.

The low humming sound faded to silence, and Lore reached out to try the door. It opened. He glanced at Shaun, then stepped out onto the crumbling blue steps.

Shaun tried to feel relieved as he followed Lore out into the grey Okui sunlight, but there was a knot of guilt coiled tight around his stomach. In less than fifteen minutes, he'd managed to get close enough to Lore to kiss him, then almost immediately driven a wedge between them.

Katou and three of his men were standing on the sidewalk in front of the house, and Katou rushed forward when he saw Lore and Shaun. "Are you alright?" he asked, grabbing Shaun's arms. "What happened? I came as soon you called, but the building was in lockdown."

"What?" replied Shaun, confused. "We didn't call you, you called me."

Katou frowned and shook his head. "I received a call twenty

minutes ago from someone who sounded like you, telling me that you were trapped inside the administration building. We got here and the house wouldn't accept my access codes."

"It was an ambush," said Lore. He had both hands tucked into the pockets of his blazer, and he was staring at the ground. He didn't look dejected, per se, but he didn't seem like himself, either. Shaun wondered if he was to blame for that. "The same person who called you also called us. We came here to find you and ended up trapped inside ourselves."

"But you were sure Katou was inside," said Shaun. He did his best to sound non-confrontational. The last thing he wanted to do was add to the unpleasant tension between them.

"An avatar linked to your user ID and serial number was inside the building," Lore explained to Katou. "I assumed that meant you were here, but now I wonder..." Lore paused and frowned at the ground, as if something had just occurred to him, then pulled his phone out of his pocket and began typing. A few seconds later, he said, "I need to examine the code for your avatar. I also need to get a closer look at the security system for the building, now that everything has been unlocked."

"Of course," replied Katou.

Shaun licked his lips and said, "Uh, so what can I do to help?"

"Log out, eat, and sleep," said Lore, still staring at his phone. He turned and ushered Katou and his men up the stairs to the house. "I'll send you a message when I'm finished here." He didn't even so much as look at Shaun as he made his way back inside.

Shaun curled his hands into fists in his pockets, then turned and walked away.

Ruby opened the door just as Shaun raised his hand to knock. She ushered him inside before peering out into the fog and then shutting the door behind him. He stood there in the front hall, feeling suddenly awkward about being there, especially when he

knew that she was in danger any time she was logged in. He'd
needed someone to talk to, though—someone he could talk to
about the case and about Lore without having to worry that he was
saying too much, and since Blake hadn't answered his phone or
responded to his text messages, Shaun had come here to the safe
house.

"Come in," said Ruby, gesturing for Shaun to follow her into
the front room. There were already two mugs of what looked like
hot cocoa sitting on the coffee table. She handed him one of them
before taking the other for herself and sinking down into one
corner of the couch with her tiny hands wrapped around her cup.
Once Shaun had settled in beside her, she blew across the surface
of her drink and asked, "What happened? You said something about
an earthquake?"

Shaun recounted the story of what had happened at the
administration building, though he left out the part where he'd almost kissed Lore in the kitchen. Ruby listened to him with a frown,
but her eyes widened and her lips parted when he told her about
the way Lore had made the shaking stop without a computer or
his phone.

"So the rumors are true?" asked Ruby.

"I don't know about all of them, but some of them sure seem
to be," replied Shaun. He took a sip of his hot chocolate, then licked
his lips and stared down into his cup. "I asked him to explain it to
me, but—well, let's just say it didn't end well. Apparently, he's none
of my business."

There was a long silence before Ruby asked, "Does he know
how you feel about him?"

"No," said Shaun, then paused for a moment and added, "Well,
he might. I don't know. I mean, it's not like I'm pining away after
him or anything."

Ruby gave him a look that reminded him uncomfortably of his
sister.

"I'm not," Shaun insisted, rolling his eyes. "What is it with
women romanticizing everything?"

"What is it with men refusing to acknowledge emotional connections?"

"Touché." Shaun sighed and put his cup down on the coffee table so he could rub his face with both hands. "It's just—I don't get him, but I really want to. I don't even know why it matters. I doubt we'd even be able to be friends after all this is over. We have nothing in common except this case."

"Sometimes that doesn't matter," said Ruby. "Sarah and I didn't have much in common either, but we ended up together anyway."

Shaun sank down into the couch cushions and let his head fall back, then rolled his head to the side so he could look at her. "I don't want a relationship with him. I'm fucking awful at them. I don't want a relationship with anyone."

"Relationships don't always have to be picket fences and minivans."

Shaun sighed and stared up at the ceiling. They sat in silence for awhile, each of them alone with their thoughts. Shaun didn't even realize his eyes had closed or that he'd started to nod off until Ruby's hand was on his shoulder, nudging him awake.

"You're exhausted," she said. "You should log out and sleep."

Shaun shook his head and rubbed his eyes. "God, you sound like Lore. I don't want to log out. That's the whole reason I came over here; I need to just be around someone." He opened his eyes and blinked at her. "Can't I just sleep here for a little while?"

"You need real sleep." Ruby frowned and squeezed his shoulder. "But yeah, you can sleep here for awhile. Not on the couch, though; you'll wake up feeling worse than you're going to anyway."

Shaun followed Ruby upstairs and down the hall to a cozy little bedroom with heavy furniture and thick velvet drapes. The double bed looked inviting, and he toed his shoes off before flopping down onto it face first. With his face still buried in the pillow, he stretched his arm out in a silent invitation for Ruby to join him. A moment later, he felt the mattress shift as she settled onto it.

"That was always Sarah's side of the bed," Ruby murmured as she stretched out next to Shaun. "Not this bed, obviously, but…"

Shaun rolled onto his side so he could look at her. She seemed so small and fragile, even more so than usual, that he couldn't resist the urge to move closer and wrap an arm around her waist. To his surprise, she burrowed up against him like she was desperate for warmth, and curled her fingers in the front of his shirt.

"I'm not usually like this," she said. "I've never really been good at the whole damsel-in-distress thing. I just miss her so much, and I feel like there's nothing I can do to make any of it make sense."

"I know," replied Shaun, stroking her hair. He wasn't sure which of them moved first, or if they both moved at the same time, but their lips touched. There was nothing sexual about the kiss; it was just a kiss between two people who were missing other people so much they couldn't think of any other way of expressing it.

They pulled away at the same time, and Ruby settled with her cheek on Shaun's chest. Shaun sighed and tightened his hold around her shoulders. She was smaller than her personality made her seem, but she was also soft and warm, and that was exactly what he needed. He kissed the top of her head, and a few minutes later, he was fast asleep.

Shaun was alone when he woke, feeling groggy and hungover despite the fact that he hadn't had anything to drink in days. There was a note from Ruby on the pillow beside his head: 'Had to log out, but email me if you need me. Thank you for talking to me last night. Now you just need to talk to him.' Shaun re-read it a few times while muzzily debating with himself, then stumbled out of bed and made his way to Lore's property. Lore had said he would send a message when he was finished analyzing the code from the day before, but Shaun wasn't feeling patient, and he wanted to at least try and mend what he'd broken between them.

To Shaun's surprise, his arrival didn't trigger the temple's security system. That made him wary, and he crept across the bridge, expecting something to rise up and grab him at any moment. When he made it all the way to the other side unharmed, he frowned and trudged up the stairs to the temple, kicked his shoes off beside the door, and knocked.

Silence.

Shaun considered that maybe Lore wasn't home, but he doubted Lore would leave the property unlocked if he was out. When Shaun knocked again and got no response, he frowned slid the door open to step inside. The tatami mats muffled his footsteps as he cautiously made his way into the living room. From where he stood, the house looked deserted, and he was about to turn and leave when a sound from the bedroom caught his attention.

The bedroom door had been left cracked open and Shaun approached it with caution, picking up a heavy wooden candle holder on the way. He wasn't sure what he expected to find when he eased the door open and peered into the room, but it certainly wasn't what he saw.

Lore was on his hands and knees in the middle of the bed, with his back arched and his fingers clawing at the sheets. A large, dark man was fucking him from behind, grabbing him by the hips and biting the back of his neck. Lore's eyes were closed, and his lips were swollen like he'd been kissing or sucking cock all night, and when the man grabbed a handful of his hair, Lore moaned deep in the back of his throat.

Shaun knew that he should leave, but he couldn't make himself move. He stood there, rooted to the spot, sick with jealousy and want, and grabbing at the doorframe to keep himself upright. It wasn't until the man behind Lore started whispering to him in French that Shaun forced himself to back away. His body still felt heavy with exhaustion, but his heart was pounding and his palms were sweating, and he was torn between the urge to run as far away as he could get or to go back into the bedroom and put the candlestick he was holding to good use.

In the end, he did neither; he trudged back outside and down the steps of the temple without bothering to put his shoes back on. He dropped the candle holder somewhere in the grass, then went to sit on a rock near the stream. He was too far away to hear them fucking anymore, but he couldn't get the sound of Lore's gasping out of his head.

Shaun pulled his knees up to his chest, wrapped his arms around them, and put his head down.

Chapter Twelve

"Mason?"

Shaun jolted awake and blinked up at the person towering over him. It took a few seconds for his vision to clear—the backs of his eyelids felt like sandpaper—but when he recognized Lore, he remembered where he was and shoved to his feet.

"How long have you been here?" asked Lore. He was fully dressed, but his hair was even more tousled than usual, and there was a darkening bruise on his neck above his scarves. He could've hidden it if he'd wanted to, but he hadn't, and Shaun hated him for it.

Shaun looked away and closed his eyes. "I don't know," he said tiredly. "Maybe twenty minutes, I guess."

"You look terrible."

"Thanks," said Shaun. He opened his eyes and tried to glare at Lore, but he could feel that he was swaying on his feet, and he wondered why it was so hard for him to stay awake.

Lore's brow wrinkled. "Did you sleep at all?"

"Almost eight hours," replied Shaun. His emotions were swinging all over the place, from angry jealousy to a weird kind of needy affection, and he stuffed his fist against his mouth to stifle a yawn. "Sorry. I don't know why the fuck I'm still so tired."

"You haven't been sleeping enough."

"I guess," said Shaun before lapsing into an awkward silence. He stuffed his hands into his pockets and swayed again, closed his eyes, and then startled himself out of a half-sleep a few seconds later. When he realized Lore was staring at him, he mumbled, "I came by to see if you figured anything about the—you know, the uhm—"

"About what happened yesterday?"

Shaun nodded.

"I wasn't able to track the data back to its original source. The computer sending it was just a ghoul. The person responsible for the attack took over someone else's computer and set it up to transmit the data. It is the same code as the car bomb, though. Our killer is playing games with us."

Shaun nodded distractedly. He was listening, but he wasn't really absorbing the information, no matter how hard he tried to concentrate. All he could think about was how much he wanted to cover the bruise on Lore's neck with one of his own, and how after doing so, he would keep Lore in bed with him while he slept for three days straight.

"Mason," said Lore, watching Shaun with narrowed eyes, "have you taken something?"

Shaun shook his head. "No, like I said, I'm just really tired. Dunno why. I hardly even remember falling asleep. One minute, me and Ruby were talking, and the next—"

"Ruby?" Lore interrupted. "You were with Ruby last night? On Simulnet?"

"Yeah," Shaun muttered and scratched the back of his neck. "Just needed some company after what happened. You were busy, it was too late to call Kim, couldn't get ahold of Blake..."

Lore's expression hardened at the mention of Blake's name, but his tone was oddly patient when he explained, "That's why you're tired. Sleeping inside Simulnet isn't a substitute for real sleep because the VR tank is keeping your brain active."

"Oh," said Shaun.

"You need sleep," said Lore. "Real sleep."

"But there's so much to do," muttered Shaun. His body was protesting the idea of staying awake any longer, though. His feet felt heavy and his legs were weak, and keeping his eyes open seemed like an impossible task.

Lore's mouth tightened. "Mason, you're useless to both of us in your current state. There's nothing you can do now that can't wait until after you've slept. Log out and sleep, or I'll force-drop your connection and block your user ID from signing on again for the next six hours."

"You can do that?" Shaun mumbled as he eyes slid closed again.
"Good night, Shaun."

Shaun was still tired when he woke six hours later, but at least he felt less sleep-deprived than he had when he'd gone to bed. He patted around on the pillow beside him, looking for his phone, then remembered that he'd dropped it on the floor when he'd trudged into the bedroom. He slid halfway off the mattress to retrieve it, rubbed his eyes to clear them, and then blinked incredulously at the screen.

There were nineteen missed calls from Hudson and two missed calls from Lore.

Shaun immediately called Hudson back, and she answered on the third ring: "You'd better have some answers for me, Mason, because we've got another one."

"Fuck," Shaun cursed and rubbed his forehead. "Who?"

"Female, mid-sixties, found by the boy who delivers her groceries every week."

Shaun sighed. "Got a positive ID on her yet?"

"Yeah, just a sec." There was some rustling of paper in the background, and then Hudson said, "Ruby Horowitz."

The L.A. Coroner's Office was an attractive, mission-style building crafted from red brick and sun-bleached concrete. It had originally housed the city's general hospital until a fire at the turn of the century killed a dozen children. It was a rite of passage for teenagers in the surrounding neighborhood to run up to the front steps of the building in the middle of the night, knock three times, and wait for the ghosts of the dead children to knock back. More than a few kids had run away screaming afterward. Apparently, no one expected morgue employees to have a sense of humor.

Shaun raced up the front steps when he arrived, bypassed the reception desk, and went straight back into the bowels of the coroner's office. Technically, since he was with Cybercrimes and not Homicide, he was supposed to sign in like any other visitor, but only a handful of people tried to stop him, and all it took was a flash of his badge to keep them from asking questions.

Hudson was standing in front of one of the exam rooms, talking to two uniformed officers. She saw Shaun as soon as he rounded the corner, and immediately waved the officers off before striding down the corridor to meet him. Shaun didn't slow down until Hudson stopped him by planting a hand in the middle of his chest.

"Where is she?" Shaun demanded. He tried to sidestep her, but she blocked his path.

"Mason, you can't go in there right now," said Hudson in a low voice. "You're not even supposed to be here."

Shaun tried again to get around her, but Hudson wasn't budging. The two officers she'd been talking to had paused at the end of the hall and were eying him suspiciously, so he stopped moving and pleaded in a whisper, "You have to let me see her. Please."

"Mason..." Hudson stared up at him for a minute, then sighed and muttered, "Look, I'll get you in to see her, but not right now. I've got three detectives and the chief coroner in there, and even if I could come up with a bullshit excuse to get you in, we can't afford to draw that kind of attention to you. You're going to have to wait."

Shaun's jaw tightened. He wanted to insist on going into the exam room right that second, but the tiny part of his brain that was still operating rationally told him that he was pushing his luck just by being there. Finally, he pulled away and took a few steps backwards, then went to sit in one of the hard, plastic chairs lined up against the wall. He rested his elbows on his knees and stared at Hudson defiantly.

Hudson watched him for a moment, then sighed and went back down the hall to where the officers were waiting. They went into the exam room together, and Hudson shot one last look at Shaun before closing the door behind her.

Shaun had heard people talk about time seeming to crawl, but he'd never experienced it quite like this. He listened to the murmur of people coming and going from autopsy rooms and checked the time on his phone every three or four minutes, expecting to see that an hour had passed since the last time he'd looked. He tried not to think about Ruby.

Eventually, he tried calling Lore again. He'd called once on his way to the coroner's office, but Lore's phone had been off. This time, the phone rang three times before going to voicemail. Shaun wondered if Lore was ignoring his phone because he was working, or if he was ignoring it because because he had company. The thought made Shaun feel sick, and he buried his face in his hands.

What seemed like an eternity later, the door to the exam room opened, and Hudson emerged along with the two officers who'd been with her earlier. Three men followed them out into the hall, two of whom Shaun recognized as Homicide detectives, and the other who Shaun guessed was the coroner. They lingered by the door for a few minutes, talking to one other, then went their separate ways except for Hudson, who hovered near the door and took her phone out of her pocket.

Shaun's phone beeped with a text message a few seconds later: 'Wait 5 min then follow me inside.'

Hudson went back into the exam room without looking in his direction, and Shaun checked the time on his phone. The next few minutes were torture. He finally broke at the four minute mark and pushed to his feet, then strode down the hall, checked to make sure no one was watching, and slipped into the exam room.

"You've got ten minutes," said Hudson.

Shaun nodded and moved closer to the table where Ruby's body lay with a blue sheet pulled up over her head. For a few minutes, he couldn't make himself do more than just stand there and stare at the outline of her face beneath the cotton fabric—the bump of her nose, and the dip where the sheet sagged between her chin and her chest. Once he'd gathered his courage, he gently peeled the sheet back.

The real life Ruby Horowitz was an older version of her Simulnet self: a petite woman in her late fifties or early sixties with the same pixie haircut and porcelain doll mouth. Her hair was grey, not blue, and her skin was dotted with age spots, but she was still Ruby, and Sean could still feel her arms around him.

The tightness in Shaun's throat gave way to a quiet, choked sob that he tried to muffle by covering his mouth with his hand.

"I'm going to step out into the hall," Hudson murmured from behind him. "Five minutes, Mason."

Shaun nodded, but he was hardly listening; he was reaching out to stroke Ruby's hair, and trying to fight the tears that stung his eyes.

Chapter Thirteen

Shaun went straight home from the coroner's office after making Hudson promise that she would email him everything from Ruby's file. As soon as he got to his apartment, he logged into Simulnet and went to find Lore. It took him three tries to enter the address for Lore's property, his hands were shaking so badly, but then he finally got it right and stepped into the chamber. Seconds later, the doors opened again and Shaun's stomach plummeted.

Lore's property was in ruins.

The tower and the endless sea were back, but the bridge that led from the arrival island to the main island was a mess of crumbling stone and bent metal. The ocean was as still as ever, but its mirror-like surface was marred with dark splotches, like someone had dropped bucketfuls of ink into the water.

Shaun's heart kicked into overdrive, and he immediately forgot about everything except finding Lore. He hurried across the bridge as quickly as he dared, climbing over rubble and skirting around gaping holes that dropped away to the sea below. When he finally made it to the other side, he came to an abrupt stop and stared up at the tower. There was an enormous crack going straight up the side, and the entire building seemed to have shifted on its foundation. The door at the base was open, and Shaun didn't even hesitate before rushing inside and running up the spiral staircase, taking the steps two at a time and ignoring the creeping fear that the tower could simply tip over at any moment and go crashing into the sea.

When he finally made it to the top of the stairs, he burst into the large, circular room that served as Lore's living space and came to a skidding halt. An entire section of the wall was missing, and the air in the room was heavy with dust. Lore was standing by the crumbling wall, silhouetted by the sun, and he turned when Shaun rushed into the room. His nose was bloody and there was a bruise on his cheek, but he looked otherwise unharmed.

"Oh thank fucking god," whispered Shaun. He was across the room in a second, throwing his arms around Lore's shoulders and pressing their cheeks together. To his surprise, Lore hugged him around the waist and clutched the back of his shirt. He closed his eyes and concentrated on the feeling of Lore's chest moving against his and the sound of Lore's soft, ragged breathing in his ear.

After just a few seconds, though, Lore jerked away and rushed over to his desk. "Stay there, I have to—there's a login code—"

"What? Hey, what are you doing? That can wait. Tell me what happened first." Shaun followed him, feeling dazed by the flurry of activity. He leaned down and tried to wipe the blood from Lore's nose, only to be pushed away again.

Lore looked half-crazed. His eyes were wide and his hands were shaking as he typed, his bony fingers practically a blur over the keyboard. While he worked, he explained, "They attacked me, they know my signature; they've analyzed my code. They've done the same thing I did to them. They attacked everything that had my code attached to it. That's how Ruby—I didn't protect her well enough because I never thought—"

"Wait, wait, what do you mean that's how Ruby—" Shaun broke off mid-sentence when he remembered that Lore had attached a tracker to Ruby's avatar, meant to monitor her vitals and keep her safe. If the killer had gone after everything that matched Lore's coding signature, then Ruby's avatar would have been included in the list of targets.

"I have to get the authentication key out," Lore was muttering as he typed, but then he shoved away from the desk and whirled on Shaun. Before Shaun could pull away, Lore reached out and grabbed his face with both hands.

"Lore, what—?"

"Shut up," whispered Lore. His eyes were closed, and his brow was furrowed. "Be quiet and let me concentrate."

Shaun's pulse was racing so fast he was afraid he might pass out. Adrenaline was making his whole body shiver, and his breathing was still ragged. The warmth of Lore's hands on his cheeks should have been comforting, but it wasn't.

When Lore opened his eyes again, he looked less panicked but still distraught. He stared at Shaun, his blue eyes more intense than Shaun had ever seen them, and then without warning, he jerked Shaun up against him and crushed their mouths together in an unforgiving kiss.

Whenever Shaun had wondered what sex with Lore would be like, he'd imagined something precise and methodical, each move planned from the start like an orchestrated game of chess. The reality was exactly the opposite. Lore kissed like it was the last kiss he'd ever have, like Shaun was the only thing in the universe that mattered. It wasn't even a good kiss, really—it was clumsy and full of more enthusiasm than skill—but it was quite possibly the best kiss of Shaun's life.

In any other situation, Shaun might have pulled away and demanded an explanation, but his brain was short-circuiting. The only thing that mattered was Lore kissing him, open-mouthed and desperate, and Lore's fingers clutching his shirt, tugging him backwards. When they collided with the table, Lore broke away to stare at Shaun for a moment as if debating with himself, and then resumed the kiss with even more intensity than before.

Shaun felt dizzy, and he stumbled a little as he grabbed Lore's hips and lifted him onto the table. Lore reached back to shove the keyboard out of the way and caught the edge of the monitor instead. The equipment teetered, then fell to the floor with a crash, but Lore didn't seem to notice. As soon as there was a clear spot on the table, Shaun pushed Lore onto his back and climbed up onto the table as well to press Lore down with the weight of his body.

When Lore turned away to catch his breath, Shaun latched on to the side of his neck, below the curve of his jaw. Lore's skin was warm, and Shaun could feel the throb of Lore's pulse under his tongue. The bruise from the day before had already vanished, and Shaun shoved the layers of scarves out of the way so he could bite the side of Lore's neck.

Lore reacted by grabbing Shaun's hair with one hand and tugging ineffectually at his shirt with the other. Eventually, he seemed to get frustrated with the angle, because he pushed Shaun over onto his back. Lore caught his mouth in another brief kiss before pulling away again and tugging Shaun's shirt up over his head.

When Shaun tried to reciprocate, Lore batted his hands out of the way and sat back to shrug out of his blazer. That was as far as he managed to get before Shaun sat up and grabbed him by the shoulders to pull him down again.

"Mason." Lore's protest was muffled by Shaun's mouth, so he turned his face away and panted, "This works better without clothes."

"Worry about that later," mumbled Shaun, pushing his hands underneath the back of Lore's shirt. He was too impatient to think about anything but touching as much of Lore as possible, and too afraid that if he stopped for even a second, Lore would have too much time to think about what they were doing.

Lore didn't seem to want to stop either, because he pressed his long, lean body up against Shaun's and leaned down for another kiss. There was no mistaking the fact that he was hard, and Shaun worked a hand down between them to tug at the front of Lore's trousers. Lore shifted, and Shaun first thought Lore was going to push him away, but then he felt Lore's fingers working at the button on his jeans.

"Tell me what you want," Shaun muttered as he shoved at the waistband of Lore's slacks. "Anything you want. Just name it and I'll do it."

One of Lore's hands had found its way into Shaun's hair, and his grip tightened when Shaun's hand brushed his cock. "I want you to shut up and concentrate, Mason."

"Trust me," said Shaun as he grabbed a handful of Lore's ass and gave it a squeeze, "you have my full attention."

Lore finally managed to get Shaun's jeans open and shoved down to mid-thigh. He pushed his hips down, and Shaun dug his nails into Lore's shoulders when he felt the hard shaft of Lore's cock against his own. He hadn't done this since high school, this rough grinding and sloppy kissing, but his hormones were in overdrive and he was so embarrassingly desperate that the mere thought of stopping made him ache.

"Jesus," whispered Shaun. "Do you have any fucking idea what you're doing to me?"

Lore bit his jaw and let out a barely audible moan. It was so soft that Shaun almost didn't hear it, and yet the fact that it had come from Lore made his dick jerk and his toes curl. He flipped them over again and tugged one of Lore's legs up over his hip so that he could settle between Lore's thighs. He rocked his hips, dragging his cock against Lore's so it left a smear of precome on the underside of Lore's prick.

Lore shuddered and clutched at Shaun's hair, then lifted his head and breathed into Shaun's ear, "Faster."

To his eternal shame, Shaun actually whimpered. The last shreds of his self-control dissolved in a white hot flash, and he grabbed Lore's hips hard enough that he was sure his fingers would leave bruises. Lore rocked against him, their movements jerky and raw with desperation. Shaun was usually talkative in bed, but he couldn't find the breath to even whisper Lore's name. They panted into each other's mouths, lips pressed together but barely moving, until Lore suddenly bit down on Shaun's bottom lip and groaned.

Watching Lore come was one of the most intense experiences of Shaun's life. Lore—twitchy, prickly Lore—was shuddering underneath him, eyes closed and cheeks flushed. His cock jerked against Shaun's belly, splattering his skin with come, and Shaun shoved a hand down between them to rub the heel of his palm against the underside of Lore's prick.

It took a seemingly impossible amount of effort for Shaun to stop moving while he waited for Lore to relax. He took his hand away from Lore's cock, knowing how sensitive it probably was, and meant to wipe it on his shirt, but Lore grabbed his wrist to stop him.

"Let me," whispered Lore, his voice ragged and out of breath. He wiped his hand across Shaun's belly to smear his fingers with his own come, then reached down between them and wrapped his long, warm fingers around Shaun's cock.

"Shit," breathed Shaun. His eyes fluttered closed, and he thrust up into Lore's hand. A shiver rippled through his body, and he grabbed hold of the edge of the table to try and steady himself.

"Mason," murmured Lore, "look at me."

Shaun forced himself to open his eyes. There was so much raw emotion in Lore's expression that Shaun almost physically recoiled, but Lore's hand on his cock made it impossible for him to do anything except stay where he was while Lore wrung hot, aching pleasure from his body. His orgasm crept up on him in measured degrees, starting at the base of his spine and radiating through his body, making his blood burn and the back of his neck prickle. Then, all at once, it sliced through him, so intense it was almost agonizing. His eyes fluttered closed, and he bit his bottom lip until he tasted blood. His cock pulsed in Lore's fist, adding to the mess on their bellies, and when Lore kissed him, he opened his mouth with a moan.

What seemed like an eternity later, his arms finally gave out, and he half-collapsed atop Lore, who tolerated his weight for a few minutes before giving his shoulder a gentle push. Shaun grunted and rolled onto his back, and lay there panting while he waited for his pulse to slow. When he'd finally caught his breath, he opened his eyes to look at Lore.

Lore was staring at him.

For one of the first times in his life, Shaun had no idea what to say. He had no quips, no playful insults. In the end, he settled for reaching up and touching the center of Lore's bottom lip with his thumb.

Lore blinked at him and said, "I thought you were dead."

"What?" Shaun stared at Lore, completely bewildered.

Lore pulled Shaun's hand away from his face and said, "I thought you were dead. You wanted to know why you didn't trigger the security system at the temple. It's because I attached an authentication key to your avatar, so you can come and go as you please."

"You attached—" Shaun broke off and thought about that for a moment, wondering in an idiotic, post-coital sort of way whether that was similar to giving someone a key to your apartment in real life, but then the full implications hit him and he whispered, "Wait, so if I hadn't logged out to sleep..."

Lore was still holding Shaun's hand, and he responded with a squeeze of his fingers.

Shaun barely even noticed. He was still looking at Lore, but his mind was a million miles away, thinking about what could have happened if it hadn't been for Lore's insistence that he go home and rest, and what had happened to Ruby as a consequence of being online at the wrong time. Thinking about Ruby made his stomach lurch, and he closed his eyes.

After a few minutes of silence, Lore murmured, "Mason."

Shaun opened his eyes. Lore was still watching him with a wistful expression. He looked so incredibly fragile all of a sudden that Shaun wanted to lean over and kiss him, though he didn't dare. He wasn't stupid enough to believe that sex had changed their relationship so much that he had free reign to kiss Lore whenever he wanted to.

"Shaun," Lore corrected himself, then searched Shaun's face for a moment before saying, "I'm glad you're here."

"So am I," Shaun muttered. He was about to reach out and touch Lore's face again when he was startled by his phone vibrating in his pocket. It was a text message from Blake that read, simply, 'Kim Lee.'

Chapter Fourteen

Kim Lee Ramen appeared to be closed when Shaun arrived, but Shaun rapped on the door and waited. A few minutes later, the door opened and Blake appeared in the doorway, his eyes bloodshot and glassy with tears. Shaun immediately pulled him into a hug.

"What happened?" asked Blake in a ragged voice.

Shaun tugged Blake into the shop and closed the door behind them, then kept his arms around Blake's shoulders while he explained. He tried to stay calm while he told the story, but he had to pause and compose himself when he got to the part about the morgue. Blake tensed when Shaun told him that it had been Lore's tracking code that drew the attack in Ruby's direction, but he didn't say anything.

Blake was quiet for awhile after Shaun finished. He stood there with his cheek pressed against Shaun's and his arms locked around Shaun's waist, and then finally he said, "She called me right before she died."

Shaun loosened his grip so Blake could pull back and wipe his eyes.

"That's actually why I sent the message for you to meet me here," Blake explained as he took Shaun by the hand and led him over to the counter, where he sat down on one of the stools. Shaun sat down beside him and squeezed his hand. Blake closed his eyes and rubbed his forehead, then said, "Ruby called me right before it happened to tell me she'd just gotten a notice that someone deposited a hundred thousand dollars into her Simulnet bank account."

Shaun's instincts prickled. "Did she say who it was?"

"No, she didn't know." Blake shook his head. "She was going to go to the bank and see if she could find out where the money came from. That's why she called me: she wanted me to come with her, just in case. She didn't want to be alone if something happened." Blake put his elbows on the counter and buried his face in his hands.

Shaun swallowed the lump in his throat and slipped an arm around Blake's shoulders.

"I think I was on the phone with her when she died," Blake whispered against his hands. "It happened so quietly I thought we'd just been disconnected."

"How'd you find out?" asked Shaun.

Blake's shoulders tensed almost imperceptibly, and he seemed to hesitate for a moment before wiping his eyes and lifting his head to look at Shaun. The expression on his face reminded Shaun of Lore, like there was something he desperately wanted to say but couldn't. Finally, he replied, "All I can tell you is that I didn't find out through any nefarious means."

Shaun felt an inexplicable flash of hurt, and it must have shown on his face because Blake reached over to take his hand again.

"I promise that if it would make any difference at all, I would tell you," said Blake. "But there are certain things about my real life that I need to keep separate from my life here, and this is one of them."

Shaun sighed. Everyone around him seemed to be keeping secrets. He gave Blake's hand a quick squeeze, then stood. "Right. I should go. Lore and I have a lot of work to do."

"You're angry at me," said Blake. His voice was calm but the look on his face was heartbreaking.

Shaun sighed again, then closed his eyes and buried his face in Blake's hair. "No, I'm not. I'm sorry. You have a right to not tell me everything. I'm not trying to be a dick, there's just a lot of shit going on and I'm not dealing with it very well." He pulled back to look down at Blake. "Will you be okay? Do you want to come with me? I can't promise it'll be much fun, but at least you wouldn't be alone."

Blake let out a shaky laugh shook his head. "No, no, I'll be fine. I'm surrounded by people all the time when I'm offline. I think I'd rather be alone right now."

"Are you sure?" asked Shaun.

Blake offered him a thin smile. "I would rather know you're out there trying to find Ruby's killer than in here, baby-sitting me."

"All right, but promise you'll call me if you need me," said Shaun. He squeezed Blake's shoulder, then turned to leave the shop. He got as far as the door before Blake said his name, and he paused.

"I know you'll find him, Shaun," said Blake without looking in his direction, "and when you do, I hope you fucking kill him."

It was strange, Shaun thought, that two people who had just finished having near death experiences and mind-blowing sex could revert to old habits so quickly. It was barely three hours after their last kiss, and they were sitting in front of the coffee shop where they'd first met, at the table where they'd first met, with Shaun drinking coffee and Lore hunched over his laptop.

"I'm having deja vu," said Shaun.

Lore just grunted in reply.

"How long do you think it'll take to finish looking through the logs?" asked Shaun. Part of Lore's security system included a tracking function that would automatically attempt to trace any incoming data back to its source, like the Simulnet version of tracing a phone call. Lore was busy combing through the security system's log files, and Shaun was busy trying to restore some sense of normalcy between them.

"Mm," Lore hummed.

Shaun sighed, then leaned forward and whispered, "Don't look, but there's a giant octopus standing right next to you."

Lore's fingers paused over the keyboard, and he lifted his gaze to stare at Shaun over the top of his laptop.

Shaun smiled. "Just seeing if you were paying attention."

"You have an unnatural obsession with sea creatures," said Lore. He looked serious at first, but then he flashed Shaun a smirk and went back to what he was doing.

Shaun watched him for a little while, but even Lore wasn't interesting enough to keep him occupied for long. Eventually, his mind began to drift, first to what had happened between them, then to Ruby, and then finally to Kim, who he suddenly realized he hadn't heard from in awhile. He debated over whether or not to try calling her; on one hand, she hated it when he got protective, but on the other hand, he was starting to get worried. Finally, he decided it was better to have her angry at him for bothering her than to have to worry over whether or not she was okay.

"Hey, I'll be right back, I'm just gonna make a phone call," said Shaun as he pushed away from the table.

Lore nodded.

Shaun walked a few yards away and dialed Kim's number. It rang four times, but just as he was about to hang up, she answered.

"Shaun?" Kim sounded out of breath.

"Are you okay?" asked Shaun with a frown.

"Yeah, yeah, I'm fine, I was in the shower so I had to run for the phone," replied Kim. "We're in a hotel in town for a few days, using the labs at the university."

A sudden flood of memories flashed through Shaun's mind: Kim as a little girl, racing all over the house in her nightgown, fresh out of the bathtub with her hair wet and her face red from the heat; Kim shoving him into the pool when they were twelve and he was still afraid of the water; Kim sitting in the window of her dorm room at college, wet from having just come in from the rain, smoking a cigarette and saying, 'Do you ever think about her? What she looked like when we found her? Fuck, if they ever catch the guy who killed her, Shaun, I swear...'

"Shaun?"

"Yeah? Yeah, sorry." Shaun shook himself and swallowed. "I was just calling because I hadn't heard from you and I was, y'know—I was starting to get worried."

Kim sighed into the phone. "You're not doing that older brother thing again, are you?"

"Maybe a bit," said Shaun with a wan smile.

"God, you really need to get a life, Shaun. I'm fine, though. Really. How are things with you? How's the case?"

"Things are—well, to be honest, they're pretty bad at the moment." Shaun let out a humorless laugh. He hadn't planned to worry Kim with any of his own bullshit, but he couldn't help himself. "There's some pretty serious shit going on. I'm starting to feel like I'm in over my head."

"But you're safe?"

"Yeah, yeah, I'm fine. I'm just—I don't know. You know how you always told me I have a habit of biting off more than I can chew?"

"Do you want to talk about it?"

Shaun sighed. "I want to, but I can't. That's one of the most fucked up parts about all this: I don't have anyone I can bounce ideas off of. I mean, I've got my partner, but—" he glanced over his shoulder at Lore, who was still typing away and seemingly ignoring him "—but he's not exactly what you'd call a heart-to-heart type."

"Wait, you have a partner?" Kim sounded suspicious. "Shaun, what the hell is going on? I thought you said you were doing this on your own. Why do you have a partner?"

"Please don't ask me to explain it right now. I promise, as soon as I can talk about it, I'll tell you everything, okay?"

Kim was quiet for a moment, but then she sighed and said, "Fine, whatever. But I swear to god, Shaun, if you screw this up—"

"I won't—at least, I hope I won't. But look, I'll call you again in a few days, okay? Will you be around?"

"Yeah, we're in town until Thursday," replied Kim. There was a pause, and then she said, "Hey Shaun? Seriously, be careful, okay? I know that probably goes in one ear and out the other, but I really mean it. I don't know what you've gotten yourself into, but you're worrying me. Keep yourself safe."

"I'm doing my best," Shaun muttered. He was pretty sure this was the first time he'd promised to be careful and actually meant it.

By the time he got back to the table, Lore had stopped typing and was just sitting there in silence, staring off into space. He was tapping the arm of his chair with one hand and holding Shaun's coffee with the other.

"That's mine," said Shaun, gesturing to the cup.

Lore looked up at him and took a sip of the coffee before handing it back. The gesture was so intimate that it sent a shiver crawling down Shaun's spine and made his cock twitch with interest. Lore didn't seem to notice the reaction, though; he pressed a few keys on his laptop and then spun it around on the table so Shaun could see the screen.

"Is that a traceroute?" Shaun pointed to a series of Simulnet addresses with times next to them, showing the path data took from one point to another and how long it took to get there.

Lore nodded. "The originating address was only temporary, so it's unreachable now, but here—" he switched to another window, which showed a map of southern California overlaid with a green circle "—is the area where the user who sent the data must have signed on from, unless they were using some sort of proxy server."

Shaun examined the map with a frown. On one hand, it would make sense for the killer to use a proxy server—a server that would essentially act as a middle man between the killer's tank and the rest of Simulnet, thereby masking the killer's real address—and it made sense that he would want the proxy server to be located in Los Angeles, where most of his victims were residents. If the killer was located elsewhere, using a proxy server in Los Angeles would provide a false link. On the other hand, proxy services for Simulnet were still experimental, and Shaun doubted the killer would risk attacking Lore using an unreliable service.

"He's cocky," said Lore, as if reading Shaun's mind (and at this point, Shaun wasn't sure he'd put that past him). "He's much too cocky to risk failure, and cocky enough to think I wouldn't survive the attack so it wouldn't matter if I had a tracking system."

"So he probably wouldn't have bothered with a proxy server," said Shaun. He sat back in his chair and sighed. "We can't just go canvassing all of L.A. though. I mean, that map is good start, but do you know how many people live inside that radius?" He gestured to the green circle on the map.

Lore turned the laptop around and stared at the screen. After a few minutes, he said, "You need to go to Ruby and Sarah's houses."

"Are you kidding me? You realize their houses are probably crawling with feds, don't you? Even if they're done inside, they're probably still keeping an eye on their buildings from outside. Besides, Hudson told me to stay away from any real life snooping."

"That was when we thought there wasn't a real world link between the victims."

Shaun frowned. "We still don't know there's a real world link. I mean, we know they're all from the same city, but if there really was a connection between them, someone would have figured it out by now. Besides, I thought we agreed that Ruby was an accident."

"Ruby was an accident, but there might be something in her house that will help us find the connection, and there is a connection," Lore insisted. "We're just looking at the data from the wrong angle."

"So what's the right angle?"

Lore's mouth tightened. "That's what we have to figure out."

"Okay, alright, I'll go. You're coming with me, though." Shaun tried to keep his tone firm instead of hopeful. If ever there were a good excuse for him to try and drag Lore off Simulnet so they could meet face-to-face in the real world, this was it.

They eyed each other for a moment. Lore's expression was inscrutable, and he opened his mouth like he planned say something, but then he closed it again and pressed his lips together. As soon as his eyes narrowed, Shaun knew he'd lost the battle. "Mason, you're more than capable of doing this on your own. Having me come with you would slow you down and be a waste of time. If you're genuinely that worried about going alone, send me a text message when you arrive and another when you leave."

"Why won't you meet me offline?" asked Shaun. He leaned

forward with his arms on the table, bowing his head close to Lore's like they were sharing a secret. He searched Lore's expression, hoping to find some kind of answer for why Lore was being so evasive. "What don't you want me to know? Huh? Or is it that real life is just too personal? Are you afraid that if we meet for real, you might actually form some kind of attachment to me?"

"Stop it, Shaun." Lore sounded tired, but his gaze was unwavering. "We don't have time for this conversation right now."

Shaun knew Lore was right, so he sighed and pushed to his feet. Rather than leaving right away, though, he tucked his hands into his pockets, stared down at Lore, and said, "I just want to know what you're like in real life."

Lore didn't look up from his laptop, but he did reply, so softly that Shaun almost didn't hear him, "So do I."

Chapter Fifteen

Despite all the other trouble he'd gotten into as a kid, Shaun had only ever broken into one house before: his own. He and his sister had been in eighth grade, and they'd come home from school one afternoon and realized they'd forgotten their keys. They'd pried the screen off of a downstairs window, wedged it open with a screwdriver, and crawled through.

Unfortunately, the experience hadn't done much to prepare the adult Shaun for breaking into a murder victim's house.

He'd parked across the street from Ruby's house in Silver Lake, and he was slouched in the driver's seat with his eyes hidden by a pair of enormous sunglasses. He was sure he looked suspicious, judging by the looks he was getting from an older lesbian couple who were out walking their dog, but he needed a few minutes to survey the area before he went inside.

Silver Lake was nestled in the hills just east of Hollywood. The neighborhood had suffered from a bad reputation for a long time, but lately, it had become a desirable spot for artists, musicians, and the gay and lesbian community. Ruby's bungalow was perched halfway up one of the neighborhood's steep hills. The exterior of the house was painted cobalt blue, the same color as Ruby's avatar's hair. There was a wooden swing on the porch and spider plants hanging from the eaves. It was the kind of house that made visitors feel at home just by looking at it.

There were cars parked along the curb in both directions, but as far as Shaun could see, they were all unoccupied. A few people were outside enjoying the afternoon sunshine, but no one seemed to be keeping an eye on Ruby's house.

Shaun took a deep breath and climbed out of his car, then tucked his hands into his pockets and crossed the street. Instead of heading straight for Ruby's house, he made his way further down the block, trying to keep his pace quick enough to look like he knew where he was going, but not so fast he'd attract attention. He took a left at the end of the street, passed the house on the corner, and then took another left down the alleyway behind the houses. He glanced around to make sure no one was watching, then broke into a jog.

Ruby's backyard consisted of a short driveway and a tiny, well-kept lawn. The property was bordered by a waist-high, chain link fence, and Shaun hopped over it before striding across the yard and up the stairs to the back porch. He slipped a credit card out of his wallet as he walked, and when he got to the back door, he glanced around before working the card in between the door and its frame. He had no idea whether or not he was doing it right—he'd found a tutorial on the Internet, but his hotel room door hadn't been a good place to test it—but he figured shimmying the door open with a credit card was less conspicuous than prying it open with a crowbar. He just hoped the deadbolt wasn't locked.

After a few minutes of wiggling the card, Shaun felt the lock give way. The door popped open, and he stared at it for a moment, surprised it had actually worked. He pocketed the credit card and pushed the door open, wincing when it gave a quiet squeak. He stepped into the brightly lit kitchen and eased the door shut behind him, then paused again and listened. When he heard nothing but the whirring of a lawn mower a few houses away, he let out a sigh of relief and got to work.

The refrigerator and cupboards were bare, which Shaun figured meant someone had already come through and cleaned them out. Other than that, there was nothing noteworthy in the kitchen, so he made his way into the living room where an overstuffed sofa faced a flat screen television. A light blue jacket was hanging on the back of the front door, and Shaun searched through the pockets. They were empty.

"Damn it," muttered Shaun as he stepped back and raked his fingers through his hair. Whoever had conducted a search of the place after Ruby's body was found had probably already gone through everything and taken anything of interest.

Shaun wasn't ready to give up yet, though, so he made his way down the hall. The first door opened into what was obviously a guest room, which Shaun gave a cursory once over before continuing to the other bedroom at the end of the hallway.

A double bed was shoved against the wall, and an SR tank dominated the rest of the floor space. The tank was a newer model, but judging by all the modifications someone had done, it had already seen its fair share of use. Shaun opened it and peered inside, and tried to ignore the mental image of Ruby floating there in the Epsom solution.

Ruby's nightstand was boring. The drawers mostly held receipts and hair elastics, but Shaun did find a picture of Ruby standing on a beach somewhere. She was wearing military fatigues and welding goggles, and she was holding a bright orange Nerf gun. She was smiling.

Shaun swallowed the lump in his throat and slipped the photo into his back pocket.

He was about to close the drawer when he spotted a flier peeking out from between the pages of a book. Anyone else would probably have ignored it—just a scrap of paper being used as a bookmark—but something made Shaun pick it up. The book itself was just a paperback horror novel, but the flier was for a women's counseling center. It gave a list of group counseling sessions, along with the names of the therapists who were hosting them.

One of the sessions in particular caught Shaun's eye: 'Sexual Abuse in Intimate Relationships' hosted by 'R. Greene.' Shaun frowned. The antidepressants he'd found in Keith and Sarah's apartment had been prescribed by a Dr. Greene. He doubted it was a coincidence.

Shaun folded the flier and stuffed it in his pocket, then headed for the master bathroom. He was reaching for the medicine cabinet when he heard the telltale creak of the back door opening. Shaun went still and listened. At first he thought he'd imagined the sound, but then he heard quiet footsteps coming down the hallway toward the bedroom.

Shaun bolted out of the bathroom and over to the bedroom window.

He could barely hear anything over the sound of his own heartbeat, and it seemed to take ages to cross the room. He shoved at the window latch, cursing under his breath, but the window wouldn't budge.

The footsteps stopped just outside the bedroom door. Shaun had no idea what the person was up to or how much time he had before they found him, but he knew loitering in the bedroom wasn't a good idea. He darted back into the bathroom as quietly as he could and inched the door closed, then glanced at the tiny window over the sink and wondered if he could fit through it.

The bedroom door opened.

Shaun froze. His breathing went shallow as he peered through the crack in the door. A tall person in a black shirt and ski mask was standing beside the SR tank, surveying the room as if they were looking for something in particular. After a few seconds, they withdrew something from their back pocket that looked like a taser and crept over to the closet.

Shaun backed away from the door and sprang into action. He climbed onto the toilet lid and grabbed the hand crank for the window. The crank turned without a problem, and Shaun worked it as fast as he could. The window seemed to inch open and he cursed under his breath, urging it to go faster. Once it was open as far as it would go, he used both hands on the window ledge to hoist himself up just as the bathroom door slammed open.

Hands grabbed his ankles and tried to drag him back inside. He kicked out, trying to dislodge his attacker, and his heel slammed into something solid. The person behind him let out a pained yelp and let go of his ankle. The taser clattered to the floor.

The metal ridges on the windowsill dug into his stomach as he fought his way through the tiny window. One of his belt loops got caught on something, and for one horrifying second he thought he wouldn't be able to break free. When a hand grabbed his leg again, though, he renewed his efforts, shoving at the outside wall below the window to propel himself forward. He finally cleared the window frame and went tumbling out onto the lawn, ripping his jeans and knocking his shoulder in the process, but he was free.

There was a muffled curse from behind him, but he didn't turn around. No matter how guilty he felt for running, the fact remained that he was alone and unarmed. For now, the most important thing was for him to get away and call for backup.

Shaun bolted for the front of the house, thinking that even if he drew suspicion, that was safer than heading for the back alley. The street was within view, and there were people roaming up and down the sidewalk. Shaun thought he was home free, but he only made it as far as the porch before he heard a sharp whine and a rapid ticking sound.

Pain ripped through Shaun's body. He thought he'd just been shot, but when his muscles went rigid and he fell to the ground, he realized he'd been tased. Electricity racked his body, and he wondered dazedly if the taser had been modified. This was nothing like being tased in basic training.

Finally, a million years later, the clicking noise stopped and the pain started to subside. Shaun lay there panting for breath, curled in the fetal position with his muscles still twitching. He was aware of someone standing over him, but he couldn't make his body move. In a ragged whisper, he managed to ask, "Who—?"

That was far as he got before a different kind of pain exploded in his skull. Red and yellow sparks danced in front of his eyes, and the last thing he thought before his vision went black was, 'So this is how I die.'

Chapter Sixteen

When Shaun came to, he was slumped in a chair in Ruby's kitchen. His wrists were bound behind his back, and his head was throbbing. The only thing keeping him from falling sideways to the floor was a rope around his chest and stomach. A dishrag had been stuffed in his mouth, and he tried to push it out with his tongue. Something warm was trickling down his forehead into his eyes, and when he looked down at his lap, he saw that blood had dripped onto his jeans.

His assailant was nowhere to be seen.

Shaun took a deep breath through his nose and tried to stay calm. He wasn't sure how long he'd been unconscious, but it was darker in the kitchen than it had been when he'd arrived. He wasn't sure how long it would be before Lore realized that something was wrong. In the meantime, he had to escape.

The chair had been placed in the corner of the room, putting him a long way from the phone on the wall. He could try and hop his way over, but that would be hard with his ankles strapped to the chair's legs. Besides, if his attacker was still in the house, the last thing he wanted to do was draw attention to the fact that he was awake. He stayed where he was and tried to think of other options.

Whatever was binding his wrists was also cutting off his circulation, so he doubted he'd be able to work his hands free. He tugged at the restraints around his ankles, but they didn't budge. He was considering trying to smash the chair apart somehow when he heard footsteps coming down the hall.

Shaun closed his eyes and let his head droop.

The footsteps paused just outside the kitchen. Shaun imagined the person had stopped in the doorway to look in at him, and he fought the urge to open his eyes. After a few seconds, the person came into the room and stood right in front of him.

Shaun really wanted to assume that if his captor wanted him dead, he'd be dead. He hoped that the fact he was still alive meant he was useful somehow. Still, he wasn't in a hurry to find out, so he figured pretending to be unconscious was the best course of action. After all, unconscious men couldn't answer questions or show pain.

The charade ended when his attacker dragged a gloved fingertip down the side of his neck, and he twitched.

"Unconscious men don't have racing pulses," said his captor. Their voice came out tinny and distorted, like the Halloween voice changers Shaun and Kim used to use for prank phone calls.

Shaun opened his eyes and looked up at his assailant. They were a little shorter than him, medium build, and wearing a black mask with a hood. Between the voice changer, the mask, and the gloves, it was impossible to tell whether they were male or female.

"Men like you are rare, Shaun. I didn't want to kill you but you're getting in the way."

The distorted voice made everything feel a hundred times more frightening. A shiver rippled through Shaun. The rag in his mouth muffled his angry grunting, and he struggled against the ropes that held him down. He'd done a million things other people called crazy, but he'd never thought he was about to die. Looking up at the hooded figure before him felt like staring death in the face.

"The problem is, Shaun, that even if you promised to stop chasing me, you'd never be able to keep that promise, would you? And if you did stop, I'd kill you anyway, because then you'd be like all the rest."

Shaun grunted again and shook his head, this time trying to get the rag out of his mouth. While he pushed at the cloth with his tongue, he wracked his brain for something to say, anything that might earn him his freedom. It looked so easy in the movies: the hero always talked his way out, or at least bought himself some time until he could wriggle out of his bonds. Reality wasn't as predictable.

"Hold still, please," the killer said as they pulled a syringe from their pocket and uncapped it. "This doesn't have to be painful for either of us."

Shaun struggled even harder, pulling ineffectually at the ropes and twisting his body in the chair.

"This is a barbiturate. It won't be unpleasant, I promise. There's no need for your to suffer. The first injection will just put you to sleep—slow your breathing, relax your muscles…Then, once you're asleep, I'll inject you with Potassium Chloride, which will stop your heart and respiration. You won't feel a thing."

Shaun had never been afraid of needles—he'd never been afraid of anything—but the terror he felt as he watched the needle moving toward him was the most brutal, primal fear of his life. The needle pricked the side of his neck, and Shaun let out a muffled scream.

He'd always heard that in near-death situations, a person's life flashed before their eyes. That wasn't the case for him. All he saw in those final moments were the faces of the people he was letting down by dying: his sister, Hudson, Katou, Kim, Blake, Ruby, Lore…. He wished he had just a few more minutes to call each of them and tell them how sorry he was.

The barbiturate took effect almost immediately. A thick, heavy warmth spread through Shaun's body, and he felt his muscles begin to relax. Fight it, he thought, don't fall asleep. But no matter how hard he railed against it, the drowsiness took him over. His head began to droop, and as he nodded off he thought to himself in a dazed sort of way that all things considered, this wasn't all that unpleasant after all.

There was a crash in the distance. The sound seemed echo through the room, like the ripples from a stone dropped into water. Shaun tried to open his eyes, but his eyelids felt too heavy. The hand that had been cupping his jaw disappeared, and his head lolled over to the side. Another crack vibrated through the kitchen, and Shaun wondered if that meant Lore was there, bringing the house down on their heads. Warm hands cradled his face, lifting his head, and the rag was pulled out of his mouth. The fabric dragged like sandpaper over his tongue.

"Shaun? Shaun, can you hear me?"

Shaun tried to reply but it came out a sloppy-sounding groan.

"Shaun, open your eyes. We need to leave now so you need to wake up."

The voice was undistorted and familiar, but Shaun was too groggy to place it. Fingers pushed his eyelids open, and Shaun tried to make his eyes cooperate. His vision was blurry, but he could make out someone with black hair and pale skin hovering over him. "Lore?" he mumbled.

"No, but I promise you can see him soon. Right now, we need to leave before a patrol car gets here."

The ropes around his wrists fell away, and Shaun's hands fell heavily to his sides. The ropes around his chest came next, and his whole body slumped forward. Someone caught him and pulled him up out of the chair, hooking an arm around his waist to keep him upright. Shaun tried to make his legs cooperate, but he ended up sliding sideways, leaning heavily against the person holding him. His eyes fluttered closed again as the person half-carried and half-dragged him out of the house, then stuffed stuffed him into the backseat of a car.

The leather was cool against his back, and the seat was well-cushioned and comfortable. Shaun slumped back against it with a groan.

Someone settled in beside him and said something in a language Shaun didn't understand, and a second later, the car pulled away from the curb.

"Who're you?" mumbled Shaun, his head drooping so his chin was tucked against his chest.

"A friend."

"Mm," Shaun hummed in acknowledgment. "Can I sleep now?"

He didn't stay awake long enough to hear the reply.

❧

Shaun woke to cotton sheets and a throbbing headache.

He lay there for a minute, trying to get his bearings and piece together what had happened. He remembered the taser, the blow to the head, and waking up bound to the chair. He remembered the syringe in his neck and the drowsiness that followed. He remembered the crash, and the commotion, and being dragged into the backseat of a car.

Shaun opened his eyes and winced when the light sliced through his skull. He was in an unfamiliar bed with the bleached linen smell of hotel rooms everywhere. The lamp on the nightstand was on, but someone had draped a shirt over it to mute the light. After his eyes adjusted, Shaun tried to push himself into a sitting position. His limbs felt heavy, but he managed to prop himself on his elbows.

A young, Asian man in a dark suit was sitting by the window, reading a newspaper.

"Uhm," Shaun croaked.

The man lowered the paper and looked at Shaun over the rims of his glasses. He was attractive in a familiar sort of way, with high cheekbones and a subdued friendliness about his face. He wasn't smiling, but he didn't need to be; there was something about him that put Shaun at ease.

"Where——" Shaun began, but his throat felt like sandpaper.

"There's water there." The man gestured to the nightstand. Shaun recognized his voice; he was the person who'd come to his rescue at Ruby's house.

Shaun picked the glass up and drank deeply from it. The water wasn't cold, but it tasted crisp and fresh, and he drained the entire glass before he put the glass down again and wiped his mouth. "Where am I?"

"The Bonaventure Hotel." The man folded his newspaper and set it aside, then folded his hands on the table in front of him. "How do you feel?"

"Heavy," replied Shaun as he pushed himself up into a sitting position. "Hung over. Like I swallowed a fucking sand dune." He rubbed his face, then blinked at the man and asked, "Who are you?"

"A friend."

"Yeah, you said that." Shaun examined the man's face, looking for any clue as to who he might be, and then he spotted the ring on the man's left pinky finger. It was the same design Katou wore.

The man seemed to follow Shaun's gaze. He glanced down at the ring and than back at Shaun. He seemed to hesitate for a moment before saying, "My name is Brian. Katou is my father."

"And he sent you out to find me?" asked Shaun, although he had no idea how Katou would have known where he was or that he was in trouble. The only person who knew where he'd gone was Lore.

Brian shook his head. "No, I got an anonymous text message with the geographic coordinates of your location. Whoever sent it said they thought you might be in trouble."

That had to have been Lore, Shaun thought, but he wasn't sure why the hell he'd contacted Katou's son instead of calling Hudson. Not that he wasn't grateful for the help, but at least if Hudson had been involved, they might have been able to make an arrest.

"I don't suppose you got a look at your attacker?" asked Brian.

"No. I'm pretty sure it was a man, but he was wearing a hood with a face mask—you know, the kind people use for Grim Reaper costumes at Halloween? And he was using a voice changer, so I couldn't even tell you what he sounded like. Hell, it might not even have been a 'him' at all."

Brian frowned. He stood and went to the window, pulled the curtain back and peered outside. It was night, and the city lights cast shadows on his face. That made him look even more familiar, but Shaun still couldn't put his finger on why. After a minute or so, Brian let the curtain drop and turned away from the window. He slid his hands into his pockets and said, "I'd like to move the tank you've been using into a suite here at the Bonaventure. It will be easier to keep an eye on you."

"Keep an eye on me? I don't need—"

"Yes, you do. You should have had someone keeping an eye on you from the start, but it's even more important now that we know you're being followed. Or did you think it was a coincidence that Ruby's murderer just happened to show up at her house while you were there?"

Shaun sighed and rubbed the back of his neck. On one hand, he didn't like the idea of being baby-sat, but on the other, the incident at Ruby's house had been a close call. "Okay fine, I'll move everything over here. Just gimme a little while to finish waking up and figure out how to get the tank over—"

"Don't worry about that. I'll have it taken care of," said Brian. "Stay here and get some more sleep. The drugs haven't quite worn off, and I get the feeling you could use the rest."

Shaun wanted to protest, but his body seemed to get even heavier at the mention of sleep, so he just sighed and nodded. Before he settled down again, though, he realized he still needed to let Lore know he was okay. He patted his jeans pocket, looking for his phone, then cursed and said, "Shit, my phone's missing. And my keys, and my—"

Brian walked closer and opened the nightstand drawer. Shaun's mobile phone was there, along with his wallet, his car keys, and the flier he'd been examining in Ruby's bedroom.

"Thanks," Shaun muttered. His phone showed no missed calls, which actually didn't surprise him. Lore wouldn't have wasted time trying to call or text him if he thought something was wrong; he would have just done something about it, which he had. Shaun smiled, just a little, and sent Lore a text message: 'attacked @ ruby's house but ok now. at bonaventure hotel w/ katou's son. thx for sending help. need to sleep a couple hours, will call u when i wake up. let hudson know what's going on plz. will tell u everythin later.' When he was done, he put his phone down and rubbed his eyes with the heels of his palms.

"Get some sleep," said Brian as he switched the lamp off, thrusting the room into darkness. "I have two men stationed in the room next door and another across the hall who's been asked to keep his door open so he can monitor activity in the corridor. If you need anything at all, just ask them. I'll be back to check on you tomorrow morning."

Shaun listened to Brian's footsteps cross the room, and waited until he'd opened the door before asking, "Hey, uhm, not that I'm not grateful or anything, but why are you helping me?"

Brian was silhouetted by the garish fluorescent light from the hallway, but Shaun didn't need to see his face to hear the anger in his voice when he replied, "The bastard who attacked you today killed one of my best friends. The least I can do is keep you safe while you find him." Then he slipped out into the hall and let the door swing shut behind him.

Shaun tried to fall back asleep after Brian had gone, but every time he started to doze off, a door down the hall would slam or a helicopter would fly overhead and he'd jerk awake again. Finally, after almost an hour of trying to sleep, he climbed out of bed. It took a few minutes before he felt he could walk without falling over, and he made his way into the bathroom for a shower.

The hot water helped. The pressure was just this side of amazing, and he spent a long time standing underneath the spray with his hands pressed against the warm tile and his head bowed.

When he was finished in the shower, he padded back into the bedroom in a hotel bathrobe and searched for his clothes. Someone had left them in a neat stack on the table near the window. Curious as to exactly how stained everything was, he picked up his shirt and shook it out. It hadn't been washed, and the sleeve and front of the shirt were stained rusty brown with dried blood. Shaun's stomach lurched and he swallowed hard to keep the nausea at bay.

He was about to put the shirt down again when something caught his eye: there was a strand of long, dark hair stuck to one of the dried splotches on the shoulder. Shaun held the shirt up to the light and squinted at the hair, then took hold of the very end and peeled it away from the fabric. It was jet black and straight, and at least a foot long from root to tip.

Shaun's heart gave a hopeful little jolt in his chest.

He carried the hair pinched tight between his thumb and forefinger as he crossed the room and knocked on the door that separated his suite from the one next door. A tall, slender man with curly blond hair and a stern expression answered the door and stared down at him.

"You're one of Brian's guys, right?" asked Shaun. When the man nodded mutely, Shaun held up the strand of hair. "Does anyone who was with you guys tonight have long hair? I'm talking long enough for a ponytail."

The guy shook his head.

"Are you sure?" Shaun pressed. "Are you positive there was no one near me who had long, dark hair?"

"Yeah, I'm sure," the man replied gruffly. "Only people who got near you were me, my partner, and Mister Katou. Trust me, I would've noticed anyone else."

Shaun's brow furrowed, and he turned away, gesturing for the man to follow him back into his room. There was a notepad on the table, along with a hotel monogrammed pen. He ripped a sheet off of the notepad and folded it around the strand of hair, then folded another piece of paper around the packet he'd made, just to be on the safe side. When he was finished, he scribbled an address on a third piece of paper and ripped that off as well, and handed everything to the guard, who was hovering behind him.

"I need you to mail that—" Shaun pointed to the makeshift envelope containing the hair "—to this address as quickly as you can get it there. Overnight if you can. It's important."

The guard was obviously perturbed at the idea of running errands, but he just nodded and saw himself out. Once the door had shut behind him, Shaun found his phone and called Kim.

"Shaun?"

"Kim, hey, listen, I need a favor."

"Jesus Shaun, what time is it there?"

"You said you have access to the labs at the University, right?" asked Shaun. "I need you to do some DNA testing for me, the kind you did for your Master's thesis. You know, the—damn it, I can't remember the name—the one where you can tell a person's sex, and whether or not they have brown hair or whatever."

"Phenotyping?"

"Yeah, that one. You can do that from a strand of hair, right?"

Kim was quiet for a moment before saying, "Shaun, bro, you know I love you, but I don't know if that's a good idea. You wouldn't be able to submit anything as evidence. Phenotyping is still a pretty new field of research. There'd be all sorts of questions about accuracy, not to mention the fact that you're asking me to use University resources..."

"I know," said Shaun. "I know it's shitty of me to drag you into this, and I'm an asshole for asking you to risk getting into trouble, but I swear I wouldn't be calling you if it wasn't important."

"It's really important?"

"It might be the most important thing I've ever asked you to do."

Kim sighed. "Fine, I'll do it."

"Thank you."

"This investigation really means a lot to you, doesn't it?" asked Kim. She sounded thoughtful.

Shaun stared down at the weave of the carpet and muttered, "Yeah, it really does."

"I'm glad. I was starting to wonder there for awhile if—you know. I worry about you."

Shaun couldn't help but smile. "Are you going to start pinching my cheeks and telling me how proud you are?"

"Ugh, you're so gross. Look, I'll get to work as soon as I get the sample. It shouldn't take more than a few hours and I'll call you when I'm done."

"I'll keep my phone on me," said Shaun, then paused for a second before adding, "Hey Kim? Thanks again. For everything. As far as sisters go, you're a pretty good one"

Kim snorted and hung up on him.

Shaun hung up and dropped his phone on the nightstand, then flopped face-first onto the bed. Just showering and calling Kim had exhausted him, and this time when he closed his eyes, he was asleep within seconds.

Chapter Seventeen

When Shaun logged in again some eight hours later, he found Lore sitting cross-legged on the floor in the center of the white tower room. His eyes were closed and his hands were resting on his knees. His hair was in disarray like he'd been tugging at it, and the circles beneath his eyes had darkened. He looked even more sleep-deprived than usual, but his eyes, when they snapped open to gaze at Shaun, were clear.

"You're safe," said Lore.

"Thanks to you," replied Shaun as he plopped down in front of Lore. He tucked his knees against his chest and wrapped his arms around them. "I'm guessing you're the one who called Katou's son? Why him and not dispatch?"

"Katou's son?" said Lore. He looked puzzled for a moment, but then he recovered and said, "He was in the neighborhood. The nearest patrol car was six miles away."

"Right, got it." Shaun frowned. He wanted to know why Lore was confused, but he decided not to ask. "Been in touch with Hudson?"

Lore nodded.

"I'm guessing she's not happy about me poking around offline? But hey, look, I think I've got something."

Lore raised an eyebrow.

Shaun told Lore about the attack, and then about the hair he'd found on his shirt. "I've already emailed Hudson about it, but I haven't heard back yet. I hate getting Kim involved, but I figure if all she's doing is some DNA analysis, it shouldn't be a problem, right?"

"Mm." Lore nodded noncommittally, then stood and went to the table to grab his laptop. "I found a few things while you were gone."

Shaun watched him and tried not to think about what had happened on top of that table less than two days ago.

"I hacked into Ruby's bank accounts," said Lore. He carried his laptop over and sat down beside Shaun so they could both see the screen. "I got into her Simulnet account and her offline accounts, and I noticed a few things..."

Hormones were rude little things, Shaun thought. They had no regard for propriety. Here he was, less than twenty-four hours after almost being killed, and he knew he should be concentrating on what Lore was saying—something about deposits, and viruses, and code signatures—but all he could think about was how he could feel the warmth of Lore's leg against his own.

"Mason."

Shaun snapped to attention and blinked at Lore, who was watching him with an odd expression—head tilted, eyes softer than usual. He expected to be reprimanded for not paying attention, so he started to mutter an apology.

He didn't expect to be kissed.

There was none of the frantic awkwardness of their first kiss. This kiss was slow and thorough, and methodical without being robotic. Lore's hands were on his face to cup his jaw, and Shaun grabbed at the front of Lore's blazer. When he felt Lore's tongue against his lips, Shaun grunted in surprise and tried to push Lore down onto the floor.

Lore gently pushed him away.

It took a few seconds for Shaun to get his bearings. He sat there in a daze, blinking stupidly at Lore and trying to figure out what he'd done to make Lore stop kissing him. Lore had already turned back to the laptop, though, and his expression gave nothing away.

"As I was saying," Lore continued without even so much as a glance at Shaun, "the deposit that was made to Ruby's account was made by wire transfer from a numbered savings account."

"What was that?" asked Shaun.

Lore finally looked at him and lifted an eyebrow. He looked as calm and collected as ever. The only indication that the kiss had ever happened was that his lips were swollen, and fuck if Shaun didn't want to grab him and kiss him again.

"The kiss," said Shaun, gesturing vaguely. "Why did you kiss me?"

"Because you were thinking about it and you weren't going to stop thinking about it unless it happened."

"Oh," said Shaun. He didn't know what kind of answer he'd expected, but he'd apparently been hoping for something more meaningful.

"May I continue now?"

"Yeah, sorry," Shaun muttered. He fixed his gaze on the laptop and tried to pay attention to what Lore was telling him.

"The account that made the deposit belongs to a real world bank," said Lore. "They have a branch inside Simulnet so that their customers don't have to set up separate accounts here. Unfortunately, their servers are set up to reject any outside queries, and I don't have enough time to find a workaround. We'll have to be inside a branch to access account information."

"So let me guess: we're taking a trip to the bank today?"

"Got it in one, Mason. I'm impressed."

Shaun was never going to get used to seeing Lore in a suit. While Shaun had donned the same trousers and blazer he'd worn to Oubliette, Lore had disappeared into the stairwell to change into a charcoal grey, three-piece suit with a matching tie and silver cufflinks. He'd hidden the tattoo on his neck, and his hair was the tidiest Shaun had ever seen it.

"You're staring."

"Sorry," replied Shaun, not feeling sorry at all. He kept his hands in his pockets because he was sure that if he didn't, he'd end up grabbing at Lore. That didn't stop him from raking his gaze over Lore's body, though, or thinking how he'd like to methodically remove each piece of Lore's suit.

"We don't have time," said Lore as if reading Shaun's mind. He looked annoyed, but something in his expression made Shaun think he wouldn't be that averse to the idea of being dragged to bed.

Before Shaun could mention the idea, Lore huffed and turned away, and gestured for Shaun to follow him to the wardrobe. Shaun waited patiently as Lore keyed in the address of the bank. Once they'd climbed inside, however, Shaun gathered his courage and reached over to let the backs of his knuckles graze Lore's hand. Lore twitched, but he didn't pull away. Shaun waited a second, then let his fingertips brush the inside of Lore's wrist.

Lore pulled his hand away and murmured, "Don't."

Shaun didn't reply. He shoved his hands into his pockets and waited, and tried not to think about how much Lore's rejection stung.

The doors opened onto a pristine marble lobby manned by six identical armed guards. Shaun and Lore stepped out of the chamber together and crossed the lobby to the revolving glass security door, designed to allow only one person in and one person out at a time. Once they were through, Lore led the way to the gleaming, black marble counter where a young bank clerk wearing a name tag that said "Gary" greeted them with handshakes.

"Hello Gary." Lore offered the clerk a dazzling smile. "My partner and I are interested in opening a joint account. Who can we talk to about that?"

"I'd be happy to help you," replied Gary, smiling with the kind of enthusiasm that only someone working on commission can muster. "I'll just need to verify the IDs embedded in your avatars against your real world IDs. We have a link-up directly to the DMV and Social Security administration, so if you'll just fill out these forms—" He licked his fingers and collected a stack of papers from underneath the counter, then put them all on a clipboard, which he handed to Lore. "Why don't you have a seat over there while you fill those out, then come on back to me when you're finished so we can talk about our different account options."

Shaun followed Lore to one of the plush leather couches and sank down beside him. After surreptitiously scanning the room to make sure no one was standing close enough to eavesdrop, he muttered, "Your partner, huh? You realize he probably thinks we're gay now?"

"He'd be three-quarters right," replied Lore as he bent his head over the forms and began filling them out.

Shaun snorted and leaned in to peer over Lore's shoulder. "I'm guessing you've made sure there's a Stephen Malone and Lee Tryton registered with the DMV?"

Apparently, Lore didn't feel the need to dignify that with an answer, because he just sighed and kept writing.

"Is that your real address?" asked Shaun.

Lore sighed again and turned his head to glare at Shaun. Shaun pulled back just in time to avoid having his nose crushed by Lore's jaw, which immediately drew his attention to just how close they were sitting to each other. Lore seemed to realize it too, because his expression shifted from annoyance to vague uncertainty.

"Uhm, better make that seven-eighths," said Shaun.

Lore didn't reply, but the corners of his lips twitched as he turned back to the paperwork.

When they were finished with the forms—or rather, when Lore was finished filling them out and Shaun was finished signing wherever Lore told him to—they took them back to the counter where Gary was just finishing with another customer.

Gary beamed at them when he saw them and held out a hand for the clipboard. "Everything all filled out?"

While Gary flipped through the paperwork, Lore put his hand on the countertop. It was a casual gesture that anyone who didn't know his secret probably wouldn't have noticed, but Shaun knew better. The sudden, faraway look in Lore's eyes confirmed his suspicions: while poor, unassuming Gary was checking their application for errors, Lore was hacking into the bank's information system.

Shaun hadn't thought it was possible for Lore to be any more terrifying or any more attractive, but he'd been wrong.

"Well, it looks like everything's in order," said Gary when he was finished shuffling through the papers. He set the clipboard down and tapped on the counter right next to Lore's hand, and the counter lit up to display an embedded control panel.

Shaun looked away politely when Gary entered his password, and he saw the corner of Lore's lips twitch.

"Now, what kind of account were you interested in opening?" asked Gary.

"Oh, that's really up to Stephen. He's the one who asked me to open a joint account with him. He just wants the reassurance that I'm really committed to our relationship, you know." Lore smiled at Shaun. "What do you think, darling?"

Shaun resisted the urge to stomp on Lore's foot. He glared at Lore for a moment, then forced himself to smile at Gary. "What kind of retirement accounts do you have?" When Gary turned away to find a list of all the account options, Shaun elbowed Lore in the ribs and hissed, "What the hell are you doing? Stop hamming it up. You're going to blow our cover."

"Just keep him occupied, Mason. I need to concentrate."

Gary came back with the list of account types, and Shaun pretended to listen while he explained each of them. When Gary was finished talking, Shaun chose one of the accounts at random, and Gary gave him a wide, salesman-slick smile. "Excellent choice, Mister Malone. Now, I just need to go through the ID verification process and you should be all set."

Shaun knew something was wrong the second Gary brought up Lore's fake DMV profile. Lore's photo appeared on the screen, along with the name and address he'd written on the application, but there was a list of codes at the bottom of the screen that Shaun assumed were bank-specific, and whatever Gary saw there made him frown. The same thing happened when he pulled up "Stephen Malone" in the Social Security database.

"I'm sorry, gentlemen, the system seems to be having some kind of problem," said Gary. His smile was tight, and he shifted his weight from one foot to the other. "I'm just going to go get my manager and see if he can help."

Shaun nodded and offered an unassuming smile, but as soon as Gary's back was turned, Shaun's smile faded and he whispered to Lore, "We need to go."

Lore's brow was furrowed and it was obvious that he was a million miles away. In a distracted murmur, he replied, "Two minutes."

"We might not have two minutes."

Gary hurried over to a tall, graying man in a navy blue suit and made a few quick gestures with his hands. The manager frowned and said something, and he and Gary looked over at Lore and Shaun at the same time.

"Right, we're leaving now," said Shaun. He grabbed Lore's elbow and pulled him away from the counter.

To Shaun's surprise, Lore didn't protest. They hurried across the room together, toward the revolving glass security door. As they approached it, the light beside the door turned from green to red, and Shaun's heart dropped to his stomach. "They're locking us in."

"No, they're not," replied Lore. He dragged Shaun over to the door and pressed his hand against the control panel. The light turned green, and Lore shoved Shaun through the door.

Shaun tumbled out on the other side, and the six security guards in the lobby turned in unison to look at him. "Fuck," he cursed as he scrambled to his feet. He looked back to find Lore throwing himself through the door. The bank manager and two more security guards were hot on his heels. When he emerged on the other side, he put his hand on the outer control panel. The light turned red, trapping everyone else inside.

The lobby guards were headed toward them, guns drawn. Shaun was sure the guns weren't lethal, but he didn't want to stick around and find out what they could do. He grabbed Lore's arm again and broke into a run towards the telechambers. There was a loud pop from behind them, and Shaun winced, expecting to feel a bullet rip through his shoulder or his leg. Nothing happened. He and Lore came to a skidding stop in front of the chambers, and Shaun glanced back in time to see the guard who'd fired the shot squeeze the trigger again. There was another loud crack of gunfire, but nothing happened.

When the chamber finally opened, Shaun darted inside with

Lore right behind him. He smacked frantically at the control panel until it buzzed in protest. The doors seemed to slide closed in slow motion, on the sight of all six guards rushing the chamber at once.

Shaun slumped back against the mirrored wall and stared at Lore.

Lore stared back. His cheeks were flushed and his eyes were brighter than Shaun had ever seen them.

"Stop the chamber," Shaun panted, still out of breath from running.

Lore didn't even ask why; he put his hand on the control panel. The light above the door had been gradually shifting from red toward green, and it stopped at a steady amber color. He took his hand away and licked his lips. "We really don't have time, Shaun. I know where the—"

"Shut up," said Shaun. He was already halfway across the chamber, and he silenced the last of Lore's protests with a kiss. Lore tried to push him away, but Shaun didn't budge. He pressed Lore against the wall and buried his fingers in Lore's hair to keep him in place. Standing with Lore trapped against him, he could feel the exact moment that Lore gave in—he felt the tension in Lore's muscles change from one type to another and felt Lore's mouth open for his—and he growled against Lore's lips.

Apparently, Lore wasn't in the mood to just stand there and let things happen. Once he decided to reciprocate, he did so with enthusiasm. He shoved Shaun away, then turned and pressed him against the mirrored wall instead. When Lore broke the kiss to bite the side of his neck, Shaun let his head fall back with a thunk.

Both of Lore's hands were working on untucking his shirt, and Shaun reached down to help. Lore batted his hands away, so he grabbed Lore's hips instead. Lore's erection was pressed against his belly, so Shaun pushed a thigh between Lore's legs and rubbed his cock through his trousers. Lore gasped, and his hands faltered on Shaun's buttons.

"Tell me what you want," whispered Shaun, sliding a hand down Lore's back to squeeze his ass.

He expected to be told to shut up. What he didn't expect was for Lore to grab a handful of his hair, tip his head back, and whisper against his lips, "Your cock in my mouth."

It took all of Shaun's self-control not to come in his pants like a horny teenager.

Lore kissed him again, hard and quick on the lips, then dropped to his knees at Shaun's feet. Shaun's eyes snapped open when he felt Lore's fingers on his fly, and he stared down at the sight of Lore looking up at him, lips swollen and a gaze so intense it seemed to burn straight through him. Having Lore stare into his eyes while tugging his underwear down to free his cock was almost too much to handle, and he breathed a barely audible sigh of relief when Lore finally looked away.

But then Lore nuzzled the shaft of Shaun's cock with his cheek, and Shaun nearly crawled backwards up the wall. "Fuck," he gasped and made a grab for Lore's hair.

Lore started at the base of his cock, grazing the bottom with his lips and then dragging the tip of his tongue up the underside. He rubbed his lips across the tip until they were shiny with pre-come, then slid his mouth over the head. He glanced up at Shaun through his lashes, and then swallowed the full length of Shaun's cock in one go.

"Oh shit—fuck, Lore, fuck—" Shaun was reduced to incoherent babbling in a matter of seconds. He tugged at Lore's hair with one hand and curled the other into a fist to slam it back against the wall. Because the walls were mirrored, everywhere he looked, he saw the image of Lore's lips wrapped around the wet shaft of his cock. Eventually, he had to close his eyes just to keep himself from losing it.

What finally did him in was Lore's quiet moan around his prick.

Shaun tried to give warning, but it was too late, and the words came out a choked gasp. Orgasm ripped through him, rendering him incapable of doing anything but shaking so hard he had to clamp his teeth together to keep them from chattering. He grabbed ineffectually at any surface he could find—Lore's hair, the wall, his own shirt. Lore sucked him through the last tremors of his orgasm, and when he finally slumped against the wall, Lore slowly pulled back and licked him clean.

"Jesus," Shaun whimpered. He squeezed his eyes shut and carded his fingers through Lore's hair, and tried not to twitch away from the feeling of Lore's tongue against his oversensitive cock. Finally, when he couldn't take it anymore, he grabbed Lore's shoulder and pulled, trying to get him to stand.

This time when they kissed, neither of them hesitated. Shaun held Lore's face in his hands and explored Lore's mouth with his tongue while Lore's fingers knotted themselves up in the front of his shirt. Tasting his own come on Lore's lips made Shaun shiver, and he ducked his head to kiss the corner of Lore's mouth, then the curve of his jaw, and the skin just underneath his ear.

Lore tipped his head to one side and inhaled sharply when Shaun's tongue found his earlobe. Every muscle in his body felt tense, and Shaun cupped the back of Lore's neck in one hand. He slid his other hand down to the crotch of Lore's trousers to squeeze his dick through the fabric.

Lore's hold on his shirt tightened. "Damn it, Mason."

"Shh, I've got it," whispered Shaun. He fumbled Lore's zipper open, then shoved his trousers down to free his cock. The length of it was heavy in his hand, and he spent a few seconds teasing it with his fingertips until Lore made an impatient sound and rocked his hips forward. Shaun grunted his understanding and wrapped his fingers around the shaft. He stroked Lore slowly at first, then harder and faster until Lore was panting and shaking against him.

It didn't take long, and just seconds before Lore came, he crushed his lips to Shaun's in an open-mouthed kiss. His cock swelled in Shaun's hand, and he moaned into Shaun's mouth.

They broke away, both of them panting for breath, and pressed their foreheads together. Lore's eyes were closed, but Shaun's were open, taking in every detail of Lore's face. His free hand was holding Lore's face, and he rubbed his thumb over Lore's cheekbone.

"Shaun," said Lore.

"Yeah?" whispered Shaun.

Lore opened his eyes. "I know where the killer is."

Chapter Eighteen

"You're sure?"

"Yes, Mason, I'm sure. Unless someone is running an unauthorized proxy server in one of the university's computer labs, this is where he signed in from."

They'd hurried back to Lore's property without even bothering to pretend they felt awkward. Lore was sitting at his makeshift desk, and Shaun was leaning down over him to stare at the map that hovered above the table's surface. A small, green circle encompassed the west side of North Hills, less than fifteen minutes away from Shaun's apartment. The epicenter of the tiny circle was California State University.

"And you're sure he was in the bank with us?"

"Yes."

A shiver rippled down Shaun's spine. He straightened and tugged his fingers through his hair with a shaky sigh. "Shit. Okay. And he's probably the one who flagged our DMV profiles, isn't he?"

"Most likely. I think he probably flagged them a long time ago and has just been waiting for us to try and use them."

"Because anyplace that would be looking up our DMV profiles would be based in the real world," said Shaun. "If we'd been caught by bank security, that would have triggered a real-life fraud investigation. Our cover would've been blown. Fuck, the bastard was probably there to watch it happen."

"Mm." Lore nodded, but it was obvious that his attention was starting to drift. He was tapping his thumb against the arm of his chair and frowning at the map.

Shaun braced a hand on the back of Lore's chair and leaned over his shoulder with a sigh. "So, the university, huh? Damn it, they've probably got a hundred tanks on campus between the classrooms and the dorms. Don't suppose you can tell me what building he logged in from?"

Lore shook his head.

"Well, it was worth a shot." Shaun sighed again, then asked, "Hey, you can access the regular Internet from here, right? Maybe the university's website will have a list of all the SR-enabled classrooms or something. That could at least help us narrow down places to check."

Lore did as Shaun asked. The university's website didn't list classrooms with SR tanks, but some of the course descriptions mentioned using SR technology.

Shaun was scribbling the class names on a notepad when his phone buzzed against his thigh, and he answered it without looking at the caller ID. "Yeah?"

"Shaun?" said Kim. She sounded upset. "What the hell happened to you?"

Shaun's hand paused over the notepad, and he frowned. "What do you mean?"

"Don't play stupid with me, Shaun. Your blood is all over this hair. Now tell me what happened."

"I just got into a tussle. It's nothing, I'm fine, I promise."

Kim was silent for a moment, and then she said, very clearly, "Fuck you, Shaun."

"What?" said Shaun, aghast. Kim almost never spoke that way to him.

"I know you're lying to me, you sorry son of a bitch. Do you think I'm stupid? Tell me what's going on, Shaun, now, or I swear to god I'm dumping these lab results in the trash."

Shaun dragged a hand over his face. "All right, all right, but first you have to promise me that you won't say a word about it to anyone."

Kim sighed, and Shaun could practically hear her rolling her eyes.

"I mean it, Kim. It's important."

"Fine, I promise. Now tell me what's going on."

Shaun told her the truth—not all of it, but enough. When he was finished talking, he asked, "Now do you understand why I said I couldn't talk about it?"

"Yeah." Kim's voice was quiet, thoughtful. He expected her to ask more questions, or at least admonish him for getting himself into so much trouble, but when she spoke again, all she said was, "I have the phenotyping done."

Shaun felt a surge of affection for her, and he smiled into the phone. "Great. Give me a second to get a pen."

A few minutes later, Shaun hung up and waved his notepad in front of Lore. "Good news: Kim got the phenotyping done. She just gave us a description of what the person we're looking for probably looks like."

"Mm," replied Lore. He was scrolling through the university's online bulletin board, where students could list events or offer services. He was in the "Tutoring Available" section, clicking through advertisements for anything related to SR technology or programming.

"Are you listening?" asked Shaun as he leaned over to look at the screen.

"Yes," said Lore. "We now have a physical description. I assume you plan to share it with me at some point."

Shaun chuckled. It came out strained, but everything about him felt strained these days. His shoulders were practically up to his ears with tension. "The guy who attacked me was definitely male, probably Caucasian with dark hair and green or blue eyes."

"A man with dark hair and blue eyes? That should be easy to find in Los Angeles."

"Look, I know it's not the most specific description, but it's more than what—wait, stop." Shaun hadn't been paying much attention to what was on the screen, but something caught his eye while Lore was clicking through notices. "Go back to that last page."

Lore went back to the on-campus events section and frowned. "What? I've already looked at this section, Mason. There's nothing—"

"No, there, click on that." Shaun jabbed his finger at the holographic screen.

Lore clicked on the posting, and they both leaned in a little closer to read it.

LGBT Abuse Survivors

LGBTAS was formed as a support group for lesbian, gay, bi-sexual, and transsexual students who have been abused by parents, partners, or friends. It exists to address the unique problems that confront LGBT abuse survivors, in a safe setting with peers who have shared similar experiences.

LGBTAS meetings are held in Room 3 of the counseling center on Tuesday and Thursday nights at 6:30PM. Sessions are hosted by Dr. Richard Greene. Students who are interested in attending LGB-TAS meetings should set up an initial intake appointment with Dr. Greene during office hours (M,W,F 12PM-4PM).

"That's him! He's the link!" Shaun pointed at Dr. Greene's name. "He's the one who prescribed Sarah's medication. There was a flier at Ruby's house that had his name on it too, for a women's counseling center in Hollywood."

"That's why the police never formed a connection," said Lore. He was staring at the screen, but it was obvious he wasn't actually reading it. "The victims were never actually connected. It was their partners who had something in common."

Shaun nodded but didn't reply. He stood there and watched Lore work, trying to imagine what was happening inside Lore's head. He imagined that Lore lifting that shiny new strand of reasoning, like picking a loose thread out of a piece of fabric, and following it rapid-fire from one place to the next, interfacing each new idea with research gleaned from his inexplicable connection to Simulnet. Just the thought of how much information could potentially be passing through Lore's mind at that moment made the hair on the back of Shaun's neck stand on end.

Finally, Lore seemed to snap back to attention, and he turned his head to look at Shaun. "He's definitely the connection. Four of the victims had partners who were patients, and one was a patient himself. Others may have been members of one of the anonymous groups that Dr. Greene hosted."

"Are you sure?"

Lore nodded.

They were both quiet for a moment before Shaun straightened and said, "Then I'm going to pay him a visit."

"What?"

"I'm going to go see him. If he's the link between the victims, I need to talk to him."

Lore was on his feet in an instant. He looked angrier than Shaun had believed he was capable of being. "Are you out of your mind? This man may be the same man who tried to kill you, and you're going to do what? Go waltzing in to his office and have a chat?"

"It's not like I'm going to his house alone in the middle of the night, Lore. I'm going to see him in his office, during the day, on a busy college campus."

"Let Hudson and her team handle it, Mason. That's what they're there for. Our job was to find the killer, not to go and confront him ourselves. Have you even considered the possibility that you showing up in his office is going to scare him into running?"

"If he's the man we're looking for, he's been inside my house, Lore. He's watched me sleep. He's not exactly shy." Shaun's jaw was clenched with annoyance, and he had to force each word out from between his teeth. "I need to see him face-to-face. I need to be able to confront him."

Lore still looked angry, but it had softened somehow, which made Shaun want to give in a little as well.

"Look, I'll call Hudson for back-up before I go, okay?" said Shaun in a quieter tone. "I won't go in there alone, but I'm not bringing a full armada with me, either. If I head in there with a S.W.A.T. team and van full of feds, and it turns out Greene isn't our guy, our cover is blown. All our hard work comes to a grinding stop."

"And if he is our guy, it may take more than just yourself and Hudson to bring him in. He's too proud to go without a fight, and too intelligent to put up anything less than a good one. If you give him a chance to, he will kill you, Shaun."

"I know."

Lore studied him for a moment, as if looking for an answer to a question he couldn't ask out loud, then he stepped forward and took Shaun's face in his hands. They looked at each other for almost a full minute before Lore pulled Shaun in and kissed him. There was nothing sexual about it; it was a hard, closed-mouth kiss on the lips. Shaun grabbed Lore's wrists with both hands and exhaled sharply through his nose when Lore's fingernails dug into his jaw.

They broke away at the same time, and Shaun pressed their foreheads together. Lore's eyes were closed; Shaun's were open. It seemed to be turning into a theme. He watched the way Lore's eyelids twitched, like his body couldn't stand to be shut off from any of its senses for more than a few seconds.

"You always have to be doing something, don't you?" whispered Shaun.

Lore's impossibly blue eyes snapped open, and he stared at Shaun for a moment before replying, "Be careful, Mason."

When Shaun logged out, he found Brian waiting for him. He was sitting by the window, reading the paper and drinking coffee, and Shaun had a flash of deja vu followed by a sudden flash of recognition. He slipped into the hotel bathrobe he'd discarded beside the tank, then stalked across the room. Before Brian could say a word, Shaun grabbed him by the front of his shirt and pressed a quick, chaste kiss to his lips, then pulled back to gauge the reaction.

Brian didn't smile, but there was an unmistakable gleam of amusement in his eyes.

"Thought so," Shaun muttered as he loosened his grip on Brian's shirt. "You could've just told me, Blake."

"Yes, well," replied Brian as he straightened his shirt and jacket. His voice had dropped to a familiar purr, and he smirked at Shaun. "I knew you'd figure it out on your own eventually, if I dropped enough hints. I don't like to be heavy-handed with that sort of thing, you know. I'm impressed, though. You got it in one."

"You sound like Lore."

"You'll find there are worse people to compare me to, darling.

Now, tell me what you've found. Luis tells me you asked him to overnight a package to France for you?"

Shaun told Brian about the phenotyping and what he and Lore had pieced together about Dr. Greene.

"Well, I'm suitably impressed—not that I ever had any doubts about the two of you, of course," Brian drawled, then examined Shaun's face and frowned. "Oh dear, you're considering going to go after him, aren't you?"

"I need to be absolutely sure it's him before Hudson brings the feds in," said Shaun. "If I go there and it turns out it's not him, my cover gets blown, I get fired, Hudson gets fired, Lore probably gets arrested, and every bit of work we've done gets wasted as soon as the feds get their hands on the case."

"So I suppose you're going to ask me if I'll have my men serve as back-up?" Brian's expression was unreadable.

"Well, I wasn't," said Shaun. "But now that you mention it... I mean, obviously you're not obligated—I mean hell, you've already saved my ass once—"

"Darling." Brian's smile was slow and full of mischief. "I wouldn't miss it for the world."

"Mason, are you sure about this?"

Shaun was standing with Hudson and Brian in the parking lot of the university's administration building. The white cargo van shielded them from view of the offices while they readied themselves to confront Greene.

"I'm sure," said Shaun as he repositioned the Kevlar vest he was wearing beneath his clothes. It was bulky, which meant he had to wear an unseasonably thick sweatshirt to hide it, but Hudson had refused to help unless he agreed to wear a vest.

Brian handed a gun to Hudson, and she checked to make sure it was loaded. Shaun had been surprised at how easy it had been to persuade her to work with Brian and his men. They didn't seem to know each other, but there had been a flash of recognition on her face when he'd mentioned Brian's last name. When Hudson was finished checking the gun over, she handed it to Shaun and said, "I hope you remember how to use one of these."

"Basic training wasn't that long ago, you know." Shaun forced a grin as he took the gun and slipped it into the side holster that was strapped to his vest, under his sweatshirt.

Hudson still looked doubtful. She pressed her lips together and eyed him for a moment before turning to Brian and saying, "Earpieces."

"Yes ma'am." Brian nodded and moved to the back of the van to retrieve the earpieces.

Shaun couldn't help but to chuckle. "Geez, you've known him two hours and you've already got him doing your bidding. I swear you were some kind of evil overlord or something in a past life." He tugged his sweatshirt down over the gun. "What made you okay with bringing him and his guys along, anyway? I was expecting to have to fight with you about it."

"I'm familiar with his father," said Hudson, then glanced over her shoulder before continuing. "Mister Katou and his family keep Triad activity in Los Angeles to a minimum. In exchange, the L.A.P.D. is willing to overlook some of his shadier business situations."

Shaun was surprised. He'd suspected that the Katou family was involved in something, of course, but he hadn't thought it extended far enough to give them control over the Chinese mafia, and he certainly hadn't imagined that the L.A.P.D. would just ignore something happening right under their noses.

"Don't look so shocked," said Hudson with a sigh. "I promise you, L.A. isn't the first city in the world to turn a blind eye to gambling and prostitution if it means keeping out bigger problems like drugs and weapons. If the Triad had it their way, everyone in L.A. would be high on meth and toting AK-47s."

"You mean we're not already?" ask Shaun with a halfhearted grin. He was trying to keep the mood light, but he knew it wasn't working. They were all tense, even Brian's men, who were waiting inside the van.

Brian came back with the earpieces. They put them in and spent a few minutes testing volume levels, and then Shaun was ready to go.

"You're sure about this?" Hudson asked again.

Shaun nodded. "Yeah, just promise you'll be ready to storm the castle if I need help."

Hudson pressed her lips together in a thin, disapproving line, but she finally huffed and said, "Fine, but do us all a favor and don't try to be a hero. The last thing I feel like doing is scraping your fucking brains off the wall because you decided to take him on alone."

"I'll be careful," Shaun promised, and for once, he actually meant it. Since he knew Hudson wouldn't accept a hug, he shook her hand instead. She gave his fingers a quick squeeze, then waved him off and climbed into the van.

As soon as they were alone, Brian put his hand on Shaun's elbow. "Remember, all you have to do is let us know you need us, and we'll be there."

Shaun gave him a tight-lipped smile and kissed his cheek, then pulled away, straightened his sweatshirt, and set off across the parking lot. On his way toward the administration building, he pulled his phone out of his pocket and sent a text to Lore: 'on my way in now. wish me luck.'

Chapter Nineteen

Dr. Richard Greene's office was in the same section of the administration building as the counseling office and the head of the university's Psychology department. The reception area was empty except for the bored-looking blonde girl at the reception desk, who was hunched over what looked like a Calculus textbook. She didn't look up until Shaun cleared his throat.

"Hi," said Shaun, trying to sound as upbeat as he could, "I was just wondering if Dr. Greene is around?"

The girl sighed and shoved her textbook away, then tapped her finger on the keypad of the computer beside her. "Name?"

"Oh, uhm, actually I don't have an appointment," said Shaun, hoping he sounded like a nervous freshman and not a grown man who was hiding almost fifty pounds of body armor under his sweatshirt.

The receptionist huffed and turned back to her textbook. "You'll need to make an appointment."

"Look," said Shaun. He leaned over the desk, planted his hand on the page she was reading, and told her very firmly, "I can't wait for an appointment. I need you to call him and tell him Stephen Malone is here to see him. Please."

The girl didn't look impressed, but she didn't argue either. She rolled her eyes and picked up the phone on her desk, and dialed what Shaun hoped was Greene's extension and not the campus police. A few seconds later, she heaved a sigh and said, "Hi, sorry for bothering you but there's a guy here to see you. He says it can't wait... yeah... no, he doesn't... I told him that... he says his name is—" She looked up at Shaun.

"Stephen Malone."

"Stephen Malone," the girl repeated. "No, he didn't say... are you sure? All right, I'll let him know." She hung up and scowled at

Shaun before turning back to her textbook. "He'll be out in a minute."

Shaun nodded and stuffed his hands into his pockets to surreptitiously dry his palms against the fabric. The girl seemed intent on ignoring him, so he wandered away from the desk and pretended to peruse the fliers that were tacked to the notice board. The earpiece was silent, but knowing that Hudson and the others were listening was the only thing that kept him from bolting. When he heard footsteps shuffling down the carpeted hallway behind him, he closed his eyes and tried to keep his breathing steady.

"Stephen?"

Shaun turned around. He wasn't sure what he'd been expecting of the cunning and ruthless killer he'd been chasing, but he was surprised to find himself looking at a man who was old enough to be his grandfather. Dr. Richard Greene was short, thin, and gray. He had kind, intelligent eyes, and a patient smile. There was a scuffed, leather bound notepad holder in his hand, which shook a little with the first fine tremors of old age.

Shaun wondered if he'd made a mistake.

Greene seemed to misunderstand Shaun's hesitation, because he smiled and said, "We don't have to talk here. Would you like to talk in my office?"

Shaun too off guard to protest, so he just nodded and followed Greene down the carpeted hall to a small, dimly lit office. The room had dusky gray walls, an overstuffed couch, and bookshelves overflowing with psychiatric journals. Greene sat in an armchair opposite the couch, and gestured for Shaun to have a seat.

"Now, how can I help you?" asked Greene once they were settled.

Shaun wracked his brain for something to say that wasn't, 'I'm here because I thought you were the serial killer who's been stalking me and I wanted to confront you.' Finally, he settled for the partial truth: "A good friend of mine passed away a couple days ago. I think you knew her and her girlfriend."

"I'm very sorry to hear that." Greene's frown looked sincere.

"What was your friend's name?"

"Ruby," said Shaun. "Ruby Horowitz."

Greene's eyebrows rose, and then his expression turned sad. He nodded. "Yes, I knew Ruby. She was a volunteer at the Hollywood Women's Center where I host group counseling sessions. She was a lovely woman. I'm so sorry to hear she's gone. Can I ask how she—?"

Shaun debated with himself—he hadn't exactly planned this out very well, he realized—and then leaned forward to reply in a confidential tone, "I know this probably sounds paranoid, but between you and me, I think she and her girlfriend were murdered."

The earpiece crackled with Hudson's voice: "Careful, Mason."

Greene looked horrified. "Murdered? By whom?"

"That's what I've been trying to figure out," said Shaun. He tried to choose his next words very carefully. "I don't know whether or not the cops are investigating, but if they are, they're not telling me anything, so I've been looking for answers on my own. Ruby was really important to me—it sounds like she was important to a lot of people—so anything you can tell me about her or her girlfriend..."

Greene look conflicted.

"I'm sorry, I know this is probably putting you in a really bad situation," said Shaun. "But I wouldn't be asking if it wasn't important."

Greene sighed and put his notepad aside, then took his glasses off to rub his nose. "From what I gathered, Ruby and her girlfriend were in a precarious situation. The girlfriend was involved in a mentally abusive relationship, and Ruby was doing her best to help extricate her from it."

"You were Sarah's therapist, weren't you?"

Greene's eyes narrowed, and Shaun knew he'd just messed up. "I wasn't aware anyone knew Sarah had been seeing me. As far as I knew, she hadn't even told Ruby."

"I figured it out on my own," said Shaun, hoping Greene wouldn't ask how he'd put it all together.

Thankfully, that seemed to mollify Greene because he visibly relaxed and shook his head. "I wish I could help you, I really do, but Sarah said very little about her relationship with Ruby. Most of her sessions with me were about her boyfriend and working through some minor childhood traumas. But if you're asking me whether or not I think her boyfriend had anything to do with her death—"

"No, no, I don't think he did," said Shaun. "I've talked to him, and he seems like a scumbag, but he's not a killer."

Greene nodded. "Keith isn't the best candidate for an intimate relationship, but from what Sarah told me about him, he isn't capable of murder." He paused, then gave Shaun a sympathetic frown. "I really do wish I could be of more help, Stephen, but I have no idea who on earth would want to kill Sarah. She had her share of problems, but I can't imagine her having enemies who would want to hurt her. As for Ruby, I wasn't close with her, but—" His face brightened as if a thought had just occurred to him. "Actually, now that I think of it, one of my interns spent quite a bit of time with Ruby whenever we were at the Women's Center, and he sat in on some of my sessions with Sarah as well. He might be able to help you better than I can. He's in the office today. I'd be happy to call him in to speak with you if you don't mind waiting?"

Shaun was vaguely aware that he was nodding, but his mind was already racing. His instincts were prickling, and the hair on the back of his neck was standing on end. He wondered if Hudson and Brian could hear Greene's side of the conversation through the earpieces, and if they could, whether either of them had just felt the same little spark of realization that he had.

Greene phoned someone from his desk, and after a brief conversation, he sat across from Shaun again. "He should be here shortly. He's just in the office down the hall."

"And you said he's your intern?" asked Shaun, trying to keep his voice steady.

Greene nodded. "He needs work-study hours to be eligible for his license, so he's has been acting as an assistant to me for the last year." There was a knock on the door, and he paused. "That must be him now. Come in!"

The door opened and a young man with a long, dark ponytail and bright green eyes stood in the doorway. He smiled at Greene first, but when he caught sight of Shaun, his expression froze.

Shaun's stomach lurched.

"Ah, Nick, there you are. Would you come in, please?"

Nick's nostrils flared. He was breathing quick and shallow like a trapped animal, and when he lifted his chin—he's going to run, thought Shaun, he knows I know it's him, and he's going to run— Shaun caught a glimpse of a tiny scar on his throat, just underneath his jaw.

Nick ran.

Shaun was on his feet in an instant. He slammed out of the room, hot on Nick's heels with Greene shouting something behind him. The receptionist was coming back to her desk with a fresh cup of coffee in her hand, and she squawked in protest when Nick shoved past her. When she caught sight of Shaun pulling his gun out of its holster beneath his sweatshirt, though, she shrieked and ducked behind the desk.

"Stop! L.A.P.D.!" Shaun shouted as Nick darted around a corner and down another hallway, but Nick didn't even slow.

"Mason?" said Hudson over the earpiece. "What the hell is going on?"

"I've got him. He's running." Shaun pushed a few terrified students out of his path. "We're on the first floor, headed toward the south end."

The administration building wasn't busy, but a handful of people had emerged from their offices to see what the commotion was. Shaun couldn't raise his gun with civilians in the way, so he shoved past people, knocking into startled faculty and confused students as he chased Nick down the hall.

Shaun had expected Nick to continue out of the building and into the quad area, but Nick caught him off guard by taking a quick left at the end of the corridor. "Shit," cursed Shaun, "he's headed west now."

The door that led outside burst open just as Shaun rushed past it, and then Hudson was at his side with her gun drawn. They sped down the hall together, and around another corner just in time to see Nick shove his way into a group of students who were coming in from the building's west entrance.

"He's outside," barked Hudson, "going west, headed toward the parking lot."

"Almost there." Brian's voice crackled. "Slow him down."

"Can't," replied Shaun as he pushed his way into the crowd. The students had finally noticed his and Hudson's guns, and the result was a trampling hysteria that slowed them down so much that by the time they made it outside, Nick had reached the parking lot.

Brian and his men were just yards behind Nick, but the parking lot was crowded with students piling in for evening classes. Shaun and Hudson ran behind the others, desperate to catch up. Nick narrowly dodged an SUV as the driver whipped it into a parking spot. The almost-accident forced Brian and one of his men to jump back, putting even more space between them and Nick.

"Fuck, we're going to lose him," said Hudson.

Brian's other man, the one with the bald head and tattooed hands, darted around the back of the SUV and sped up. Nick glanced back at him and strafed right, ducking between two parked cars and into the next lane of the parking lot. The man who'd been chasing him grunted something in Japanese and vaulted over the hood of moving car to try and catch up, but Nick had already put considerable distance between them.

Shaun, meanwhile, was cursing the weight of the Kevlar vest he was wearing. Without it, he might have stood a shot at catching up, but he wasn't used to running with fifty extra pounds strapped to his back. Even the short distance he'd run so far had him panting with exertion, and he was almost grateful when Hudson slowed beside him and grabbed his arm to make him stop.

"We're not going to catch him," Hudson panted and pulled her phone out of her pocket.

Brian and his two men were still chasing Nick across the

parking lot, but Shaun could already see that they didn't stand a chance. Nick was too far ahead.

Hudson dialed a number and pressed her phone to her ear. A second later, she said, "Dispatch, this is Detective Lisa Hudson, Homicide. I need units on the lookout for a white male..."

"I should be out there," said Shaun, pacing across his hotel suite for what had to have been the millionth time. A brilliant sunset of the sort that can only be the byproduct of wildfires and L.A. smog had set the room ablaze with tones of gold and red. Shaun hardly noticed.

Brian was sitting in his armchair near the window with his legs crossed and his fingers steepled against his lips while he watched.

"I should be helping," said Shaun. "This is my investigation."

"I know, darling. But I also know that if the federal government catches wind that this was your investigation, you could lose your job at best or spend time in prison at worst."

"That's such bullshit," Shaun spat. He raked his fingers through his hair and stopped beside the window to glare out at the city skyline. He couldn't smell the fires, but he could see the smoke. He wished the whole fucking city would burn. "I've spent two weeks working on this, and I don't even get credit for it. Anonymous tip my fucking ass."

"You knew from the start you wouldn't get credit for it," said Brian.

Shaun didn't reply. They was nothing he could say, because Brian was right. Besides, it wasn't the credit that bothered him the most; it was the fact that he wanted to be out there doing something, not cooped up in a hotel room under armed guard. He wondered if this was cabin fever.

"Would you like a drink?" asked Brian as he stood and went over to the minibar.

Shaun shook his head. "No, thanks." He closed his eyes and

rested his forehead against the cool glass for a moment, then opened his eyes and watched the afternoon traffic crawl down Third Street. He'd been part of that world just two weeks ago, just one of billions who woke up every morning and drove to the same office building, sat at the same desk, drank the same shitty coffee, and listened to the same stupid co-workers share the same stupid gossip. Shaun had never been happy with that life, but the thought of going back to it now was downright unbearable.

"I'm logging in," he mumbled. "I need to debrief Lore."

He pushed away from the window and went over to the SR tank, tugging his off as he walked. The truth was, he'd already sent Lore several text messages to let him know what happened, and there was no reason for him to log in right that second, but the thought of just standing there in his hotel room, waiting, was making his skin crawl.

Brian watched him with a frown, hand poised over his freshly poured drink. "You should eat something first."

"Not hungry," replied Shaun as he shucked his jeans and kicked them away.

Brian moved closer and stood between the tank and Shaun. He looked troubled, and his tone was soft when he said, "Shaun, I know what it feels like to come back to the real world after spending so much time in Simulnet."

"What it feels like—?" Shaun had bent over to take off his socks, but he paused and looked up at Brian with a frown. Then he looked away again and muttered, "No, that's not it. I just need to talk to Lore. I sent him a couple text messages, but I'd rather talk to him in person."

"Shaun."

"Look," said Shaun as he straightened and stared at Brian, "I get what you're trying to say, okay? And I get it. I do. But right now... I can't just sit around while that asshole is out there roaming the streets—"

Brian held his hands up in surrender.

Shaun softened and gave Brian's shoulder a squeeze. "Hey, look,

I really do appreciate you looking out for me. I just need to not be here right now."

Brian nodded and sighed, then leaned in and brushed a lingering kiss across Shaun's lips.

Shaun's eyes widened, and when Brian tried to pull away, Shaun grabbed his arm. He searched Brian's face and said, "Hey, you don't—do you?"

"I don't what?" Brian frowned, but then comprehension seemed to dawn, and he gave Shaun a tight smile. "No, Shaun, I don't. But I would have, maybe, if things had been different for us."

Shaun's throat tightened, although he wasn't sure whether that was from relief or regret, and he pulled Brian into a hug. "Yeah, me too."

They stood there for a moment, with Shaun's hand on the back of Brian's head, until Brian broke away. He cleared his throat and straightened his tie, then gave Shaun the same knowing smile he'd given him the first day they met and said, "Tell Lore I said hello."

Chapter Twenty

The temple was back.

There was a gate at the end of the footbridge this time, but it opened as Shaun approached. He made his way across the grounds and slipped his shoes off at the door before padding into the temple. He found Lore kneeling on a cushion in front of the Buddha statue, wearing a dark blue kimono. Shaun approached him as quietly as possible, then knelt beside him on the tatami mats.

Neither of them said a word. Shaun listened to the wind in the trees outside and marveled at how relaxed he felt just being there with Lore.

After awhile, Lore opened his eyes and looked at Shaun. "Has there been a development?"

"No." Shaun shook his head. "Hudson stuck me in the hotel room under armed guard, though. I know she's just trying to look out for me, but being cooped up in there was driving me crazy."

"Mm."

Shaun tipped his head back and looked up at the statue. "I didn't know you were Buddhist."

"I'm not," said Lore as he pushed to his feet and walked toward the bedroom, untying and shedding his kimono along the way. He was naked underneath, and the tattoos on his back seemed to slither across his skin while he walked.

Shaun watched him leave and wondered if he'd ever not want to shove Lore against a wall.

When Lore came back a few minutes later, he was fully dressed in his usual ratty blazer and scarves. It was strangely comforting, Shaun thought, that as mercurial as Lore had proven he could be, he never changed himself for Shaun's benefit. He seemed as prickly and distracted as always, and he didn't bother to sugar coat the question when he asked Shaun, "Why did you come here?"

"Like I said, I got tired of being cooped up in the hotel. On Simulnet I can go anywhere I want, whenever I want. Seemed like a good solution for cabin fever." Shaun shrugged.

Lore hummed in acknowledgment and sat down on the floor near the coffee table. His laptop appeared in front of him, and he immediately opened it and started typing.

"Hey, I've been meaning to ask you," said Shaun as he pushed to his feet and wandered closer. "I know you're not gonna tell me how you can do the shit you do with Simulnet, and that's fine, but how come you still use this when I'm around?" He pointed to the laptop. "I mean, you already know that I know. Seems like a waste of time to go through the motions."

"There's a limit to how many things I can do at once," Lore explained without lifting his gaze from the screen.

"Ah, right," said Shaun as he plopped down into one of the armchairs.

"Mason," said Lore, his fingers pausing on the keyboard, "of all the places you could have gone, why did you come here?"

Shaun was quiet for awhile, trying to think of an answer that wouldn't sound ridiculous or girly, or both. Finally, he replied, "I dunno. I just wanted to see you."

Lore's silence wasn't encouraging, and when he slammed his laptop shut, Shaun actually jumped. The look on his face was hard to decipher, but the way he gathered his laptop and stalked out of the room without a word left no doubt in Shaun's mind that apparently, his answer had been the wrong one.

"Wait, whoah, what the hell?" said Shaun. He scrambled to his feet and hurried to catch up with Lore, who had stepped out onto the porch and was shoving his feet into his boots. "Hey, what's going on?"

"Go home," said Lore.

Shaun frowned. "What? Why?"

Lore didn't reply.

"Look, whatever I said, I'm sorry," said Shaun as he followed Lore off the porch and into the grass. "Lore wait, listen—" He reached out and caught Lore's sleeve.

Lore jerked away and whirled to face him. For the first time since Shaun had known him, he looked properly angry. "Get away from me, Mason. Go home."

"Not until you tell me what the fuck I did wrong." Shaun could feel the anger welling up inside him, and he grabbed at Lore's sleeve again only to be physically shoved away.

"Don't touch me," Lore hissed. "You shouldn't have come here. What made you think I'd want you here?"

A slap to the face would have hurt less. Shaun was so stunned that for a moment, he couldn't even speak, and when he did, it came out as a croak. "Because—I thought—I mean, we're partners. Why are you—?"

"We were partners." Lore's eyes were bright with fury, and Shaun physically recoiled. "The investigation is over, and so are any ties we had to each other. Now get away from me and stay away from me."

"Lore," Shaun began, but he didn't know what else to say.

Lore made a disgusted sound and turned away. Without even so much as a backwards glance, he vanished, leaving Shaun barefoot on the temple lawn with only the wind in the trees as company.

Shaun was drunk when he got the phone call.

After Lore had left him standing in the garden, a little bit broken and feeling like a fool, he'd gone back inside and helped himself to the rum on the side table. It was good. It burned the way he wanted it to burn, and it was heavy in his stomach.

Once he was numbed by the alcohol, he'd picked the bottle up and shuffled into the bedroom. Lore's bed looked untouched, but Shaun couldn't stop thinking about him clutching at the blankets while a stranger fucked him from behind. The memory made Shaun sick, and he had to turn away.

The top of the dresser was littered with stuff: receipts that looked like they'd been stepped on, a silver button, a ticket to an

amusement park in one of the entertainment districts, a handful
of nails... Shaun sorted through the mess with a frown, and
wondered why Lore was keeping it. He was hardly the type to be
sentimental, and he didn't seem like a hoarder, and yet the only
thing in the whole goddamn place that had any personality at all
was a collection of random objects that looked like things Lore had
found on the streets.

"You fucking confusing bastard," said Shaun. He sighed and
walked backwards, stumbling a little, until he could flop down on
the bed. He stared up at the ceiling and tipped the bottle toward
his mouth, spilling rum on the bedspread in the process. He
scowled at himself, and then at Lore, and then shouted, "You
fucking prick. You cowardly fucking asshole."

He knew, in the back of his mind, that he was making a disgrace
of himself. He knew he'd be horrified later, when he was sober and
thinking about Lore watching the video feeds. For the moment, he
didn't care.

Shaun tossed the bottle off the side of the bed and rolled over,
burying his face in the comforter. He wanted to sleep until Lore
came to his senses, and he was almost asleep, too, when his phone
buzzed against his thigh. Thinking it might be Lore, he fished it out
of his pocket and blinked at the screen until the number came into
focus. It was Kim.

He considered ignoring the call—she'd probably just lecture
him about drinking—but then he realized she might be calling to
give him more information about the phenotyping. He fumbled at
the phone with clumsy fingers and answered the call with a
grumbled, "Yeah? Hello?"

"Shaun," said a too-familiar voice.

Shaun's eyes snapped open as his heart stopped dead in his
chest. "Nick?"

"Indeed. I think we need to have a little chat, don't you?"

Chapter Twenty-One

"Where are you calling me from? How are you calling from Kim's number?" Shaun sat up and closed his eyes when the room spun around him.

"Oh, don't worry about your sister. She's right here beside me. Say hello, Kimmie."

There was a muffled voice in the background, followed by Kim's voice yelling, "Shaun? Shaun, he's m'mgh—"

Her voice went muffled again, and Shaun snarled, "You fucking asshole, let her go."

"Mm, you do make a convincing argument, but no. I'm afraid I can't do that until you do something for me."

"What?" Shaun felt sick, and it wasn't because of the rum.

"Well first, you're going to hang up and log out. I hope you have your phone handy in real life, because you'll have thirty seconds to answer it. Oh, and Shaun? I wouldn't bother calling Hudson if I were you. This needs stay our little secret."

The line went dead, and Shaun cursed. He hated logging out anywhere but in his own Simulnet apartment, but there was no way he'd make it there in time, so he lay back and typed the logout command into his phone.

Seconds later, he was opening his eyes inside the SR tank and ripping the electrode cap off of his head. He shoved the tank open and scrambled out of it. The room was empty. His cell phone was already ringing, and he bounded over to the bed, dripping wet, and grabbed his phone off the nightstand.

"I knew I could count on you," said Nick. "Now, I need you to get dressed. You're going to be taking a little trip."

Now that Shaun was sober and thinking clearly, he realized there was a problem: even if Nick had driven straight from the University to the airport with no traffic (not a likely occurrence in

Los Angeles), there was no way he could have already flown to Paris
to kidnap Kim.

"I'm not going anywhere just yet," said Shaun, surprised at how
steady his voice was. "First, I want better proof that you actually
have Kim. Anyone can fake a voice for a couple of a seconds. Put
her on the phone and let me talk to her."

Nick sighed into the phone, but then he replied, "All right,
brother dearest, but only because you asked so nicely."

There were a few muffled sounds, and then Kim's panicked
voice came on the line. "Shaun? Shaun, are you there? Oh god,
please tell me you're there."

"Kim? It's me, I'm here."

"Oh god, it's you. Thank fucking god it's you."

"It's me," Shaun repeated. "And I'm coming to get you, okay? Just
hang on for me. But I need to ask you a couple questions first, okay?"

"Shaun—"

"Where did he get you?" Shaun cradled his phone against his
shoulder so he could tug his jeans on. "Where did he pick you up?
I need to know where you are."

"I was just coming to see you. I was worried about you, so I
flew in, but when I got to the airport he was—I thought he was a
cab driver. God, I'm so stupid. I'm so sorry."

"Shh, it's okay. Are you in L.A. now?"

"Yeah—yeah, I am, I think, but I don't know where."

"That's okay. Are you hurt?"

"No, I'm not, but Shaun, he said he's going to kill me if you
don't—"

The sentence ended with another muffled protest, followed by
an indignant scream, and then Nick's voice asked, "Are you satisfied
now?"

"You bastard," said Shaun. "If you hurt her—"

"I'll only hurt her if you don't cooperate. Now, if you're ready
to do as I tell you..."

"I can't go anywhere. I'm under armed guard." Shaun was sure
that at least one of Brian's men was keeping an eye on his room,

and he considered writing a note to tell them what was happening.

"Actually, your guardians seem to have deserted you for the moment," said Nick. "The two men in the room across the hall just stepped out for a cigarette, and the man in the room next door is sleeping."

Shaun's chest tightened. "How do you know that?"

"The hotel's security cameras are on the hotel's wireless network—which is unsecured, I might add."

Shaun finished buttoning his jeans and took the phone away from his ear long enough to pull on a shirt. Then he put the phone back to his ear and asked, "Fine. Tell me where I'm going."

The V.A. hospital in Westwood was a sprawling complex of medical buildings situated right next door to the Los Angeles National Cemetery. Shaun had always thought it was in bad taste to have a military cemetery so close to a military hospital.

There were no guards at the gate when Shaun arrived, so he drove to one of the visitor lots and parked. It was almost midnight according to the clock on his dash, and unlike regular hospitals with emergency rooms, this one seemed eerily quiet. Shaun still had the gun Hudson had given him, which he took out of the glove compartment and stashed down the back of his jeans. "I'm here," he said.

"Good. Now, get out of the car and go to the large white building to your right."

Shaun had switched to a wireless headset for his drive to the hospital, and Nick's voice drawled right into his ear. It made his skin crawl, but he forced himself to ignore the roiling in his stomach. He needed to concentrate.

He'd wracked his brain during the entire thirty minute drive, but so far, he hadn't come up with a single way of letting the others know exactly what was happening. Nick was monitoring Brian's text messages, and he claimed to be keeping a similar eye on the

L.A.P.D. He hadn't told Shaun where he was going, he'd just given turn-by-turn directions that made Shaun suspect he was tracking Shaun's movements using the GPS in his phone.

"You do realize I'm about to walk into a military hospital with a gun, don't you?" said Shaun. The parking lot was deserted, but he knew the buildings wouldn't be.

"They won't search you," said Nick. "I've made sure your name is on the list."

"The list?"

"Just show the M.P. your badge. You do have an L.A.P.D. badge, don't you?"

Shaun frowned. His experience with military hospitals was limited, but he was pretty sure he'd never had to pass through a security check to get into one of the buildings. Sure enough, though, there was an armed M.P. standing just inside the glass door of the building, and he eyed Shaun as Shaun made his way up the steps.

"Identification," the M.P. demanded as soon as Shaun stepped into the building.

Shaun was sweating. He knew that the worst case scenario was that they would search and detain him, but even for an L.A.P.D. employee—especially for an L.A.P.D. employee—getting caught with a concealed, loaded firearm inside a military hospital was bad news. He fumbled his badge out of his pocket and handed it to the M.P. who examined it, glanced at Shaun, and then handed the badge back. "Go ahead, Sir."

Shaun nodded and ducked his head as he started down the hallway, trying to look like he knew where he was going. When he was far enough away that the M.P. couldn't hear him, he whispered, "What the fuck was that about?"

"I told you: you're on the list. You're tonight's registered visitor. He only gets one per day, you know."

"Who only gets one per day?"

"Go to the elevators at the end of the hall. Take one to the sixth floor."

Shaun jabbed at the call button and shoved his hands into his pockets while he waited. After glancing around to make sure no one could overhear, he murmured, "You still haven't told me why you're doing this."

"Patience," said Nick. "You'll need to show your badge again when you get to the sixth floor. If they ask who you're visiting, tell them you're there to see Lee Tryton."

The elevator chose that moment to arrive, and the doors opened just in time for Shaun to catch sight of his own wide eyes in the elevator's mirrored wall. For a second, he couldn't move, but when the elevator doors started to close again, he darted forward and pressed the floor button. Once the doors were shut, he asked, "You're taking me to meet Lore?"

"I think you already know the answer to that."

Shaun's heart was pounding. The elevator doors opened, and he showed his badge to a series of M.P.s while Nick directed him to a heavily guarded room at the end of the hall. This hospital was unlike any other he'd ever seen—it was swarming with security, and the rooms were full of bizarre machines—but he didn't stop to take a closer look. He felt like he was drifting instead of walking, but when he got to the room at the end of the hall, he snapped back to reality so quickly it left him dizzy.

Lore was lying motionless beneath the starched white linens. His eyes were closed, and his eyelashes barely covered the dark blue circles beneath them. His cheeks were sunken, and his paper-thin skin was stretched tight across his cheekbones. The machinery in the room almost drowned out the sound of his shallow breathing.

"Oh my god," whispered Shaun as he moved closer to the bed. The door swung closed behind him.

"Do you want to know what happened?" asked Nick. "The U.S. government happened. He's their favorite dirty little secret. It's a pity that he had to be involved in this. He's been through so much already, and it would be a shame to waste such a brilliant mind."

Shaun sank down onto the edge of the bed and stared at Lore. He looked the same as he did in Simulnet, but the harsh fluorescent lighting made him seem too fragile to even touch.

"You've heard the rumors, haven't you?" said Nick. "My favorite story is that he was born connected to Simulnet. He wasn't, of course, but I'm sure you figured that much out on your own."

Shaun didn't reply. He slid his hand across the blanket and rubbed the backs of Lore's knuckles with his thumb.

"He wasn't always Lore, you know. Once upon a time, he was just Lee Tryton. His parents died when he two, and he became a ward of the court. The poor lamb. He spent most of his life in foster care, until a middle school teacher noticed his remarkable aptitude for technology. He started programming when he was six, you know. Anyway, this well-meaning bitch of a teacher mentioned him to her husband, a military neurosurgeon. Lee had been seeing a therapist twice a week—foster care issues, you know—so the doctor made friends with Lee's therapist and had him brought to the research center for some tests. Needless to say, he passed with flying colors, and when he was just twelve years old, he was chosen for an experimental surgery."

While Nick talked, Shaun noticed a wire that ran from underneath Lore's head across the pillow. It coiled across the floor, and then up again to a machine that reminded Shaun of the processor of an SR tank. Shaun's breath caught, and in a horrified whisper, he said, "Oh god, they hardwired him to Simulnet."

"You're smarter than you look," said Nick. "But yes, they hardwired him to Simulnet. They pushed him down the rabbit hole and he never made it out again. They've spent the last twenty years trying to figure out how to extract him without frying his brain."

"God, the public didn't even know about Simulnet twenty years ago," said Shaun. He tried to imagine what it must have been like for Lore, wandering through a Simulnet that was still in its infancy. He wondered what it looked like then, before millions of users in cities worldwide had begun to build and create.

"You're looking at one of Simulnet's first architects, Shaun. For all intents and purposes, you're staring at the face of a god."

Shaun closed his eyes. He didn't want to think of Lore as a god any more than he wanted to think of Lore as this fragile creature in a hospital bed. "So is that why you brought me here? To find a way to save him?"

"Maybe, but not in the way you think," said Nick. "Before I tell you what to do, though, I want to tell you another story."

Shaun's patience finally snapped. "No, god damn it, I don't want to hear any more stories. Just tell me why I'm here."

"Choose."

"Choose what?"

"Choose who, you mean. Whose life are you going to save tonight, Shaun? Lore or Kim?"

Shaun swore his heart stopped beating.

"Are you ready to listen to my story now?" asked Nick. When Shaun didn't speak—couldn't speak—he said, "Yes, I thought that might shut you up. Now, once upon a time in a land called London, a little girl was born to two proud, loving parents who named her Nicholas Theodore Cole. No one knew she was a little girl at first— she'd been born with a penis, after all—but she knew what she was."

Shaun's stomach dropped even lower. He was sure he knew where this story was headed, but he listened in absolute silence.

"One day, when she was five years old, she tried to explain to her parents that they'd gotten it all wrong. She was a girl, not a boy. Her mother laughed and told her she was being silly, but her father got angry. That night, after her mother had gone to bed, her father came upstairs to her room. He took the little girl by the hair and told her, 'You upset your mum, Nicky. You upset your mum with all that queer talk, and I won't stand for it.'"

"That wasn't your fault," said Shaun, trying to make his voice as gentle as possible. "Whatever he did to you, it wasn't your—"

"Shut up," Nick snarled. "Shut the fuck up, Mason."

Shaun stopped talking, but his heart was pounding so hard he was surprised Nick couldn't hear it over the phone.

When Nick spoke again, his voice was calm. "Now, this little girl—we'll call her Nichole—she loved her mum, so she tried to be a boy for a very long time. She played sports, and chased girls on the playground, and did everything a little boy should do. When she went to university, though, she decided her parents couldn't be disappointed by what they couldn't see, so she started changing from the boy her mum wanted into the girl she really was. And it was brilliant, Shaun. It felt like lying in the sun after spending eighteen years in a cave. But it didn't last.

"For the first year, she only dressed like a girl when she was alone, or when she was going out with friends she trusted, but at the beginning of her second year, a friend convinced her to go to a party as herself. She didn't want to—she didn't think she was ready for it, and she didn't think the other students were ready for it either—but her friend finally convinced her. Some people stared, and some people whispered, but everyone else was surprisingly nice. In fact, one chap even chatted her up, and at the end of the night, he invited her upstairs."

There was a long pause, and Shaun hardly dared to breathe. He kept his eyes squeezed shut, as if that could somehow block out the images that Nick's story was creating.

"You can't imagine what it was like," said Nick. His voice had lost its nonchalant, conversational tone, and was now rough with emotion. "I had no idea, Shaun, no idea what he'd do to me. He raped me. He shoved his cock into me, and he held a knife to my throat, and he raped me. And do you know what he said to me while he was raping me?"

Shaun couldn't make his voice work. He opened his eyes and stared at Lore. A lock of hair had fallen across his forehead, and Shaun reached over to push it away.

"Answer the fucking question, Shaun."

"No," whispered Shaun. "No, I don't know."

"He said it was my fault." Nick laughed, but it was humorless. "He said I brought it on myself, that I was a faggot and a freak, and that if I wanted to be a woman, I deserved to be fucked like one."

"Is that why you kill them? The men in female avatars?"

"They're disgusting. They're the abominations. They'll spit on two men holding hands, go home and hit their wives, and then log in and let other men fuck them while they're pretending to be women. They're the sick ones, not us."

"But I'm not one of them," said Shaun, trying to choose his

words carefully. "You know I'm not one of them, Nick, and neither is Kim and neither is Lore."

"But you've been trying to stop me. I understand why. I do. But that doesn't change the fact that you've led the police to my doorstep, and we both know it's only a matter of time before they find me now that they know who I am. You need to be punished for putting a stop to my good work."

"Then deal with me," said Shaun. "Leave Kim and Lore out of this."

"Make your decision, Shaun."

"They have nothing to do with any of this!"

"They have everything to do with this. Now which is it, Shaun? The boy or the girl?"

Shaun twisted his fingers in the pillowcase beside Lore's head, and his jaw was clenched so hard his teeth hurt. There was no right answer, and he knew it, and not just because it was impossible for him to choose between two people he cared about. In Nick's mind, choosing to let Kim die would make Shaun no better than the men Nick had been preying on, but killing Lore would make him a murderer. And even if there had been a right answer, he wouldn't have been able to give it. Not when he couldn't imagine a world without one of them in it.

"Your time is running out, Shaun. I have a gun in my hand and a program that will cut main and backup power to the building you're in. If you don't make a decision soon, they both die. All it takes is a bullet and a keystroke."

Shaun closed his eyes and wracked his brain for another solution, but there was none. With his heart pounding, he said, "Fine, I choose me."

There was silence on the other end of the line.

"I can't choose," said Shaun, staring at Lore and thinking of Kim. "I can't choose, and if this is supposed to be my punishment, then I'm the one who should die."

"You'd die for them? I understand your willingness to die for your sister, but for Lore? A man you haven't even known for a month?"

Shaun swallowed hard. He'd thought about exactly this scenario—in fact, the night before he applied to Homicide the first time, he'd sat down and made a list of people he would die to protect—but what he hadn't expected was that if the time ever came, it would be such an easy decision to make.

But that didn't mean he was going down without a fight.

"Yeah," said Shaun, making the plan up as he went along. "I'll die for him, for both of them, if you'll let me."

"And what does it feel like to say that?"

Shaun stroked Lore's cheek with his fingertips. "I don't know."

"Are you only telling me you'd die for them because you think I won't hold you to the promise?"

"No," said Shaun. It must not have settled in yet, he thought, that if all of his plans backfired, he was going to be called upon to kill himself. That was the only explanation he could think of for why he wasn't terrified.

"Well I have to say, Shaun Mason, I didn't see this coming. You never stop surprising me."

"Do you accept or not?"

"As a matter of fact, yes," said Nick, "I do accept. I've never actually seen an act of martyrdom before, and I can't imagine a more fitting punishment."

Shaun closed his eyes and swallowed. If the next part of his spur-of-the-moment plan didn't go the way he hoped, he didn't know what else to do. "Can I ask for just one thing before I do it? Can I at least say good-bye to Kim?"

"No, I'm afraid that can't happen, Shaun."

Shaun's heart plummeted into his stomach. The plan had been a long shot anyway—trying to subtly question Kim about where she'd been taken, then using his phone to post the information on the Internet—but he'd at least expected Nick to let him talk to her. Now he was really out of ideas.

"Interesting, I would have expected you to beg me," said Nick when Shaun didn't reply right away. "For what it's worth, she's tied to a chair and she has no idea where she is, so whatever it was you were going to try to have her do, I doubt it would have worked anyway. At best, it would have bought a few extra minutes, but then you would have found yourself right back where you are now. Now, are you still prepared to die for them? Because I intend to hold you to your word."

"There has to be another way," said Shaun. He'd never been trained in hostage negotiation, so he tried to imagine what he would want to hear if he was in Nick's position. "There's still a way out of this."

Nick let out a bitter-sounding laugh. "Don't ruin my perception of you by lying, Shaun. We both know it's only a matter of time before they find me."

"I led them to you, right? So I can lead them away." Shaun knew that wasn't the right thing to say as soon as it came out of his mouth.

"Would you do that?" Nick asked. "Would you really set a killer free and let him keep murdering strangers if it meant saving the lives of two people you care about?"

Shaun wasn't sure what bothered him most: the fact that Nick had no qualms about referring to himself as a killer, or that fact that Shaun would happily set him free if he really thought it would save Kim and Lore.

"We're out of time, Shaun. I need an answer."

"Nick, look, I know you're—"

"Ten."

"Stop, wait, just talk to me for a—"

"Nine."

"Damn it, just hold on a second!" Shaun's heart was racing and he tugged at his own hair out of pure frustration.

"Do you know what this sound is, Shaun?" There was the unmistakable click of a gun being cocked, followed by Kim's muffled screaming. "Eight."

"Stop," Shaun choked out. "Please stop, Nick, please."

"Let me hear yours or I'll kill her now. Seven."

Shaun fumbled the gun out of the back of his waistband and

flicked the safety off, then held it up to the headset in his ear so Nick could hear him cock it. The noise seemed too loud in the otherwise silent room, and he let out a quiet, choked sound into the phone as he begged, "Please don't make me do this."

"Six. If you can't muster the courage to do it yourself, just step out into the hallway and take aim. I'm sure the M.P.s would be happy to help you out. Five. In fact, I'd almost rather you did go out into the hall, really. The security cameras out there are at a much higher resolution."

Shaun leaped off the bed and scanned the room for cameras, and finally found one mounted in the corner, pointed at Lore. Shaun looked directly into it, pulse thundering and stomach roiling, and said, "Please, Nick, stop. Just stop and talk to me about this. Just a few more minutes, that's all I want."

"You've already had a few more minutes. Four."

Shaun had heard the phrase, 'time seemed to slow down,' but he'd never actually experienced it. The next few seconds crawled by. Though his heart was still racing and a cold sweat was trickling down his spine, a strange calm settled over him. His hand was steady when he reached down to squeeze Lore's too-thin shoulder, and his voice didn't waver when he murmured, "Tell Kim I love her."

"I will. Three."

Shaun closed his eyes and rested the barrel of his gun against his forehead like an war-torn movie hero, and whispered a prayer to whichever gods might be listening. Then, he took a deep breath and reached for the door handle.

Time exploded into a dizzying blur of sound and movement like someone had just hit fast forward. A commotion in the hallway made Shaun jerk away from the door, and a siren went off overhead. Nick shouted something unintelligible, followed by the crack of gunfire and the sound of Kim screaming.

Chapter Twenty-Two

There was a blue smear on the wall of Lore's hospital room. It was two inches long, and it looked like it had been made by a tiny, paint-covered finger. Shaun stared at it.

A man in a suit was asking him questions, and he could hear himself replying in a dull monotone, though he wasn't conscious of what he was saying. People drifted in and out of the room. Some came over to talk to him, and others checked the machines around the bed. None of them tried to make him let go of Lore's hand.

Shaun didn't snap back to reality until the door opened and Kim flew into the room. She was in his arms in an instant, fingers twisted in his shirt and face buried against his chest. She wasn't crying, but her shoulders were heaving, and Shaun gave up his deathgrip on Lore's hand to wrap both arms around her.

Hudson and Brian appeared in the doorway a second later. Some of the agents tried to block their way, but Hudson flashed them her badge and a scowl, and they quickly stepped aside.

"Oh god, Shaun—Shaun, are you okay?" Kim's voice was muffled against Shaun's chest. "God, I was so worried. I had no idea—"

"I'm okay, I'm okay," said Shaun, stroking her hair. He'd never been so relieved to see her in his life, and he drew back just to look down at her face and make sure she was really there. He pulled her into another hug and mumbled into her hair, "I thought I'd lost you."

Hudson kept her distance until Shaun and Kim were finished hugging, then moved closer and squeezed his shoulder. "Okay there, Mason?"

Shaun nodded. Now that the shock was wearing off, he felt shaky, and he pulled away from Kim to sink down into the chair beside the bed. Kim perched on the arm and put a hand on his shoulder, apparently unwilling to be separated from him just yet. Shaun rested one hand on her knee and curled the other around Lore's wrist

"How'd you find us?" asked Shaun. He vaguely remembered one of the agents saying Hudson had tipped them off, but Shaun had no idea how she'd known where they were.

"A text message."

Shaun arched an eyebrow. "A text message?"

"Well, technically almost a thousand of them," said Brian. He looked like he was trying to keep his expression neutral, but there was warmth in his eyes when he looked at Shaun.

"Everyone in the department got two hundred messages in a row, all at the same time." Hudson pressed her lips together and darted a glance at Lore. "I'm guessing whoever sent them wanted to make damn sure we were paying attention."

Shaun's gaze drifted to Lore. He wondered where Lore was right now and what he was thinking, and whether or not he knew how close they'd all come to dying. "Have you talked to him?"

"He's safe," said Hudson.

Shaun nodded, then swallowed and asked, "Nick?"

"Shot twice in the leg, but he's stable," said Hudson. "As soon as the doctor gives the okay, we'll move him into lock-up and hold him until trial."

"Who got the honor of taking him down?"

Hudson gave him a look, and Shaun's gaze darted to Brian, who stared back at him without even so much as blinking. After a heartbeat of silence, Hudson said, "We're not sure, and I don't intend to pursue the matter."

"Wish you'd killed the son of a bitch," said Kim.

Shaun squeezed her knee.

"Shaun Mason?"

Shaun looked up to find a balding man in a navy blue suit standing over him. There was an American flag pin on the lapel of his jacket. Shaun wondered if it was some sort of requirement that federal agents advertise themselves with that particular piece of jewelry.

"I'm Agent Larson." The man stuck his hand out for Shaun to shake. "Agent Moore tells me you're responsible for identifying the suspect." He jerked his chin at one of the agents near the door, who Shaun vaguely remembered talking to while he'd still been in shock.

Shaun took a deep breath and nodded. He already knew where this was going.

"Would you mind telling me what the hell an off-duty Cybercrimes employee was doing snooping around a federal homicide investigation?"

"Well technically, I wasn't really snooping around the homicide investigation," said Shaun. "I went to the houses of a couple victims, but for the most part, I did most of my snooping in Simulnet."

"I'm assuming I don't need to tell you that Simulnet is outside your jurisdiction."

"Yeah, but that's the problem. As far as I know, Simulnet is outside all our jurisdictions." Shaun stood so he could face Larson instead of looking up at him. "I figured while you guys were sitting around playing politics, I'd get a head start on my own time."

Larson's eyes narrowed. "You realize this could cost you career? The Bureau doesn't like having their toes stepped on."

"I know," said Shaun. Whenever he'd imagined having this conversation, he'd expected to be more nervous. Then again, he hadn't expected to be having this conversation less than an hour after facing his own death.

"Sorry, but did you just threaten to have my detective fired?"

Shaun and Larson both turned to look at Hudson. Her arms were crossed, and she was scowling. It was the kind of look that had probably sent a hundred rookie detectives fleeing her office in tears.

"Your detective?" Larson's eyebrows shot up toward his receding hairline.

"My detective," said Hudson. "I'm the one who asked Shaun to take this investigation, and I'm the one he's been answering to, so if there's a problem, take it up with me, not him. Mason was just following orders."

"Well," said Larson, "then I guess you'd be the one to go to if I wanted to tell Detective Mason what a fine job he's done?"

Shaun's eyes widened, and he glanced at Hudson, who looked

similarly surprised. Kim reached over and squeezed his hand.

"Mason, I don't need to tell you how fucked up this could have been." Larson still looked stern, but he also looked less foreboding than he had just a few minutes ago. "But if it hadn't been for you, Nicholas Wade would still be out there. I don't want to think about how many more people would have died before we found him. Now, obviously I can't speak for the Bureau director—he'll need to review everyone's statements and come to his own conclusions—but I've been around long enough to know a good cop when I see one, and I doubt he'll come down too hard on you." He stuck his hand out.

"Thank you, sir," Shaun managed to croak. He wiped his sweaty palms on the fronts of his jeans and shook Larson's hand.

"As for you." Larson pulled his hand away and turned to Hudson. They stared at each other for a moment before Larson arched an eyebrow and said, "Don't supposed you'd consider coming back to work for us? The Bureau needs some good, old-fashioned, manipulative agents."

"Not on your life, Larson," said Hudson.

Shaun turned to Kim and Brian while the others carried on in the background.

"He was right," said Brian. "You did an amazing job, Shaun."

Kim nodded her agreement and slid her arms around Shaun's neck.

"Thanks," Shaun muttered. He let Kim pull him into another hug, but he was staring over her shoulder.

Lore lay motionless in the bed while the others milled around him, talking and making notes. Only a few people even bothered to glance in his direction. The others avoided looking at him. It was like he made them uncomfortable, or worse, like they'd forgotten he was there. It seemed so unfair that Shaun could hardly stand it, but at the same time, he couldn't help but to wonder if maybe it wasn't more fitting this way, that instead of standing in the spotlight at Shaun's side, Lore would be hovering in the background, lingering in the collective unconsciousness of everyone in the room like a silent, watchful sentinel.

Shaun held Kim's hand all the way back to the hotel.

After they'd given their statements to no less than five different agents, Hudson had come to their rescue by escorting them out of the building and into a cab. Shaun hadn't wanted to leave his car at the hospital, but Hudson had been firm, and Brian had promised to bring it to the hotel the next morning. Hudson bid Shaun and Kim good-night, then sent them off with instructions to sleep, as if that was something either of them would be capable of doing.

Neither of them said a word for the entire ride.

Once they were alone in Shaun's suite, Kim crumpled. They sat there on the floor together, just a few paces away from the door, and Shaun held her while she sobbed against his chest. He couldn't remember the last time he'd seen her cry—he thought it might have been the night after they found the body in the canyon—and it was scarier than he'd ever admit.

Almost an hour later, when her choked sobbing had quieted to the occasional hiccup, Kim lifted her head to look up at him with bloodshot eyes. "I'm sorry, Shaun."

"What? You've got nothing to apologize for."

"Yes I do," Kim insisted. "If I hadn't come to L.A.--"

"If you hadn't come to L.A. he would have found another way to fuck with me," said Shaun. "What happened tonight wasn't your fault."

Kim stared at him for a moment, then looked away, down at the fraying knee of his jeans, and picked at a loosening thread. "You need new pants," she muttered.

"Yeah."

There was a long silence. Shaun pressed his lips to the side of her head and stared blindly at the other side of the room while he wondered what Lore was doing, what he was thinking, whether he had any idea how close Shaun had just come to dying for him. He wondered if Lore would answer the phone if he called. The last time they'd seen each other, Lore had made it clear that he never wanted to see Shaun again, but Shaun had a feeling circumstances had changed.

"Do you love him?" asked Kim.

"What?" Shaun spluttered. "How did you—what?"

Kim just gave him a look. "How did I what? Pick up on you mooning over him back at the hospital?

Shaun let out a strained laugh. "No, I don't love him. God. Why do people keep asking me that? Just because I was worried about him—"

"My brother, the emotional retard."

Shaun huffed and looked away. He didn't love Lore. He was pretty sure of that. But he had to admit he cared about Lore a lot more than he was ready to say out loud.

"So," said Kim after a long silence, "what now?"

"Well," said Shaun, "I, for one, can cross 'chasing a serial killer' off my bucket list."

Kim snorted.

"Ditto getting drunker than I've ever been in my life, watching an anthropomorphic panda bear give a blowjob to a dragon—"

"What?"

"Yeah, we have a lot to catch up on," said Shaun, but he didn't elaborate. He stared at the tank humming softly in the corner, its control panel lit up like a welcome sign.

"You know, maybe I'll just take a nap," said Kim.

Shaun jerked to attention and looked at her with a guilty expression. He couldn't believe his sister had just been kidnapped, and he was busy daydreaming about a man he'd only known for a couple of weeks.

Kim laughed tiredly at him and climbed to her feet. "You're such an idiot," she said, offering him a hand up. "You're head over heels for this guy, and you're going to fuck it up because you're a pansy."

"I'm not—"

"You are, Shaun, and it's gross. Stop being such a wuss."

Shaun's jaw clenched. "It's complicated."

"Oh, bullshit." Kim sighed and rolled her eyes. "You just saved each other's lives. I'd say that makes things pretty goddamn clear, wouldn't you? Now stop being such a moron and go see him."

Shaun frowned and stuffed his hands in his pockets. He eyed Kim, who stared right back at him, and suddenly they were six years old again, having a staring contest to decide who had to take out the trash. As usual, Shaun lost.

"Oh Jesus Christ, fine," said Shaun.

"That's my boy," said Kim.

Lore's world hovered in twilight. The tower stood high and bright against the dark purple sky, and the air around it was so still that Shaun's footsteps seemed like the only sound in the universe. The bridge had risen, and its gates had opened for him at a touch, and he wondered what that meant. He wondered if that was Lore welcoming him back, or if it was just a leftover privilege that Lore had forgotten to take away.

Shaun hurried up the stairs, but he paused beside the doorway. He'd picked his way through a lot of unfriendly situations in the past, but this one actually meant something, and he was terrified of fucking it up. He knew he had to try, though, so he took a deep breath and rounded the corner.

Lore was sitting on the floor in the center of the room, facing the rack of monitors on his makeshift desk. His legs were crossed underneath him and his hands were on his knees. He looked like he might be meditating until he turned his head so Shaun could see the ridge of his cheekbone.

"I know you told me to stay away, but we've got some unfinished business," said Shaun. He put his hands in his pockets and leaned against the door frame. He was pretty sure he didn't look as calm as he hope.

Lore didn't reply.

"Can we talk?" asked Shaun. "I'll beg if you want."

Lore twisted around to look at him, then pushed to his feet. For a second, Shaun was worried he would say no, but then Lore crossed his arms and said, "Talk."

"Oh—uh, okay," said Shaun, caught off guard by the lack of argument. "Well, I guess first of all, I just want to know how you knew where me and Kim were."

"I've been tracking the GPS on your phone since the day we met," said Lore. Judging by the look on his face, he really thought that Shaun had known.

Shaun sighed.

"When I realized where you were going, and that you'd been on a call since you left the hotel, I knew something must be going on. I traced your call to Kim's location, then sent text messages with the coordinates."

Shaun knew he should probably be irritated at the invasion of his privacy, but it was hard to be angry when the invasion saved people's lives. Besides, Lore was still keeping an eye on him. That said more than anything either of them could say out loud. Shaun shifted uncomfortably. There were a million things he wanted to say. He'd even practiced some of them in his head. But now that he was actually standing in the same room with Lore, everything he'd planned to say felt so trite it made him cringe. Finally, he settled for muttering, "Thanks."

"You're welcome."

They stared at each other for a very long time. Shaun wanted to draw it out a little longer, just in case Lore kicked him out again. He knew this might be the last time they saw each other. The thought made his stomach hurt.

Eventually, after what must have been five minutes, Lore turned away and said, "I have work to do. If that's all you wanted, you should—"

"Wait," said Shaun. Lore's dismissal made him angry, and he took a few steps forward to grab Lore by the shoulder. "That's it? Really? You're okay with saying, 'nice working with you, thanks for saving my life,' and never seeing me again?"

"What do you want from me?" Lore snapped and pushed

Shaun's hand away. "If you came here expecting me to sing your praises for saving my life—"

"You know what I want," said Shaun. He wondered if Lore could see past his irritation. He wondered if Lore knew how fast his heart was beating or how hard it was to keep his hands from shaking. He wondered, not for the first time, if Lore could read his mind.

"That isn't how I do things," said Lore. "Working with you was educational, but everything else that happened—I don't know how you got it in your head that we could have any kind of relationship. In case you hadn't noticed, we literally exist in two different worlds. There's no way we could—"

"Oh fuck you, Lore," said Shaun, and kissed him.

To Shaun's surprise, Lore didn't try to pull away; he went into the kiss at full speed, grabbing at Shaun's hair and opening his mouth for Shaun's tongue. They hit the table, sending two monitors crashing to the ground, and then stumbled toward the bed without ever breaking apart. Lore's nails were scraping Shaun's scalp, and it was hard to believe that just a few seconds ago, he'd been naming all the reasons they shouldn't do this.

"Tell me to stay," Shaun panted as he shoved Lore down onto the bed and held him there with a hand on his chest.

Lore stared up at him, his unnaturally blue eyes as wide as Shaun had ever seen them. His lips were swollen and his hair was disheveled, and he looked so wonderfully human. Shaun slid a thumb into his mouth just to feel the wetness of his tongue. Lore made a soft noise, maybe a protest, and pulled his mouth away to say, "You're more self-conscious than you need to be."

"What? I'm not—"

"Tell me to stay," Lore mimicked, then grabbed the front of Shaun's shirt to haul him down again. Their kisses turned filthy, and by the time they broke away again, they were both panting through their noses. "You knew I wanted you here before you logged on," he said. "You're just wasting time by pretending otherwise."

"Actually, I didn't," said Shaun, but the point seemed moot

when Lore squirmed up against him.

Lore's fingers were bunched in his shirt. Shaun pried them away so he could pull his shirt off and toss it aside. As soon as Shaun was naked from the waist up, Lore lifted his head to lick the hollow of his throat. The heat of his mouth made Shaun's cock twitch, and he reached down to pull at Lore's zipper.

"You drive me fucking crazy," whispered Shaun.

Lore huffed against his collarbone. "You don't need to sweet talk me. You're already in my bed."

"Who's sweet talking? You really do—fuck, that's—"

"Shut up," muttered Lore.

"Say my name again."

"I said shut up."

Shaun laughed and closed his eyes while Lore wriggled down the bed underneath him, licking and biting his stomach along the way. Lore had his jeans open before Shaun could even think to do it himself, and he dug his fingers into the sheets when Lore pulled the waistband of his underwear down. He wasn't surprised anymore that Lore could be so passionate, but he still twitched when Lore growled against his hipbone. The vibrations from it rippled through him, and he tried not to rub himself against Lore's cheek.

When Lore mouthed the head of his cock, though, Shaun gasped and pulled away. Lore pulled away to look up at him, and Shaun shook his head. "I'm not gonna last five seconds if you do that, and I think I'd rather fuck you." He licked his lips, and when Lore didn't reply, he hesitantly said, "Unless you don't want to."

Lore crawled back up the bed and crushed his mouth to Shaun's.

"I was hoping you'd say that." Shaun gasped and dug his fingers into Lore's hair.

Lore laughed—a real, throaty laugh that made Shaun's toes curl. As far as Shaun was concerned, that was the hottest thing Lore had ever done.

Lore pushed Shaun's jeans down, then wriggled out of his own.

Shaun barely even registered that they were finally naked together
before Lore was biting his lip and curling a leg around his waist.
Their cocks rubbed together, first by accident and then because
Lore was shoving up against him.

Shaun grabbed at Lore's hip to keep him still and muttered,
"D'you have anything?"

"In the drawer," replied Lore. His voice was rough, and he
sounded out of breath.

Shaun fumbled in the nightstand until he found the lube. He
uncapped the bottle and slicked his fingers, spilling some on Lore's
belly in the process. He knew he could get Lore to do this part for
him with a few quick changes to code, but he wanted to do it
himself. He wanted to sink his fingers into Lore's body and feel
around inside him until he was begging for it. He was so distracted
by the push of his fingers into Lore's ass that he almost didn't
realize Lore had a hand over his eyes. Shaun reached up and Lore's
hand down.

Lore didn't try to resist, but he did close his eyes and turn his
face away.

"Does it hurt?" Shaun frowned.

Lore pushed out a laugh like the air had been forced from his
lungs. "If it did, I would just make it stop."

"Oh, right," said Shaun. He couldn't be expected to think
clearly when he was knuckle deep inside Lore's body. He twisted
his fingers and watched Lore's brow furrow. "What's it feel like?"

"You know what it feels like."

"Not for you," said Shaun. He pulled his fingers out nice and
slow, then shoved them back in fast.

Lore gasped and threw an arm over his face. Seeing him that
way, so vulnerable and trying to hide it, made Shaun's blood boil.
He leaned down for a kiss and thrust his fingers into Lore's ass
until he felt Lore open up around them. "God damn it," he
whispered. "You have no idea how much I want you."

"You—you sound like a'mm—" Lore trailed off when Shaun
pulled his fingers out, and he reached down to grab Shaun's

forearm, the tendons of his inner wrist flexing with impatience.

"Easy," muttered Shaun. "Easy, just gimme a second." He fumbled with the lube again, quick and messy, then grabbed at his slippery cock and rubbed the head against Lore's hole. Even after his fingers, Lore was impossibly tight, but he didn't get a chance to say so, because Lore planted his heels in the small of Shaun's back and jerked him forward.

"Stop fucking around," said Lore. His voice was ragged like he'd already been screaming.

Shaun growled and bit the patch of skin underneath Lore's chin. The head of his prick nudged Lore's ass, and he guided it inside, nice and slow. Lore moaned, and Shaun could feel the vibrations from it against his lips. The sound made his whole body weak. He'd gotten off with dozens of people in dozens of ways, but no one had ever made him feel like this: a little scared and a little desperate, and so fucking grateful he could cry. Lore's thighs were shaking and his fingers were buried in Shaun's hair, and Shaun whispered, "thank you, thank you, thank you," against the hollow of Lore's throat.

"Shut up," Lore moaned and pulled himself up onto Shaun's cock. "Please just—"

"Yeah, all right," said Shaun before pressing their mouths together. He pulled his hips back and shoved forward again, hard enough to make Lore skid across the blankets. Lore whimpered into his mouth, and Shaun almost came on the second thrust.

"Shaun, I need to—"

"Okay, okay, it's okay," said Shaun. He tried to make his hips stop moving so Lore could adjust, but Lore was squirming underneath him, and his body refused to obey.

"No, it's not—I don't need—"

Shaun finally got the hint and lifted up. Lore worked a hand in between their bellies, and when Lore groaned, Shaun sat back on his heels so he could watch.

Lore's cheeks were flushed, and his hair was sticking to his forehead. His eyes were closed, and his lips were parted, and every time Shaun thrust into him, the muscles in his belly tensed. Looking at him was driving Shaun out of his mind.

"Shit, you need to hurry," Shaun panted. He hauled one of Lore's legs up over his shoulder so he could get his cock even deeper. His thrusts turned slower but determined, and he dug his toes into the mattress for leverage. His balls were slapping Lore's ass, and between that and the way Lore was squeezing him, he knew he only had a couple of seconds left.

Lore didn't reply. His brows were furrowed like he was concentrating, and his quiet, hitching moans were vibrating through his body. He buried his free hand in his own hair, and the muscles in his arm flexed when he gave it a pull. That edge of pain seemed to be all he needed, because a second later, he was coming with a startled-sounding gasp. The muscles in his stomach tensed, and his eyes snapped open to stare up at Shaun as his cock jerked and he came all over his belly.

"Oh Jesus fuck," Shaun cursed, staring wide-eyed at Lore. He dug his fingernails into Lore's hips and used his grip to haul Lore down onto his cock one last time before his orgasm ripped through him. He shoved in as far as he could go while his cock emptied itself into Lore's body. It seemed to go on for hours, and by the time it finally started to subside, his come was leaking out around his cock and trickling down Lore's buttocks.

Shaun collapsed atop Lore, gasping for breath against the curve of Lore's shoulder. One of Lore's hands was still trapped between their bodies, but he used the other to stroke Shaun's back. Shaun smoothed the hair away from Lore's forehead and turned his head to kiss the patch of skin behind Lore's ear. "Too heavy?" he mumbled.

"You're fine," replied Lore. He sounded fucked-out and relaxed, and if Shaun hadn't just come, that would've been enough to get him hard again.

As it was, the most he could manage to do was twine Lore's hair around his fingertips and say, "Give me a chance." Lore stiffened underneath him, but that wasn't enough to make Shaun back off. He lifted his head to look at Lore, who was staring up at him warily. Shaun rubbed his thumb over one of Lore's eyebrows and said, "Look, I'm not asking for much. I'm not even asking for a relationship. I just want to see you again, that's all."

"You're a masochist," said Lore in a frustrated tone. It seemed like he was about to say no, but then he sighed and wriggled his hand out from between them so he could wrap his arms around Shaun's back. He dug his fingers into Shaun's lower back like he was trying to hold Shaun in place, and said "You'll just bother me until I say yes, won't you?"

"Probably," said Shaun, trying not to grin. "Might as well just give in now and save yourself the headache."

Lore's mouth tightened in obvious irritation, but then he slid one hand up into Shaun's hair and pulled him down into a kiss.

Chapter Twenty-Three

Stackston was sunny and warm, and overflowing with college students on spring break. Shaun dodged a group of translucent fairies who giggled at him when he pretended to tip his hat. "Excuse me, ladies." He grinned and turned to walk backwards, watching to see if any of them glanced back. A growl from behind him made him jump, and he whirled around just in time to not collide with a large, black worg.

"Watch it," the worg grumbled.

"Sorry." Shaun grinned and stepped aside to let him pass, then made his way down the block. He stopped on the sidewalk and shielded his eyes from the sun to squint at the cafe across the street. A lone figure in a dusty black blazer was sitting at a table outside. Shaun pulled his phone out and sent a text message: 'what are u wearing?'

Across the street, Lore's cell phone jangled, and Shaun stifled a laugh when he saw rather than heard Lore heave an annoyed sigh. He watched Lore shove his laptop away and pull his phone out, then stare at the text message before typing a reply.

A second later, Shaun's phone beeped. 'You already know what I'm wearing. Stop being a child and come here if you want to talk to me instead of skulking around across the street.'

Shaun laughed and shoved his phone into his pocket, then ambled across the street to plop down across from Lore. "Got another tracker stuck to me?"

Lore didn't look up from his laptop. "I could see your reflection in the shop window."

For some reason, that made Shaun laugh. The glare Lore shot him over the top of the laptop just made him laugh even harder, and once he caught his breath, he grinned. "Have I ever told you how funny you are?"

Lore grunted and turned back to whatever he'd been doing.

Shaun let him work for awhile before reaching over to push the laptop closed.

Lore pulled his fingers out of the way just in time, and he lifted his gaze without raising his head so he was looking at Shaun through his lashes. He was stupidly attractive.

"You're having lunch with me, not your laptop," said Shaun.

Lore pressed his lips together in obvious annoyance, but then he sat back in his chair in a mimicry of relaxation. "All right, I'm sorry. What do you want to talk about?"

"There doesn't always need to be some kind of agenda for conversations, you know," said Shaun, although the truth was, he did have something he wanted to talk about. He just wasn't ready to bring it up yet.

Lore didn't look convinced, but he didn't press the issue. "How is your sister?" he asked.

"Still a little shaken up, but she'll be fine. She's on a plane back to France at the moment. I took her to the airport this morning."

"And Brian?" asked Lore.

"Busy." Shaun shrugged, then quirked a smile. "Why? You're not still jealous, are you?"

Lore rolled his eyes, but the way his mouth tightened made Shaun think he wasn't as nonchalant as he was pretending to be.

"So," said Shaun in an attempt to change the subject. They hadn't really talked about what they were doing, but even though Shaun was dying to put a name to it, he'd promised not to press. "I got a call from Hudson this morning. They finally found some middle ground with the feds regarding Simulnet jurisdiction, and she's putting in a recommendation for me to the new Simulnet Security division. We're gonna answer to the Department of Homeland Security. Pretty cool, huh?"

"Mm." Lore's brow furrowed, and he looked away. He used his fingernails to tap out a nervous rhythm against the arm of his chair.

Shaun licked his lips before continuing. "So uh, I'm gonna need a partner, and Hudson asked me if I knew anyone I'd like to work with."

Lore stopped tapping, but he didn't look at Shaun. "We've been over this, Mason. Us working together was a one time thing."

"Yeah, yeah, I know, you're a lone wolf, blah, blah, blah," said Shaun. The rejection stung, but he wasn't going down without a fight. "Look, we both know Hudson's not gonna leave you alone now. Everyone knows that once you do one thing for that woman, she keeps coming back for more, and she can be a real pain in the ass when she wants something."

Lore didn't reply, but he darted a glance at Shaun from the corner of his eye.

"We're good together," said Shaun.

"It would end in disaster."

"You don't know that."

"Name one way in which it wouldn't end in disaster."

"I can't, but—" Shaun held up a finger "—that doesn't mean it will end in disaster. We made it work for two weeks, right? And if I can put up with your egotistical, manipulative ass for that long, I can put up with anything."

Lore's jaw clenched.

"Come on, what else are you gonna do? Go back to building shit you'll never show to anyone anyway? Spying on people just for the hell of it? You've gotta get bored once in awhile, yeah? That's why you took the case with me in the first place."

"Mason, I can't—"

"Oh for fuck's sake, Lore, it's not like I'm proposing we go out and get hitched. I just don't wanna get stuck with some asshole rookie fresh out of academy—"

"How long ago did you graduate?"

"I'm going to ignore that."

Lore scowled.

"Come on, I'll let you sneak up on me whenever you want," said Shaun in a singsong.

Lore huffed and looked away again, off into the distance. The late afternoon sunlight made his coat look even dustier than usual, but it glinted off the silver hoops in his ear and made his blue eyes seem brighter than ever.

"Lore," said Shaun, and when Lore turned back to look at him, he swallowed and added, "Please? I don't want to work with anyone else."

A long silence stretched out between them. They held each other's gaze, and Shaun imagined he could see Lore's mind at work, following each possibility to its conclusion, all starting with a simple yes or no.

Finally, what seemed like an eternity later, Lore closed his eyes and sighed.

Shaun grinned. "I was hoping you'd say that."

Lore sank back down into his seat with out another word, and after glaring at Shaun, he slowly reached over and opened his laptop. Within seconds, he was typing, his slender fingers flying over the keyboard while his boot tapped a staccato rhythm on the sidewalk. Shaun watched, elbow propped on the table and chin resting in his hand, and grinned every time Lore shot an annoyed glance in his direction.

Their knees bumped underneath the table.

Normal people wouldn't be so excited about something so simple, Shaun thought. Normal people wouldn't care so much about a touch so innocent it could almost be accidental.

But that was fine.

Sometimes, the things normal people overlooked were the things that mattered the most.

About the Author

Rian Darcy is the real life alter-ego of fan fiction author Nishizono Shinji. Once upon a time, she wanted to be an archaeologist (or an astronaut, or a librarian, or a dinosaur), but writing has always been her one true love. She likes coffee, Sherlock Holmes, and things that make her laugh until she cries. Rian's work has appeared in *Spellbinding: Tales from the Magic University*, published by Ravenous Romance, and she is editing an anthology of gay fairy tales for Circlet Press entitled *Charming*.

QUEERPUNK edited by Cecilia Tan & Kelly Kinkaid
ISBN: 978-1-885865-59-5 $4.99

Queer sexuality has long defied the conventional standard of sexual expression; intersecting with the tech-driven backdrop of cyberpunk, it has now rewritten the rules completely. Queerpunk, with its collection of stories that revel in a near-futuristic vision of our own time, investigates the evolution of Queer sexuality under the smog-covered umbrella of urban and technological advancement.

THE VELDERET by Cecilia Tan
ISBN: 1-885865-27-9 $7.49

The Velderet is the story of Kobi and Merin, two roomies on the peaceful world of Bellonia, world where "equality" rules. But they each harbor taboo fantasies of BDSM, and when they world is colonized by the warlike Kylar, who worship the gods of dominance and submission, everything changes.

MATE by Lauren P. Burka
ISBN: 978-1-613900-30-7 $2.99

Three short stories of erotic science fiction with a BDSM edge. Terry Montiero and d'Schane Grey are techies whose relationship is fueled by their chess game--a power game. Originally published in 1992 as a chapbook, the stories have been unavailable for years until this eBook revival. Fans of m/m will enjoy these characters thoroughly.